WILL TO SURVIVE

FEAR GOD AND
KEEP YOUR BOWELS CLEAR

A NOVEL

MIKE J READ

To family

WILL TO SURVIVE
FEAR GOD AND
KEEP YOUR BOWELS CLEAR

PROLOGUE

EUROPE, 1939 - 1946

Peter Greene answered the call and joined the Canadian Armed Forces. Three months passed, and on December 22, 1939, the twenty-two-year-old embarked for Great Britain with the Princess Patricia's Canadian Light Infantry. Based on his previous experience in telecommunications, he was tasked as a communications specialist attached to Rifle Company C. The Patricias were part of the 2nd Brigade in the 1st Canadian Infantry Division.

*　　*　　*

World War II victory celebrations began on May 8, 1945, with the unconditional surrender of Germany at Reims, in northeastern France. On the Eastern Front, fighting ended with the surrender of Germany's last remaining forces on May 11, 1945. In a radio address, Prime Minister Mackenzie King spoke to Canadians: "You have helped rid the world of a great scourge."

*　　*　　*

Peter Greene was granted five days' leave. He borrowed a military jeep and, with Vivian Grey by his side, travelled to a small Inn on the White Cliffs of Dover, where a local minister performed their wedding ceremony on June 23, 1945. Three days later, Peter returned to mainland Europe and caught a transport back to the Netherlands.

*   *   *

By late September 1945, due to the lack of transatlantic ships, thousands of Canadian servicemen had yet to return home. It was Peter's last day in Amsterdam. He aimlessly wandered the city, whiling away the hours. He settled on a park bench to enjoy a coffee and a cigarette. While he sipped the lukewarm black coffee, across the narrow street, among the shops, he noticed an art gallery. A minute later, he dropped his coffee cup in a bin, dropped the cigarette butt and extinguished it under his dull, tired army boot. He crossed the street and, on a whim, entered the gallery. The narrow lobby was quiet and empty of patrons. Walking through another doorway, he discovered a well-lit inner chamber. He walked around, impressed with the variety of paintings covering the walls. After a few minutes, his eyes fell on a Dutch landscape painting displayed on a wooden easel.

A ceiling light cast a circle on the floor, illuminating the artwork. Standing within the circle, his eyes travelled across the canvas. While Peter studied the painting, images of a world at war, scenes of human suffering and despair, loss of life and innocence played out in his mind's eye.

The painting surreptitiously reached out, pulling him back from the dark place. It awakened in him a sense of mystery, wonder…and hope. Peter waved to the gallery proprietor. A minute later, the two men had settled on a fair price that included a carton of cigarettes and two pairs of silk stockings.

*   *   *

Vivian Grey was born in East London, England, during the spring of 1921. As a child, she exhibited an optimism and belief in the habitual goodness of humanity that would fuel her inner strength throughout her life. Vivian and her older sister, Rosemary, experienced a rich and joyful childhood in the tight-knit community. She relished her time in school, and while attending classes, she felt fortunate knowing that many girls and boys her age seldom had the same opportunity. By the age of fourteen, most children had left school to help support their families by working in the textile factories or the coal mines. Life could be arduous and unyielding in East London.

Every Sunday, Vivian, Rosemary and their mother enjoyed an evening meal of beef served with Yorkshire pudding drenched in beef drippings, and a vegetable when in season. Every Saturday morning, the local butcher put aside a discounted cut of beef, wrapped and ready for the girls' mother when she entered the butcher's shop.

Vivian cherished Sundays. She attended church in the morning, played on the street with neighbouring children during the afternoon and at night, exhausted, she tumbled into bed her stomach full of beef and pudding. She also experienced days when her belly ached from emptiness; however, she never complained, it was just one of life's inconveniences. Many years later, while living in Canada and raising her own children, she would often reminisce about her wonderful life as one of the working-class poor of East London.

In 1930, Reverend J. W. Graves founded the first female marching pipe band, the Dagenham Girl Pipers, in the town of Dagenham. In 1934, while attending Sunday School, Vivian was introduced to Reverend Graves. She lived a short bicycle ride from Osborne Hall, where, with her mother's blessing, she was accepted as an apprentice with the Girl Pipers.

Five years hence, eighteen-year-old Vivian, in a Highland dancing uniform complete with kilt, tartan socks, velvet jacket, and tam o' shanter, played the bagpipes, touring with the pipe band throughout England, Scotland and Wales.

By late summer 1939, the grey clouds of war had coalesced and were rapidly descending on Europe. On September 3rd, Britain and France declared war on Germany in response to its invasion of Poland. Seven days later, on September 10th, Canada declared war on Germany.

*   *   *

By the end of the War, 44,000 women, mostly from Great Britain and other parts of Europe, had married Canadian servicemen. These remarkable women were known as war brides. In February 1946, Vivian Greene said a tearful goodbye to her family and boarded the *Lady Rodney* for the transatlantic voyage to Pier 21 in Halifax, Nova Scotia. Nine days later, the ship docked in Halifax. As she stepped onto Canadian soil, she noted in her diary that she had been separated from her husband for five months. A deep uneasiness settled in her stomach as she contemplated the magnitude of her union with a Canadian boy, living in a far-off land five thousand six hundred kilometres from her family.

In step with thousands of Canadian soldiers, Peter had boarded one of the few remaining British transport ships and arrived home in the waning days of October 1945. He was granted two weeks' leave to reacquaint himself with civilian life before resuming his career with the Bell Telephone Company of Canada. Four months later, on the last day of February 1946, he left home and drove east to Montreal's Central Station, where he met Vivian as she disembarked from the west-bound train that had transported her from Halifax Harbour to Montreal, Quebec. The couple drove westward back to Millington, a small farming community in southern Ontario, on the shores of Lake Ontario and Peter's birthplace.

*   *   *

The federal government enacted the Veterans Charter to assist veterans by supporting their reintegration into postwar society. In early September 1946, after lodging with his parents for six months, Peter secured a low-interest loan and bought a one-and-a-half-story three-bedroom Victory home in a new subdivision in north Millington, surrounded by other veterans.

On December 29, four months after moving into their new home, Vivian and Peter welcomed the first of five children.

*   *   *

The morning light poured through the living room's bay window, bathing the chesterfield in warmth as the light scattered across the interior wall. A Dutch oil painting hung slightly askew above the chesterfield. The light mingled with the windmills, their lattice-frame sails shimmered in contrast to the dreary grasslands and the isolated buildings sheltered among the barren craggy hills. In the foreground, a lone tree cradled a nest on its upper branches. A large bird stood watch—a sentinel witnessing dawn's early blush of bronze and orange as it touched the golden horizon.

CHAPTER

ONE

The local TV news anchor/weather prognosticator assured his audience that Friday's forecast was for clear skies and balmy temperatures, with a high of 48 degrees. He urged the viewer not to get too comfortable, as the weather system was unusually mild for late November. With winter right around the corner, it was sure to be a day that enticed the housebound to venture beyond their front doors. A last gasp to take advantage of the final days of autumn before winter's bite blanketed Ontario with four months of bitter cold and waist-deep snow.

*   *   *

A soft tapping at the side door caught Timmy's attention. He stopped mid-chew, dropped his spoon, stood up and walked over to the door. He opened the door and waved vigorously at the milkman's back as he descended the driveway. He resumed chewing and hoisted both plastic milk jugs by their red handles. Timmy closed the door quickly with his butt and then struggled to lift one jug onto the kitchen table. He moved to the refrigerator and slid the second jug onto an empty shelf, then returned to the table and popped off the milk jug cap. A splash of milk painted the linoleum floor. Not to worry, Mildred will clean up the mess. Timmy drenched the dry cornflakes in milk and shovelled a heaping spoonful into his mouth. He devoured the flakes with renewed vigour. He was like a contestant at the annual hotdog-eating contest held at the town's Fall and Harvest Fair.

He dropped the spoon into the empty bowl and wiped his mouth with the back of his hand. He walked into the living room, belched loudly, much to his own satisfaction, and gazed out the bay window. Across the narrow two-lane street, he watched Mr. Wright, briefcase in hand, walk toward his 1957 Ford Fairlane 500 sedan. Timmy admired the two-tone car with its swept-back roof and chrome that stretched from the headlights to the tips of its rear tailfins. He enjoyed the loud rumble escaping the big V8 engine. He watched the red-and-white car back down the driveway and slowly drive along the centre of the street toward County Road 3, leaving behind a trail of swirling blue smoke.

He dreamed that one day he would have a shiny and noisy car just like Mr. Wright's. A noise interrupted his dream; he whirled around to see William, his older brother by three years, sitting at the end of the chesterfield, his legs crisscrossed under his butt. He had his left hand around her waist, and with his right, he was touching her breasts.

William had been staring at him the whole time, watching his *little* brother drool over the big Ford across the street. With a smirk, he began to use the tips of his fingers to circle each of her breasts.

"Wha' ya doin'?" Timmy asked in a bewildered voice.

"What do you think I'm doin'?" William mocked as he continued to fondle her breasts that, clearly, were much too large for her slight frame.

Timmy watched his brother poke and prod her parts. A moment later, losing interest, he moved on and began to touch her buttocks. Timmy walked over and settled on the opposite end of the chesterfield. He was engrossed and confused as he watched his brother.

"Will'am, wha' ya doin'?"

William laughed and continued to plod away, fondling her body parts. He quickly realized, however, that it was not as much fun as he had imagined. He held her out to Timmy, "Hey, do you want to touch her bum…or her titties?"

Timmy inhaled and hooted with laughter, then asked, "Why?" He hesitated, looked at his grinning older brother, "Ya…'kay…will me be in t'ouble?" He pulled his legs up and crossed them under his butt, imitating his brother. His indecision kept him from reaching out and participating in his brother's anatomy lesson.

Loose floorboards groaned in the hallway. Someone approached. William wheeled around and stared at the entranceway. With surprising agility, he forced the doll on his brother.

Timmy jumped off the chesterfield and dropped his arms by his sides, unaware that the undressed doll hung stiffly in his left hand, arms raised overhead. Her curly blonde ponytail hung loosely, masking the doll's eyes. He stared sheepishly at the figure standing in the living room, blocking the only exit.

The morning light accentuated their sister's flushed, sunken cheeks. With narrowed eyes, she glared at her younger brothers. Twelve-year-old Mary Lynn stood motionless, hands-on hips, obstructing their escape. She stared at the boys with a scowl that would prompt a dog to scramble and hide under a table.

With an abundance of hostility, she hissed in a shrill voice, "You little bastards, you perverts…you two…are in so much trouble."

A couple of days before, she had wondered if someone had been mucking around in her bedroom. Honestly, she didn't care what her brothers were up to today, or for that matter, on any day. And besides, she had outgrown Barbie at least three years ago. They could keep her whole Barbie collection for all she cared. On the other hand, they had invaded her bedroom and rummaged through her stuff, her private stuff. She was steamed.

As her mind wrestled with the knowledge that her privacy had been violated, she quickly concluded that she had no choice but to squeal. Surely, she thought it would be to her benefit to unload, tell Mum that these little brats, without her permission, messed around in her bedroom, searched through her closet and stole her Barbie doll.

Feeling a warm, surging sense of exhilaration, she imagined that her brothers would be forever forbidden from stepping over the threshold into her bedroom. Hiding her excitement, she glared at the two losers. Today, she thought, would be a good day. She bellowed, "How dare you go into my room, invade my privacy and trash my stuff…Mum."

Timmy withered before her eyes.

William weighed his options. A queasiness erupted in the pit of his stomach. He vaulted off the chesterfield, leaving his brother standing by the armrest holding the evidence. "It was Timmy, he went into your closet and took your Barbie! I tol' him not to…" he confessed.

Mary Lynn scowled and subjected him to her best pissed-off squint.

Timmy, eyes wide, turned to his brother. His shoulders slumped as a tear slid down his cheek. His face puckered, and he let out a high-pitched "guffaw," startling his siblings.

Surprised, William thought he had laughed.

"It's not funny," said Mary Lynn.

Timmy's anguish then erupted into tears streaming down his cheeks.

William looked sideways at Mary Lynn as it struck him that he was in big, big trouble. He held his head up, sniffed, and wondered how he would get out of this predicament.

Hearing Mary Lynn's scream, their mother left the bedroom and walked to the second-floor landing. Vivian leisurely descended the stairs, wrapped in her housecoat and slippers, wondering what sort of drama was unfolding so early in the morning. Mary Lynn's cry for help undoubtedly was one of exasperation. Her brothers were doubtless up to their *no-good* shenanigans. As she entered the living room, Timmy's sobbing swelled as William fought to hold back his own tears. Oh, my goodness gracious, she thought, eyeing her three distraught children.

Mary Lynn trumpeted that she had walked in on the boys playing dirty games with her Barbie doll. In a high-pitched voice, she screeched: "Mum…they were on the chesterfield feeling-her-up—they were playing with her boobs." A smirk slid across her face as she looked sideways at her brothers.

Vivian felt an uneasiness, igniting low in her stomach. She loosened her robe as the sunlight cast a spotlight on William. My Lord…surely, he is too young to be entertaining such thoughts. She believed he was still years away from *the talk*.

With slippers on, Vivan stood five feet tall. Despite her small stature, she seemed taller when she routinely exhibited selflessness and compassion for both people and animals. Moreover, if someone thought her ministering was a sign of weakness, they were sorely mistaken. In her home, she was the conductor of a five-child orchestra. To her friends and neighbours, she was a comely and devoted war veteran's wife who spoke with a funny accent.

*   *   *

A clamour from the corner of the living room drew Vivian and the children's attention. The family's black Labrador Retriever yawned, pulled her body into an upright position, then stared at Vivian.

"Mary Lynn, please take Mildred outside so she can do her business."

"How dare they go into my bedroom *without* my permission," she fumed. Mary Lynn summoned the dog and retreated toward the back door with Mildred trailing behind.

She moved quickly, determined to witness her rotten brothers getting a proper dressing-down.

Vivian turned her attention to the boys. "Well, what do you pair have to say for yourselves?" she demanded.

With tears trickling down his cheeks, Timmy tossed the doll onto the couch. "Will'am did it. He…tol' me ta get Mary's Barbie." He shuffled his feet, inhaled heavily and went on, "Mum, me din't…touch Barbie's parts. Will'am, he dirty." He turned his head and noticed the stunned look on his brother's face.

William fell back onto the chesterfield and crossed his arms, "…Mum, Timmy's… the doll was here when I walked into the room." He looked down at the undressed Barbie sinking between the seat cushions, a doll-sized pink dress beside her. He looked wide-eyed at his mother, "I didn't take off her clothes," he whined with little conviction.

Vivian glanced at Timmy, then set her eyes on William. If the boys were a little older, they might have noticed a hint of a smile. She said, "I want you pair to know that what you were pretending to do with Barbie, had Barbie been a real woman, is not dirty. It is normal for a husband and wife to show affection toward one another."

Then, in a stern voice, she said, "But," and it was a heavy *but*, "you boys know better than to go into your sister's bedroom when she's not there. Mary Lynn is a young woman, and she is entitled to her privacy. Do you understand what I am saying to you?" She paused. She was clearly not in the mood to deal with their antics, especially first thing in the morning.

Heads down, eyes fixed on the turquoise broadloom, the boys silently waited for their mother to drop the other shoe.

"Do I make myself clear?"

"Yes, Mum." They said in unison. Relieved, the boys exchanged stealthy grins.

"Now, I want you to promise your sister that you will stay out of her room." And then to reinforce the order, she repeated, "I will say again, you are not allowed in Mary Lynn's room except when she gives you permission."

Vivian placed her hands on her hips, "Any more trouble today and I'll be sure to tell your father tonight when he gets home from *the* Bell!" She stared at the boys, "Again, do I make myself clear?"

Mary Lynn came around the corner, breathing heavily, "That's it, you are going to do nothing, you're not grounding them?" She stared at her mother in disbelief. "Mum!" she said, exasperated.

Vivian ignored Mary Lynn and went on, "William, I want you to march upstairs and put the Barbie doll on Mary Lynn's bed, then quickly get ready for school. It is getting late, the school bell will be ringing soon, and you do not want to be late for class."

William slumped under her piercing glare. He then noticed his sister's shiny red face and her stern, disapproving look. To his surprise, it was directed at their mother. Mary Lynn was in a tizzy. She could barely contain her anger. While she was distracted and prancing around the room, he plucked the doll and her dress from the chesterfield before they disappeared between the seat cushions. He exhaled, knowing full well he was getting off lightly and scurried to exit the room with Timmy close on his heels.

Shaking her head in disgust, Mary Lynn blocked their escape and then raged, "Never you mind, give me the doll." She looked menacingly at her brother and added, "If I ever catch you…little perverts, in my bedroom again, I will—"

"Mary Lynn, that is quite enough, young lady," Vivian chastised. She watched the boys push past their sister and run for the stairs. She sighed and peered through the bay window, then stepped into the hallway. "It's a cold morning, so don't forget to wear your toques and mitts to school."

"William…," the boys screeched to a halt on the upper stairs and looked back at their mother, "…after school on your way home, I want you to go into McGregor's store and buy today's newspaper. I will send you to school with a dime. Please do not lose it." Vivian turned her attention to her youngest and said, "Timmy, I will see you at lunch time, and we will walk home together." She closed her eyes for a moment and said, "Now, where did I leave my purse?" She paused at the bottom of the stairs. "William, what day of the week is today?"

He met his mother's gaze with a puzzled look. "Is…is it Friday?" he asked, tentatively.

"Yes, it is…Friday, November 22nd. When you are in the store, be sure to check that the date on the newspaper is today's. You will find it printed at the top of the folded newspaper," she said, looking sternly at him. "Please do not bring home yesterday's paper. Understood?"

"Uh-huh," William nodded. He considered his situation and thought this may be an opportunity to ease his way back into his mother's good graces. "Mum, today is Friday…the last day of school. When I wake up yesterday, er tomorrow, it will be Saturday and cartoons will be on TV." He looked keenly at her, "And I know what year number it is…1963," he said in an authoritative voice, visibly pleased with himself.

Vivian surveyed her son's innocent face. "Yes, yes, it is dear. Now, hurry and get ready for school. The pair of you."

Once upon a time, the firm mattress afforded Will and Veronica Greene a restful night's slumber. However, any chance of a tranquil night's sleep on the old lumpy mattress was now just a figment of their past. It noticeably sagged in the middle, forming a crescent-shaped depression stretching from the pillows to their feet. Thinking he was quite clever, Will had nicknamed the mattress Mariana.

A sliver of morning light pierced the drawn curtains and settled across his face. He rolled over onto his left side to avoid the intrusion, causing a collision between his bony elbow and his sleeping wife's tender nose.

Veronica winced, grimaced in pain and groggily said, "Goddamn it, Will." She gingerly dabbed at her nose. "Ouch. That hurt." She pulled her hand away and focused on her fingertips. "Is my nose bleeding?" she said, distressed.

Will drowsily sat up, studied her nose for a moment and replied. "Nope. I see *nu…thing,* no sign of blood." He reached out and held her face for a more thorough inspection.

"Hmmm…well, your nose is still intact and sitting nicely between your eyes."

He then noticed a red mark on the side of her nose and said, "Sorry 'bout that, babe. I was rolling over to escape the sunlight." He then conceded, "You know, this damn mattress doesn't help. We always end up fighting over who owns the middle ground." Will leaned in, squeezed his lips together and purred, "Slide over and give us a big wet one, you…You, Goddess of the morning light."

"Stop it. God…No! Stay away." Veronica stuck out her hand, nearly poking him in the eye. She grimaced and grumbled, "Morning breath…gross!" She then added, "You're right, though, we seriously need to consider saving for a new mattress. I am so tired of rolling into the centre or inadvertently being assaulted." She looked at him and twitched her nose like Elizabeth Montgomery in *Bewitched*.

"I wholeheartedly agree, and this time we should purchase the bigger Queen-size mattress." Will rolled onto his back and stretched just as their son, Adam, sprinted through the bedroom doorway and leapt into the air in full Superman flight. He landed on the bed between his parents.

"Hey, Champ, how'd you sleep?" asked Will.

Veronica stared at the two of them. "Well, now I know why our bed is falling apart."

"You think that's the reason, do you…" Will grinned and winked oddly at his wife. He turned his attention to his son. "Hey Champ, what would you like for breakfast?" He smiled at his son and thought about the immeasurable love he felt for his two children. Adam was a typical three-year-old with gangly appendages and a head too big for his scrawny frame. He was at the age where the little boy had outdistanced the baby. He was a good-looking kid with hazel eyes and a mop of sandy blonde hair. Will honestly hoped that his son's big head also encompassed a big brain.

"Well, should we have eggs and bacon on this fine Saturday morning, or do you want the same old thing you have every other morning?"

"Cereal," Adam replied.

"Cereal it shall be." Will slid out of bed, pulled on a T-shirt, tucked it in his pajama pants, then scooped up his son. "To the bathroom we go, young apprentice." Again, he winked oddly at his wife, then produced the requisite swooshing sounds as he flew Adam across the bedroom, into the hallway, past the children's bedroom and into the bathroom.

Adam pushed his pajamas down to his ankles, leaned against the basin and pointed his penis at the blue toilet water. Just as he had been instructed. Father and son waited, but nothing happened. They continued to wait. He looked up expectantly at his dad. Will slowly turned the faucet until a burbling stream of water ran into the sink.

Adam began to fidget as he peered into the toilet. "My penis *breaked*, Daddy," he said apprehensively.

"Listen to the running water, try to relax, be loose." He looked down and smiled as Adam twisted and wiggled to his own internal beat. They waited. "Hmmm…well, Champ, we can try again after breakfast—"

"Tinklin'," Adam said exuberantly, laughed and threw his arms up. A surging yellow stream of piss splashed on the toilet seat and showered the toilet reservoir.

"Oh, shit…shit," Will stammered. He slid across the floor and, with only one thought on his mind, tried to block the spray. Too late.

With his pajamas around his ankles, his arms raised above his head, Adam excitedly twisted his tiny body toward the wall and to his astonishment, the stream of piss followed. He was elated. He then swung his body to the left and watched as the yellow stream played catch-up. He laughed with abandon at this new game.

"Oh Christ," Will murmured. Palms out, he reacted like a goalie attempting to block the spray; however, he lacked the hand-eye coordination.

Adam laughed at his dad's wildly animated circular hand motions.

Will frowned as he suddenly pictured himself as Mr. Miyagi's apprentice—wax on, wax off.

Adam dropped his head and watched the weakening stream of urine. He dropped his arms and said, "Done." He hauled up his pajamas to his belly button and said again, "Done, Daddy." He yawned and stared happily at his dad's shiny red face and sopping wet T-shirt.

Will shook his head, disgusted with himself; clearly, his defensive moves had been pathetic and futile. His T-shirt and pajama pants were soaked with urine. While still in a semi-crouched position, he slowly turned and inspected the bathroom. He shook his head again; he had forgotten to lift the toilet seat. Piss pooled on the seat and then trickled down the basin. A yellow puddle moved across the linoleum floor toward the low corner.

While he scrutinized the mayhem, he accepted that swinging his own arms to block the spray had obviously compounded the chaos. He sighed, looked down at his wet T-shirt, then eyed Adam standing in a pool of urine. Will tried but couldn't hold back; he erupted in laughter. Adam, confused, watched his dad, and then he, too, burst out laughing.

Will looked over his shoulder as he heard the *plink, plink* of piss as it travelled down the vanity and splashed on the floor. He groaned; a twinge in his back forced him to reach for the vanity as he stood up. He then struggled to remove the wet T-shirt. Once removed, he dropped it on the floor, stepped to the sink and copied the technique made famous by *Medical Center's* Doctor Joe Gannon, washing his hands and arms up to the elbows. He cautiously picked up Adam, set him in the sink and washed his hands and feet. To his surprise, Adam's pajama bottoms were dry. He lowered him to the floor and said, "All right, Adam…you go to the kitchen, I will be there in a minute."

Adam left the bathroom and skipped along the hallway. Will dropped the bath towel on the floor and, using his foot, dragged it along the base of the vanity, around the toilet and along the baseboard. He carefully picked up the urine-soaked towel and T-shirt and pitched them into the sink. He surveyed his handiwork, nodded at his reflection in the mirror, and thought Job well done.

He walked down the hallway and into the children's bedroom. Ellie was asleep, cradling her Cabbage Patch doll. On the floor beside the bed, a Care Bear and a purple My Little Pony were cuddling. Protruding from under the bed, a Speak and Spell hummed quietly. Will dropped to one knee, winced and flicked the *off* switch. He suspected he would need some Ben Gay ointment on his aching lower back. With the assistance of Ellie's bed, he gained his feet, then stepped on a Transformer as he moved over to Adam's bed. The blankets hung off the side, twisted and bunched together. He laid a hand on the mattress sheet. Disappointment washed over him.

He strode down the hallway into the bedroom and gawked at the motionless lump curled up under the blankets and said, "Once again, *your* son did not manage to make it through the night—his waterworks soaked the mattress." While waiting for a reply, he absently scratched his genitals. He then reminded his wife, "Last night, I mentioned it was a mistake to give *your* son that drink of orange juice before bed." The lump remained motionless.

Finally, there was a rustle of sheets. Veronica sat up, yawned, then patted her nose. She looked at her fingertips, relieved to see no evidence of blood. She eyed Will, mustered her best indignant look, then lay back and pulled the covers tightly around her shoulders. She closed her eyes.

"Nice try. Good morning, Ronnie," Will said. He smirked, "I do not want to belabour the point, my dear, but…we both know why Adam's bed sheets are wet…" He inhaled and waited for her to challenge him. He stared at his bride of nine years, then decided to move on, take the high road. "Oh, and by the way, your son made a mess in the bathroom, so watch where you tread." He chuckled and went on, "I tell ya, the kid has a bladder like a racehorse."

He walked to the tallboy dresser where he owned the bottom two drawers. After a struggle to get his jeans on, he moved to the closet and retrieved his favourite green-and-yellow striped golf shirt. A year ago, he was wearing the same golf shirt when one of Ronnie's girlfriends commented that he looked like a young Arnold Palmer. While he sauntered along the hallway to the kitchen, he imagined life as a professional golfer.

Adam stood patiently by the table waiting for his dad. Will entered the kitchen, carefully picked up his son, put him in the booster chair and said, "Well, let's see what we have in the way of cereal." He opened the cupboard, "Froot Loops or Franken Berry?" He looked at his son for a reaction. Nothing.

Adam was preoccupied watching a spider slide down its web. The spider tentatively reached for the table surface. Will decided on a different tack. He looked into the cupboard and said, "Oh, here's my favourite cereal made with whole grain wheat…yummy and healthy for your tummy." He reached for the Shreddies box.

"Loops, p'ease."

Will sighed, "Froot Loops it is."

Ellie walked into the kitchen, yawned mightily, and flopped down in the chair opposite her brother. She leaned forward and put her elbows on the table.

"Good morning, Ellie," Will said.

Meanwhile, the large spider had descended and planted all eight legs firmly on the table. Houston, we have touchdown. It was inspecting the large impediment in its way—Ellie's arms.

Will poured the Froot Loops into the special bowl with suction cups for feet and drenched the cereal with skim milk. As he moved from the counter to the table, his thoughts were on keeping the bowl's contents from landing on the clean floor.

Adam grinned and pointed, "'pider."

Will stuck the bowl to the table, looked across at Ellie and said, "What would you like for breakfast…" His eyes refocused on the enormous hairy spider squaring off against his daughter's forearms. He gasped and recoiled, stiffened, then lunged for the tissue box on the counter. He quickly realized the sensible move would be to pounce and capture the spider—he smirked—he planned to contain, then extinguish the enemy.

Ellie shrieked, "Daddy, don't hurt it." With youthful vitality and precision, she scooped up the spider and casually carried it to the side door. She opened the door and put her new pet outside, against the snowdrift by the house.

Will watched and grudgingly acknowledged that his daughter didn't care whether it slithered, slimed, or squawked; she would come to the creature's rescue. He exhaled and stuck the crumpled tissues in his jeans' pocket.

"Ellie. Hurry and close the door; we want to keep the cold air from getting inside."

"I' goin' to name my spider…Esmerelda," she said with conviction as she closed the door.

Adam watched excitedly, clapping and laughing as his sister rescued the spider. Milk sloshed and splashed from his bowl, chunks of Froot Loops, like multicoloured sticky little projectiles, escaped his mouth. An intact orange Froot Loop found refuge on his chin.

Veronica shuffled into the kitchen with the weekly flyers tucked neatly under her arm, took in the scene, poured a cup of coffee, added cream and two heaping teaspoons of sugar, then sat next to her daughter.

Adam had removed the Froot Loop from his chin and was attempting to slide it onto his finger.

Veronica sat at the table, wrapped in a yellow bathrobe cinched tight around her waist—her favourite birthday present from Will. And she wore pink furry slippers—her favourite birthday present from the children. She peered into her mocha-coloured coffee, took a slow sip, and enjoyed the warmth of the mug in her hands. She reflected on their worthwhile purchase of the sleek and shiny perk-coffee machine with its adjustable brew strength and automatic timer—modern technology, she mused. She exhaled and said, "Well…well, what on God's green earth just happened in my kitchen?" She brought the warm mug to her lips.

Will's head popped up. He mulled over a response while he wiped up the milk and cereal chunks stuck to the table.

"Daddy was goin' to 'quish Esmerelda, but I stopped him," Ellie said, pleased with her good deed. "It's my friend. It's outside to catch insects, then I goin' to put it in a jar, in my bedroom."

"Now, Ellie," Will began, "we should leave the spider outside where he can spin a new web and catch lots and lots of insects. Don't you agree he'd be happier outside and free, not in the house, trapped in a jar?" Will gauged his daughter's facial reaction and knew he was unlikely to win her over.

He decided he needed to implement Plan B. Any dad worth his salt should have a fallback plan. He leaned back against the counter, crossed his arms and said, "Listen, Ellie, that spider…that huge spider, is not like the friendly neighbourhood spiders we usually get in the house. I wouldn't be surprised if it were one of those non-radioactive spiders."

Will looked beyond Ellie and fixed his gaze on Veronica, sipping her coffee. He attempted to wink. She was having none of it. He shook his head, refusing to accept her dismissal and said, "Besides, young princess Ariel, I was concerned that it would jump on your arm and crawl up to your face."

Ellie stared wide-eyed at her dad. Confused, she glanced at her mum and felt reassured by the smirk on her face. With renewed confidence, she said, "Daddy, spiders don't do that. They are more 'fraid of us."

"Oh, Ellie, I don't know about that. Spiders are always looking for secretive places to lay their eggs—"

"Will!" Veronica interjected. She regarded her husband quizzically, then anxiously looked at her daughter.

Ellie appeared aghast or excited at the thought of spider eggs.

Adam had both hands firmly cupping his ears.

Veronica raised her head, through narrowed eyes, her voice taut with frustration, "What is your deal! Are you trying to traumatize our children?" She noticed Ellie nervously fidgeting on the chair. "Ellie, don't listen to him, he's just being silly and not very funny. I am so happy you saved the spider and put it outside. That was the right thing to do, sweetie."

Veronica looked across the table at Adam as he scraped the last of the cereal from the side of his bowl. She held the coffee mug to her lips and sipped as the tight, thin furrows across her brow slowly retreated. She put the mug down, shifted the chair closer to Ellie and said, "What would you like for breakfast, my love?"

Rather than change the subject as Veronica obviously intended, Will doubled down and said, "Just last week, Ronnie, we watched an old episode of Rod Serling's *The Night Gallery*. It was a spellbinding and unsettling story about an earwig that slithers into the deplorable Mr. Macy's, E-A-R, and by the end of the episode, remember? …the insect burrowed through his grey matter, only to emerge from his opposite E-A-R."

With his gaze fixed on her, eyebrows raised, he taunted, "Come now, you must remember, Mr. Macy believed he'd beaten the grim reaper, but discovers the *little beastie* had laid eggs mid-journey." He opened his eyes wide, "You know, come to think of it, this story may have been based on actual behaviour observed in the animal kingdom. Well, Ronnie…what do you have to say now?" he asked, not expecting a response. Satisfied, he puffed out his chest.

Veronica scowled at him, "Hey, bub, what side of the bed did you get out of this morning?"

"That's just TV. It's made b'lieve," Ellie said with the determined conviction of a five-and-a-half-year-old.

"That's right, sweetie. It's make-believe. It's just fiction. Daddy was pulling your leg," she said reassuringly.

Ellie looked down and scrutinized her legs.

Chinook padded into the kitchen, noticed the tablecloth leaking milk, cereal on the floor, and scurried over to mop up the mess. She was a Heinz-57, a mutt rescued years before the children had entered the picture. She was an amiable dog, but as she aged, she developed troubling habits that concerned Veronica.

Adam leaned forward and watched Chinook clean the floor beneath his booster chair. He reached out and grabbed her ears. The dog raised her head, bared her teeth, and snarled at the intrusion. Glimpsing a snout full of yellow canine and incisor teeth, Adam howled, pulled back, and muttered, "Oh shit, oh shit." Satisfied the threat had abated, Chinook lowered her head and happily resumed mopping the floor with her tongue.

Veronica almost spilled her coffee as she leapt up and rushed to position herself between Adam and the dog.

With the floor wet and glistening and not a Froot Loop in sight, Chinook flopped down beside Adam's chair, licked her muzzle, then eyed her approaching master.

Looking dismayed, Veronica looked to Will for a reaction. He was deep in thought and seemed unconcerned about what had just happened. She exhaled, "Some time soon, we need to discuss our four-legged family member. And, secondly, someone used a bad word, and now it is part of Adam's vocabulary…and I do have my suspicions." Veronica challenged.

Ellie giggled. "Daddy, did you say a bad word?"

Veronica helped Adam out of the booster chair, picked up her coffee mug and moved to the counter next to Will. She looked at Ellie and said, "My money is also on the other *adult* in the kitchen." Smiling, she looked down at *sticky* Adam. "Ellie, please take your brother to the bathroom and wash his hands and face for mommy." She then cautioned, "Be careful, you don't want to get soap in your brother's eyes." Ellie sprang into action, took Adam's hand, and led him out of the kitchen.

THREE

Will watched and waited until the children left the kitchen. He turned his head and eyed his bewildered wife. At that moment, the morning light burst through the window above the sink, casting an amber glow across her shoulders and face. The sight of his wife bathed in a blaze of light caught him off guard. A warm smile crossed his lips.

Veronica loosened her yellow robe, oblivious to his stare. Underneath, she wore her favourite X-Large, orange T-shirt with a crusty decal of a toothy Garfield the cat. Pink and yellow knee socks covered her shapely legs.

Will broke the silence, "Well, my dear, I think the *shit* is on me…not literally, of course," he deadpanned.

She whirled around in a blur of colours. "What the heck was that?" she whispered through her teeth, "talk about out of the frying pan and into the fire, sheesh." She threw her arms up in frustration. "Like, what were you thinking, Will? Tell me, what the hell is up with you this morning?"

"What do you mean?"

She exhaled, drained her coffee, placed the mug in the sink and then rubbed her temples. "For Christ's sake, Will…telling Ellie that a spider could burrow into her head!"

"Oh, that. I panicked. As I was saying it…I knew it was a fuckin' dumb thing to say."

"You think!"

"In my defence, you know I have a…a spider thing. I don't want to say phobia, but yeah…ah, besides, the damn thing was about the size of a frisbee with brown fur and eight legs—could've been ten legs." He nervously shifted his feet, eyed his beautiful yet perturbed wife, "Jeepers, Ronnie, I could have worn it as a toupee and tied the legs under my chin—not that my hair is thinning, mind you." He flashed an ingratiating, toothy grin.

She looked sideways, obviously not ready to be *Will-charmed*.

"I could see Ellie was keen to adopt a new pet and damned if I wanted her to know that her six-foot-two, strong and macho—"

Veronica snorted derisively, "Six foot-two!"

"Alright, let's not be nasty. I suppose I was…a wee bit apprehensive to corral a spider high tailin' it across the table…" He sighed. "So, I reacted. I deflected. Happy now? I messed up. However, on the bright side, neither of us wants our daughter to think her dad is a wimp, right?"

Veronica walked over to the table, sat down, and ignored his efforts to win her over. "Whatever," she said in her best Who are you trying to bullshit voice. With her elbows on the table, she used both hands to massage the pressure building behind her eyes. "You would rather your daughter have nightmares about spiders laying eggs in her ears." She exclaimed.

"Granted, point made." He then confessed, "I should have thought about the possible repercussions before belching out a crazy story concerning insects depositing eggs in human brains." He watched her for a moment, then said, "Ronnie, I hold Rod Serling personally responsible."

She did not offer a reply.

Will noticed Adam's empty cereal bowl and realized Ellie had not eaten breakfast. He went on, "She's a bright kid and resilient. I'm sure there won't be any lasting negative effects on her psyche."

He raised his voice, "Ellie, how 'bout Froot Loops for breakfast?" Without waiting for a reply, he walked to the cupboard and reached for the bag of Quaker oatmeal. By the time Ellie entered the kitchen, a steaming hot bowl of porridge was on the table waiting for her.

Adam, with wet hands and a clean face, ambled in behind his sister, knelt at the refrigerator, and began to rearrange the coloured magnetic letters clinging to the fridge door.

Will grinned. The letters were in alphabetical order in five rigidly straight rows. He knew she would deny it, but to his eye, Veronica must have used her obsessive-compulsive ruler to align each row.

Ellie sat down and peered into the porridge.

"Sugar or maple syrup?" he asked, then added, "I don't understand why my daughter prefers oatmeal over Franken Berry with its dee…licious marshmallow bits in chocolate and strawberry flavours." He shook his head in mock disbelief.

"Sugar p'ease…cause, Daddy, other cereal is full-a bad 'gredients," she replied. Her brow knitted together as she looked earnestly at him. She was a five-and-a-half-year-old replica of her mother, both in appearance and in temperament. He sprinkled a heaping teaspoon of sugar on top of the steaming oats.

Will grinned, "You are just too smart for your age, young lady."

Chinook pulled herself up from under the table and padded across the floor until her wet nose touched the side door.

Will walked over and opened the door. Chinook scurried outside as a rush of chilly air burst into the house. He quickly closed the door, then turned to Veronica. "Well, my dear, what's on the Saturday agenda?"

She eyed him warily, then decided it was time to move beyond the spider kerfuffle. She sighed, "Well, the other day I said to Ellie that we'd get started on her summer dress."

Will appeared confused.

"You know, the yellow and lime green print dress." She looked at him and shook her head, "Just last week, I showed you the pattern. Anyway, Ellie's been pestering to wear it. The poor girl says she can't wait until summer. It may hang on her a bit now, but fingers crossed…it will fit her by summer."

She smiled at Ellie, "Porridge not too hot, sweetie?"

Ellie nodded.

"This morning, we'll pin the pattern to the material and get it all cut out, ready for sewing. Once that's done," she put her hand on the grocery flyers, "I'll check the flyers and plan my route to the grocery stores based on which stores have the best deals."

"Interesting," Will said.

"Grocery shopping is a science, bub." She exhaled, "Once back home, the groceries will need to be unpacked and stored away in their designated spots."

"Designated spots?"

"Piss off," Veronica mumbled under her breath. "Then…there are five overflowing loads of laundry waiting to be sorted, washed, delicates in the dryer, towels, sheets and pants on the clothesline." She caught his eye and sighed heavily, "Finally, I will disinfect the sorry mess you left in the bathroom."

"What do you mean, I cleaned the bathroom?"

"I noticed." She exhaled again, "FYI, the wall and floor need to be scrubbed with Mr. Clean—yellowish streaks are already noticeable on the wall." She pursed her lips, "Oh yes. I neglected to mention…with the kids' help, we will change the bed sheets and tidy up their bedroom." She took a moment to survey the kitchen. "And if that is not enough…someone has to plan and execute dinner."

"Hmmm…well…vegetarian tonight?"

She smirked, then looked expectantly at him. "And you, William, what do you have lined up for today?"

"Oh, William, is it?" He abruptly realized that during all the excitement, he had forgotten to pour his morning coffee. He filled a mug with coffee, added a hint of milk and stole two quick swigs. He leaned back against the counter, smiled, and said, "So, my dear, your day really isn't too busy…unlike mine,

I have a full schedule. While you're doing your thing in the house this morning, sewing and such, I will be changing the engine oil on the Tempo."

Veronica lifted her head.

He answered her silent query, "Don't worry, I will have the oil changed before you're ready to grocery shop. Now. Let me see…after lunch, I'm thinkin' the plan is to take the kids and Chinook for a walk at the conservation point."

"All that fuss, you get your clothes oily and grease under your nails. Why not just take the car to a garage for an oil change?"

Will tilted his head and said, "Come on, Ronnie. You know why I prefer to change the oil myself, and besides, I like tinkering with the engine, changing sparkplugs, cap and rotor, filters—your basic weekend mechanic stuff." He sipped the coffee and met her gaze. "Saves us a few coins for the piggy bank too." He laboured to wink.

"Well then, we need to buy you cheap coveralls. At least then, I'll be able to wash them by hand, so I don't get grease in my washing machine." She opened the first grocery flyer, smoothed out the creases, and began the search for weekly deals.

"Deal," Will said. "Hey, if you're not too busy this aft, you should accompany us to the park. It will be fun—exercise and fresh air." He sat down on the closest chair, "Hmmm…come to think of it, after our outdoor adventure, if time permits, I'll swing by Blockbuster Video and rent *The Little Mermaid* and pick out a new release for the adults."

Two muffled barks momentarily distracted him.

"Now, where was I…Oh yes, a movie we missed when it played at Satellite Cinema, *Raiders of the Lost Ark* was just released to video. It's Steven Spielberg's latest, set in the 1930s, about an adventure-seeking, globe-trotting archaeologist racing against the Nazis to find a religious chest that contains mystical or sacred objects. According to one review, the action during the first fifteen minutes alone is worth the price of admission."

Through narrowed eyes, he peered across the table, waited a moment for his offer to settle, and then tried to comprehend Veronica's demeanour. Her attention was squarely focused on the flyers. A scraping sound, like fingernails on a blackboard, followed by two shrill barks, signalled Chinook's eagerness to come in from the cold. Veronica looked up, glanced at the side door, then nonchalantly eyed Will before resuming her inspection of the grocery flyer.

Her disinterest in his movie choice was undeniable. He pushed on, "It stars Harrison Ford." He punctuated the actor's name with a wonky wink. He sipped his coffee, watched, and waited. Head down, she appeared indifferent and replied by flipping to the next page of the flyer. Will exhaled loudly, "Well then…obviously, you are not interested in Spielberg's latest masterpiece." With little enthusiasm, he said, "There is, however, another movie that's causing an awful lot of Oscar buzz in Tinseltown, *The Dead Prophets Society*. It stars Mork, you know, ah, Robin Williams."

Veronica looked up and, with a glimmer in her eye, corrected him, "The movie is *The Dead Poets Society*." Then in a lively voice she added, "Cindy at work saw it at the movie theatre, and she raved about it, said it's one of the best movies of the year. She went on and on about Robin Williams and his outstanding acting."

Taken aback, Will said, "Okay…great. *Dead Zombie Poets*, it is." Finally, he had her attention, he thought. Wasting little time, he went on, "On the way home from the conservation point, maybe I'll swing by the liquor store and pick up a bottle of Inniskillin's finest Niagara red." He dropped his head, eyed her, and whispered conspiratorially, "You know what, babe?"

"No…what?"

"It just occurred to me that I should take the kite to the point—supposed to be plenty breezy this afternoon. After a walk through the woods, I'll take the kids over to the open field. The little rascals and Nook will get plenty of exercise chasing after the kite." He noticed Veronica's curiosity was rapidly waning. She was peeking at the flyers.

"Hear me out, we're getting to the good part. Then, after a warm bath on a full stomach, our two precocious and precious offspring will be exhausted." Will grinned knowingly and said, "According to my abacus, by 6:30 p.m., it will be time to load the VCR and fire up *The Little Mermaid*." He peeked over the mug at her. She appeared more receptive. He continued, "I reckon, nay, I am confident that after watching Ariel and Flounder swimming the seven seas for 90 minutes, the little scoundrels will be dog-tired and asleep before we can get them tucked in."

Will chuckled mischievously and rubbed his hands together. "Then, my dear, we will have the rest of the evening to ourselves." As Veronica contemplated his elaborate scheme, he sipped coffee, took stock, and tried to wink at his wife.

Veronica scrutinized her husband and then said, "Will Greene, you are devious. And, for your wife's sake, please stop trying to wink. You look deficient." She then smiled, "Hmmm…and when did you consummate this plan?"

Will professed ignorance and then said in his most persuasive voice, "Oh, you are nimble. You may not know this, Ronnie, but whenever people comment on your beauty, I set them straight and say: 'I married her *not* for her beauty but for her superior intellect.'"

"Wonderful. And pray tell, who are these admirable people?"

"Who are these people, you ask. Well, they are not your garden-variety, plain vanilla type, they are the influential, the upper-crust, the blue bloods—"

The dog barked and continued her assault on the side door. Will sprang up, boogied across the kitchen, and opened the door. Chinook charged into the house, shaking vigorously from head to tail. She padded over to the refrigerator, leaving a slushy path from the door to her snow-covered snout. Sitting quietly on the floor, Adam had rearranged ten magnetic letters on the fridge door.

Will eyed the dog, then spotted Adam's handiwork. He muttered under his breath, "DOG, EAR…SHIT, oh man, here we go again."

FOUR

Twenty-five years before William's parents moved into their new home on Gilwood School Drive, Albert and Tilly McGregor converted the lower level of their home to a general store. The McGregors enjoyed their simple life in the small town of Millington. With the influx of World War II veterans and their families moving into the new Gilwood family-planned community, the elderly couple's desire to escape the hustle and bustle became a topic of nightly discussion. By 1950, Millington's population had surpassed six thousand.

Well into their seventies, with rounded backs and creaky knees, the couple had had enough. Retirement beckoned. During the summer of 1953, a buyer interested in continuing the McGregor tradition purchased the property. While packing up their belongings, Tilly suggested keeping the outdoor sign, McGregor General Store, as a memento of their happy, prosperous life on Gilwood School Drive. Albert, however, reminded his wife that he had repaired and repainted the sign more times than he had fingers—it held no sentimental value, only hardship. At the end of the day, he decided, it was a decision best left to the new owners.

In August 1953, young buyers from Vancouver, British Columbia, moved into the home and reopened the general store on the ground floor. The couple used their meagre savings to extend the parking lot and to spruce up the store's interior with new shelving and a coat of paint. With their savings exhausted, the weathered sign remained above the entrance where it had endured the elements for three decades.

*   *   *

The general store was adjacent to Gilwood Public School, situated at the intersection of County Road Three and Gilwood School Drive. From the school, it would take William ten minutes to walk home, assuming he didn't doddle.

The door's hinges groaned as he entered the general store.

"Hello, William. School out already?" asked the store's proprietor from behind the counter.

"Hi, Mrs. Gregor," William said. He stood in the doorway, inhaling the sweet and musty smells while marvelling at the clutter and the overstocked shelves. The general store was crammed from floor to ceiling with a broad range of products: garden tools, vacuum tubes for radios and televisions, plumbing materials, a variety of widgets, school supplies, last-minute groceries, and more.

William eyed the rickety three-tier cabinet. Each shelf held four two-quart Mason jars filled to the rim with a variety of candy: Chupa lollipops, Pixy Stix, Peeps, Atomic Fireballs, Saltwater taffy, and an assortment of hard candies and soft chews. A faded handwritten sign taped to the cabinet offered: '3 Candies for One Penny.' His eyes lingered on the sweets as he reached for the stack of newspapers.

Leaning over the counter, the proprietor said, "That's today's paper, just arrived." The proprietor produced a small brown paper bag from under the counter. She blew into it, reached into a mason jar and dropped several black balls into the paper bag. "Here, you are, hon," she smiled, handing William the bag. He laid the dime on the counter, tucked the newspaper under his arm, and thanked her for the candy.

Outside the store, he spied the contents in the bag, counting six black balls. He gave each of his Gilwood school friends one black ball; that left one for himself, and the last one he dropped in his pants' pocket.

Scottie, who disliked licorice-flavoured candy, pitched the black ball to his twin brother. Stuart, wearing mitts, moved to intercept, but failed to catch the projectile. He turned and watched it vanish into a snowbank alongside the two-lane street. He kicked around the snowbank, hoping to find the black ball. He looked back at Scottie, shrugged and held up his empty hands.

Stuart rarely got upset with his *younger* brother. At birth, he beat him to the finish line by eighteen minutes. Stuart was quiet and studious, while Scottie was expansive and spirited. By the time the boys reached school age, Scottie was repeatedly getting mixed up in some predicament and would inevitably drag his brother along for support. Stuart, however, relished his role as *older* brother and was always prepared to defend Scottie.

"Sorry, Stu," said Scottie. He then jumped over the snowbank into the ditch. He straddled the frozen stream at the bottom of the ditch. On milder days, the runoff would flow westward along the ditch to the end of Gilwood School Drive, spilling out into the old orchard of a bygone era.

Jimmy Henderson popped the candy into his mouth. "Thanks, man." He walked over next to the ditch, looked around, and decided the black ball was lost to the snow.

William, Stuart, Jimmy, and Turtle jumped over the ditch and began walking along the middle of the street toward their homes. Scottie slid along the frozen stream, keeping pace with the other boys.

Turtle nudged Stuart, then nodded his head toward Scottie and said, "For twins, you two sure look different."

"That's 'cause we're not identical twins," Stuart said, exasperated. "I've told you a bazillion times, we're dizygotic twins."

"It's funny when you say dizzy…gothic," Turtle laughed.

William glanced at Turtle, his next-door neighbour, and said, "Hey, when is your dad home from Green…land?"

"Mom told us he gets home on Saturday. He's been in Greenland on the DEW line for six months," Turtle said.

"Today is Friday. Tomorrow is Saturday," William informed him.

Turtle's face lit up.

*   *   *

Turtle's mother had been part of the Canadian war effort, working in a retooled factory assembling portable radios for the military. In 1947, she quit when it was time to welcome their first child. It was, in fact, a mutual decision between employer and employee, as the company was again retooling for domestic sales and male labourers were preferred for production lines and shift work.

During the Second World War, Turtle's father enlisted and was trained as a heavy machinery mechanic. During the three years he spent overseas, he enjoyed his time as a mechanic and appreciated the camaraderie of military life. Once back in Canada, he married his high school sweetheart and reenlisted with the Canadian Armed Forces.

David and Hillary Tuttle accepted the challenges inherent in military life. Lengthy overseas assignments and postings to the Canadian Arctic were integral to his military career. During his father's absences, on the first day of each month, Turtle would spring out of bed, barrel into the kitchen, and flip the page on the wall calendar to the next month. He would then count the number of weeks until his father's return. Hillary Tuttle operated a strict household and spared no effort to keep her children busy with school and household chores. She also insisted that one night a week would be designated as family board game night.

*   *   *

Scottie grew tired of sliding along the frozen stream. He plowed through the snowbank, caught up with the gang, and asked, "Do you guys want to hang out at the towers?" Stuart nodded at his younger brother, then turned and walked up the gravel driveway toward their home.

Jimmy looked at Scottie and said, "I'll meet you guys at the hydro towers. I'm going to change out of my school clothes and drop off my knapsack." Due to a summer growth spurt, Jimmy had one pair of pants and two shirts that still accommodated his expanding girth. Jimmy persevered.

"Hey, Jimmy, what books did your teacher give you today?" William asked confidentially.

Scottie overheard. Concerned, he said, "You got homework?"

"No. Not really. Mrs. Thorpe lent me a couple of interesting books to read," Jimmy said.

"Oh…I don't like reading or rithmetic," Scottie laughed and went on, "I like comic books—Batman and Fantastic Four." Relieved, he waved, lurched to his left, and followed his brother up the driveway.

William sidestepped and moved closer to Jimmy. He was too young to comprehend how special his friend was, but he knew Jimmy was smart-as-all-get-out.

*   *   *

Mrs. Thorpe had taught at Gilwood Elementary for twenty-three years, teaching students from grades one to eight. When Jimmy entered her grade three class, he was the third Henderson child, after Karen and Dean, assigned to her classroom. Within weeks, she recognized his *potential.* She was so enamoured with his intellect that she arranged a series of provincially sanctioned intelligence tests. Six weeks later, the test results arrived at the school.

Mrs. Thorpe then found herself in a quandary. After poring over Jimmy's extraordinary test results, for reasons known only to Mrs. Thorpe, and knowing it was inappropriate and contrary to elementary teachers' pedagogical rules of conduct, she, nevertheless, did not enlighten Mrs. Henderson.

When she privately shared the results with Jimmy, she grinned broadly and said he was a bona fide genius. She could hardly contain herself as she gushed and told her star pupil that he might very well be the *most intelligent boy in all Upper Canada*. Jimmy, uneasy with the accolades, had shrugged, looked sideways at her, and said the multiple tests were easy-peasy.

She immediately set in motion several extracurricular activities designed just for her star pupil. Jimmy especially enjoyed the two books Mrs. Thorpe assigned to him every Friday. She picked books from her own collection, borrowed books from colleagues, and from the public library. Jimmy, the genius of Upper Canada, never failed to read both books from cover to cover.

In her heart, she believed it was her civic duty to guide Jimmy's intellectual growth for as long as he was a student at Gilwood Public. Secretly, she wished to maintain their relationship well beyond eighth grade.

*   *   *

William watched Jimmy slowly walk along the middle of the street. He waited, then again asked, "What books did Mrs. Thorpe give you this week?"

"She gave me a Farley Mowat book, *Owl's in the Family*. It's about a boy named Billy who saves owls." Jimmy inhaled, looked sideways at William, and said, "I told her you might like to read it too, and she said, 'That is a grand idea…tell William there's no need to rush through the book, reading is not a race.'" He then peered into his knapsack and said, "The other book is *The Apprenticeship of Duddy Kravitz*. Mrs. Thorpe said it's about a boy growing up poor in a Montreal neighbourhood."

He hesitated, glanced at William, and said, "Tomorrow, I'll give you the *Owl's in the Family* book if you want to read it?"

William nodded, "Far out. Sure, man." He was confident Jimmy would devour the *Owl* book that night and knock off *Duddy Kravitz* by Monday.

Jimmy threw the knapsack back over his shoulder, jumped over the ditch and said, "See you guys at the hydro towers."

A minute later, Turtle pointed at William's house. Leaning against the front door, his head barely visible above the bottom panel of the screen door, Timmy watched and waited patiently for his brother to get home. Turtle saluted, then ran home.

William stepped into the house, dropped his winter gear, pulled off his boots, eyed Timmy, and said, "Where's Mum?"

"Ou'side doin' clothes 'tuff," said Timmy.

He nodded and remembered that Friday is laundry day.

"Is that you, William?" Vivian asked as she entered from the kitchen side door, carrying a basket of cold, stiff bed sheets fresh from the clothesline. She glanced at the clock, "Oh my…my show is about to begin."

William thought about how much his mum enjoyed her *Soap operas* and how his dad referred to the television as the *boob tube* and just a waste of time. He walked into the kitchen and dropped the newspaper on the table. His mum laboured under the heavy basket of clean laundry. He offered to carry the basket to the living room.

"That's all right, dear. I've got this. If you would scamper upstairs and bring down the blue hamper filled with clean clothes from my bedroom, that would be an immense help."

He retreated and galloped up the stairs as organ music blared from the TV. From the second floor, he yelled, "Mum, your TV show is starting..."

Vivian limped into the living room and dropped the heavy basket next to the ironing board. She wondered if her son might be showing an interest in *As the World Turns*. She was enthused about the day's episode: Penny still has amnesia, Lisa's extra-marital affair with Bruce was about to fail, as well as her marriage to Bob, and Lisa's son Tom, who is sick…she stared up at the ceiling and whispered, "Now what else is going on in their world?" She closed her eyes, "…Oh yes, poor David is mourning the death of his wife, Betty." She sighed, "My goodness, so many story lines."

William shuffled into the living room, dropped the full hamper and dragged it to the ironing board.

Vivian cheerfully said, "Thanks, dear. Are you going to watch *As the World Turns* with me?"

"I can't," he answered between breaths, "I tol' my friends I'd meet them over at the hydro towers."

With a whiff of disappointment, she said, "Oh, very well. I will tell you all about the episode later. You go now and have fun at the old Gilwood orchard. And William, please take your brother along. The poor boy has been cooped up in the house all afternoon. A little exercise and fresh air will do him wonders."

William felt a warmth moving up his neck into his cheeks. His shoulders slumped. He felt doomed. He didn't want Timmy hanging with him and his friends. It just wasn't cool.

Vivian sensed his internal struggle and said, "You should be thankful that you have a brother who looks up to you and wants to be by your side. And William, dinner is at six…sharp. That means inside the house by 5 o'clock. Do not be late."

William had no choice; his mother had spoken. He turned to leave the living room. A glint from the chesterfield captured his attention. A tiny black object protruded from between the cushions. A momentary sense of shame washed over him as he recognized Barbie's black stiletto shoe. He stealthily reached out and, with his index finger, pushed the toy shoe deeper into the separation between cushions. He then looked sideways at his mother. Vivian absently slid the iron over one of Pete's white work shirts while she watched the TV daytime drama. He exhaled, relieved.

The boys walked west along Gilwood Street, shading their eyes from the lowering sun. William tilted his head back, exhaling a mouthful of air, then said, "Look, Timmy, I can see my breath." Timmy watched the plume of moisture slowly ascend before dissipating above their heads. A moment later, an exposed culvert marked the end of the road. William stopped and squinted ahead at the big tree and the old orchard in the distance. He thought of his teacher, who had just discussed Millington's most famous family, the Gilwoods. The boys jumped over the culvert into the old meadow overgrown with juniper and sumac shrubbery. They stumbled along the snow-covered trail that would guide them to the old Gilwood orchard.

*　　*　　*

In the 1860s, on the northern outskirts of Millington, the Gilwoods purchased a two-hundred-acre parcel of Crown land. The Gilwood clan installed fencing around a seventy-acre section for grazing livestock, and the arable land to the south was cleared to grow cash crops. An apple orchard, planted by first-generation Gilwoods, bisected the two sections.

Following the Great War, Thom Gilwood, the third-generation patriarch, secured a loan from a Toronto Bay Street bank to expand the family's dairy enterprise. He continued to invest heavily, and by the late 1920s, the Gilwood Dairy was known throughout southern Ontario for its milk, butter and exceptional cheeses. Within the small rural community of Millington, the townsfolk routinely discussed the Gilwood family, their success story and their charitable contributions.

Thom Gilwood was considering further expansion when the stock market crash of October 1929 rocked the world's financial centres. Almost immediately, the Canadian economy experienced a widespread decline in activity: exports collapsed, industrial production plummeted, and businesses faltered, bringing about massive job losses and pervasive poverty across large segments of the population.

By 1933, Canadians, mired in the depths of the Great Depression, struggled to maintain a semblance of pre-Depression life. As a last resort, with no end in sight to the widespread unemployment, hungry and desperate, family after family abandoned their homes for places unknown, harbouring wistful memories of greener pastures.

The Gilwoods also struggled to weather the economic fallout. The family's dairy business limped along, then suffered a precipitous drop in sales. As the months dragged on, their reserves dried up. In a last-ditch effort, Thom Gilwood sold the livestock to service the bank debt. Nonetheless, financial ruin was imminent. Within days, two bank agents cautiously approached their home, foreclosure papers in hand.

The family matriarch, Eve Gilwood, ever the good neighbour, donated her book collection to the Millington library. Moreover, she offered Mrs. Gordan, the head schoolmistress, a variety of children's books for the one-room schoolhouse built on the Gilwood property.

The sprightly Mrs. Gordan, an avowed gossip, enjoyed bending the ear of anyone willing to listen to her long-winded, drafty yarns. In her vast mental loft where she stowed and catalogued her yarns, she savoured the intimate story of the Gilwoods' fall from grace. For anyone who would lend an ear, she would begin her story with their slow drip to financial ruin, then end with the family pulling up stakes, departing town in their gleaming 1930 Cadillac Fleetwood seven-passenger sedan, towing their most treasured possessions stacked high in their wood-sided trailer, painted Forest Green to match their automobile.

The Gilwoods' journey carried them eighteen hundred miles to Saskatoon, Saskatchewan, where relatives promised to lodge the family until they got back on their feet. Eve Gilwood confided to Mrs. Gordan that by the Grace of God, the Gilwood clan would return to Millington, reclaim their possessions and once again produce the best cheese in southern Ontario. For the rest of her years, Mrs. Gordan held Eve Gilwood in contempt simply because she never received a letter from the Gilwood matriarch. Mrs. Gordan was of the feverish belief she was entitled to know the conclusion to the Gilwood saga.

By the latter half of the 1930s, various levels of government implemented a series of plans to galvanize and breathe new life into urban and rural economies. One plan was to augment the distribution of hydroelectric power throughout Ontario. Transmission towers were erected across the vacant Gilwood land and continued westward, supplying electricity to rural areas. The economy slowly strengthened. Although unemployment and hardship remained widespread, a renewed sense of optimism blossomed across the land—the next decade would be one of growth and prosperity.

*   *   *

A smattering of pine and spruce trees surrounded the old Gilwood orchard. Row upon row of sixty-year-old Macintosh apple trees had withstood time, the elements and the pruners' clippers. Although the trees had not been pruned in decades, each autumn, they would be heavy with worm-infested fruit.

Approaching the orchard, William could see a small group of kids milling around the old maple tree.

"Wha' me hear, Will'am?" asked Timmy as he skipped along the snow-covered trail behind his brother.

William listened as he drank in the frigid air. "I hear it. It's *Wipeout*. Donna must have brung her radio," he said.

"Wipe…?"

"It's a song," William said. He slowed, faced his younger brother, "Timmy…don't embarrass me in front of my friends."

"Wha' ya' mean?"

He mumbled incoherently, sighed loudly and said, "Just don't talk to anyone besides Jimmy, Turtle or the twins."

Timmy forced his hands into his pockets, his shoulders slumped, and his head dropped. He paced back and forth along the narrow trail. "Me goin' home…you' not nice."

William breathed in the fresh autumn air and, for a moment, stared at his brother, then said, "Hey, do you smell that?"

Timmy tipped his head skyward, opened his mouth and tried to smell the air.

William yanked out a handful of sweet grass, shook off the clingy wet snow, sniffed it and said, "Here, smell it…the grass smells like candy."

Timmy held the clump of wet grass against his nose and breathed in deeply.

"Jimmy tol' me all about the long grasses that grow here. When the hot sun melts the snow on the grass, it smells like licorice."

Timmy wrinkled his upended nose. The clump of grass tickled his nose and chin. Again, he inhaled deeply, then grinned widely.

"Oh yeah, I forgot. Mrs. Gregor at the store gave me some candy after school." He reached into his pocket and retrieved the lint-covered black ball.

"Oh boy, t'anks Will'am." Timmy plopped the fuzzy candy onto his tongue. He then happily trailed after his big brother.

The magnificent maple tree with its billowing canopy seemed to hold dominion over the old orchard. Several teenagers were gathered beneath its outstretched limbs. William looked around and spotted Jimmy standing next to his seated brother, Dean, who always brought three folding stools. A sullen Randy Cooper was kneeling beside the trunk of the maple tree, adjusting the volume on Donna's portable radio. Sitting off to the side, John and Judy, heads pressed together, huddled under Judy's thick woollen Hudson Bay blanket with its characteristic dyed bands of green, red, yellow and indigo. The couple were, as usual, holding their own private conversation.

Frankie Malone threw an overhand pass to Donna Moore. William was impressed as she laughed and nimbly caught the football, even though she wore bulky mitts and a stylish, new winter coat with ten ivory buttons and a hood accented with white rabbit fur.

Once a month, Donna and her mother would drive into the big city of Barriston to shop at Eaton's spacious five-story department store. She didn't boast about her monthly trips to the clothing and furniture store; nonetheless, her Eaton's shopping adventures invariably cropped up in conversation. William admired the coat and wished one day he could shop at Eaton's.

Donna tossed the football back to Frankie, the de facto leader of the orchard gang. Built like a linebacker, he could hardly wait for next September when, as a grade nine student, he would be eligible to try out for the high school football team, the Blue Crows.

Frankie was a huge Angelo Mosca fan and dreamed of following his hero into the pro leagues. He had watched Mosca play twice during the season, and now the Tiger-Cats would be playing in the 51st Grey Cup game against the B.C. Lions at Empire Stadium in Vancouver on November 30th. He had told the gang he would give anything to see his idol play in the championship game.

Donna spied the two Greene boys approaching and said, "Hey there, William." She shot him a quick peace sign. She then looked down at Timmy, reached out and adjusted his togue. "That's better, now both ears are covered." Timmy stood comfortably in Donna's shadow, grinning as he looked up at her. She laughed, displaying metal on her teeth, "William, who is this cute little man?"

William sighed. His mind raced. His cheeks burned red. He tried to act casual and even attempted to lower his voice, "He's my little brother, Timmy, and…I have to *babysit* him." As soon as he had spoken, he regretted it. He sighed again, looked at Donna and thought she was so pretty—even with tracks on her teeth.

Timmy eyed his brother, looked up at Donna and said, "Mum made 'im…" He then gleefully added, "Ya smelt the grass?"

Donna looked quizzically at him, smiled, and felt an instant fondness for William's younger brother. Sticking out her hand, she said, "Come on, Timmy, we'll follow Turtle and that other kid to the old orchard and see if any apples are still hanging from the trees."

William quickly announced, "That's Scottie. He's Stuart Murphy's twin brother." Donna looked sideways at him, turned to Timmy and said, "Come on, buck-o," and walked away. William was deflated. He wondered why she never called him *buck-o*.

With the football tucked under his arm, Frankie quickly closed in on the twosome. He looked down at Timmy, then slowed his pace to match Donna's stride. He leaned in and whispered, "Hey, why don't you ever call me buck-o?"

Donna squinted at him and said, "Because this little man's less demanding."

William glanced over at the maple tree. Jimmy was on one knee, turning the radio dial in search of another station. A moment later, a sunny, surfer-type melody rode the breeze. He guessed the song was by The Highwaymen or The Beach Boys. His older sister, Susan, would know; she was in love with The Beach Boys and could recite the lyrics to all the band's songs.

Meanwhile, Randy Cooper, leaning against the tree trunk, was staring menacingly at Jimmy.

*   *   *

At school, the younger children kept their distance from Randy Cooper, and especially on Hot Dog Fridays, when lunch money was kept out of sight, buried deep in pockets. Every Friday during morning recess, the hulking Randy would prowl the school playground, sniffing out potential victims. As he stalked and then cornered his prey—it was beneath him to pick on girls—spittle spewing from the corners of his mouth, he would offer the petrified boy an ultimatum—pay up or eat a fist sandwich.

Randy didn't enjoy Friday recesses. Moving around the playground caused havoc with his back, his leg throbbed, and his foot played catch-up, often causing him to shuffle or stumble, thus hastening his fury. Deep down, he suspected his limp was growing more pronounced. Regardless, he did his utmost to hide his symptoms in school and at home. Years later, at the age of twenty-two, persuaded to seek medical help by a graphic arts friend, he is diagnosed with an advanced case of lumbar scoliosis.

*   *   *

An ominous cloud of condensation circled Randy and Jimmy's heads. Randy narrowed his eyes and subjected Jimmy to his signature move, the hairy eyeball, honed through many sessions in front of the bathroom mirror.

Jimmy's after-school peanut butter sandwich invaded Randy's nostrils. He snorted loudly then grunted, "You comprehend…dummy?" He raised his fists. He had decided that Dean's brother needed to be schooled.

Jimmy boldly held his ground against this goon who was threatening to punch his lights out. He stared into Randy's moist red eyes.

John and Judy pulled the blanket tighter and attempted to block out the annoying intrusion.

Dean jumped up, knocking over his stool. His head swivelled between contenders as he tried to gauge his best friend's intentions while weighing his younger brother's welfare. "Come on, Coop, Jimmy don't mean nuthin'," he begged. He tepidly moved to position himself between the two boys and implored, "Come on, man, Jimmy talks shit—just gotta ignore him. You know how he is…how he's…ahh, too smart by half." He then removed a pack of cigarettes from his coat pocket, plucked a cigarette and thrust it toward Randy. "Here, buddy, have a fag." After a moment, with his arm outstretched, peace offering in hand, Dean sighed and dropped his arm by his side. The cigarette slipped from his fingers and fell to the ground.

William guardedly moved next to Jimmy. He slipped his hands into his bomber jacket pockets and tried to silence his wobbly knees. He wondered if the other guys could see his knees shaking.

The four boys formed an impromptu circle.

Dean reached out, put a hand on Randy's shoulder and pleaded again, "Come on, Coop, let's go back to my place…hey, Karen should be home." Randy had a thing for Dean's eighteen-year-old sister.

Randy glanced at him, "Get outta my face…step off, unless you're cruisin'…"

Dean quickly stepped back and said, "Please, man, don't hurt 'im."

Jimmy silently studied his opponent.

William held his breath and wished he could grab his friend and run home, leaving Randy Cooper in their dust.

A pleasant folk melody frolicked in the light breeze slicing through the tense stillness of the moment.

A hush had fallen over the four boys as all eyes waited for Randy's next move.

William recognized the song, "Puff the Magic Dragon" by Peter, Paul, and Mary. He glanced over his shoulder at Donna's radio by the maple tree. His mind shifted gears—her radio was a new state-of-the-art Panasonic 2-band transistor radio with its own leather case and carrying strap. He recalled that his oldest sister, Caroline, had asked their parents for one

Christmas present this year, a Panasonic 2-band radio for her dorm room at the Nursing college.

Meanwhile, the rest of the orchard gang were on their way back to the old maple tree. A soaking wet Scottie Murphy, recognizing an old-fashioned impasse, tramped over to the circle of four and then furtively nudged William. Cracking the silence, he asked, "Hey, what is you all doin'?"

"Randy is some mad at Jimmy," he whispered.

Scottie's head pivoted from side to side. "Outta sight," he said excitedly. He took a last bite of an apple, threw it as far as his spindly arm would allow, then settled in for the show. He stood rigidly in place as if he were in school, at attention, listening to the morning broadcast of "The Maple Leaf Forever." Captivated, he waited for the bell to signal the start of round one.

Turtle and Timmy arrived next, coat pockets stuffed with small apples. Turtle bit into a misshapen McIntosh apple. His face puckered. He liked sour apples. His sister once told him that there's nothing worse than biting into an apple and finding half a worm. One day, he'd ask her what she meant. He wheezed, sized up the situation and wondered why loony Randy was in Jimmy's face? He took another bite, dropped his eyes to the half-eaten apple—still no worms.

William glanced around at the growing crowd and then saw Timmy sitting by the trunk of the maple tree, eating an apple. The fragrant grasses he had picked earlier dangled from his little brother's coat pocket. He turned and watched Donna and Frankie, still holding a football, trudging through a deep snow drift.

Tommy Roe's "Sweet Little Sheila" welcomed the couple back to the maple tree.

Randy grimaced and grunted. His eye twitched as a burning sensation deep within his hip pulsed down his leg. Numbness crept along his toes. He was confused and cold. His indomitable extortion tactics had bombed.

William sized up the two opponents. It was readily apparent that Jimmy was as tall as Randy and, in his estimation, twenty pounds heavier. He then had a strange premonition that genius-Jimmy was toying with Randy. William thought of a phrase his dad would summon on occasion, 'when it came to utensils, he was not the sharpest spoon in the drawer!' Could his friend wallop Randy? Could he conquer the schoolyard bully? He was not keen to find out.

Judy stood up, wrapped herself in her Hudson Bay blanket, glanced sideways at John, who then bolted upright, and together they strolled away toward the road without speaking, without looking back, leaving two empty chairs.

His eyes bloodshot, Randy wiped his snotty nose with the back of his hand. Mucus continued to leak toward his mouth. His tongue slid across his upper lip. He was befuddled by Jimmy's inaction and apprehensive about his own next move. He exhaled heavily. A stream of musty breath blanketed Jimmy's face.

Oh man, here we go, William thought.

Jimmy stared at Randy, then slowly but deliberately reached into his pocket, pulled out a tissue and offered peace. Randy stared at the tissue, perplexed. He struggled to fathom what this fat kid was up to; he blinked repeatedly until a flickering of understanding ignited behind his morose dark eyes. He sighed heavily through clenched teeth, snatched the tissue from the outstretched hand, then half-heartedly shoved Jimmy and sneered: "Stay outta my way, shit-stain or I'll knock ya into next Tuesday."

"Randy Cooper," Donna called. "Everything copacetic over there?"

"…Nuthin' to see here," Dean said quickly, folding chairs, losing no time to pack up and leave the orchard before his buddy Coop reconsidered.

"I'm cold…I'm goin' home," said a reanimated Scottie, begrudgingly acknowledging that the dustup went up in smoke.

William breathed a sigh of relief. He eyed Scottie— shivering and looking like he had just pulled himself out of an icy pond. "Scottie, how'd you get so wet, anyway?"

Donna answered, "He was crawling and rolling around in the snow trying to catch mice."

William nodded. That sounded like something Scottie Murphy would do. He smiled at Donna. She smiled back. He felt a sudden warmth in his gut. It felt invigorating.

Timmy wandered over to Randy and offered him a shiny, bruised apple. The offer was ignored.

Frankie left Donna's side, walked over to Randy and said, "Come on, buddy, let's get out of here. I don't know about you, but I'm friggin' cold." He threw an arm around Randy's shoulder and, with his other hand, pressed the football into his stomach. With his head bowed, Randy accepted Frankie's offer and the football.

Twenty minutes later, William and Timmy walked into the house. The boys removed their toques and mitts, unzipped their coats, and yanked off their boots, leaving wet socks buried within. A wet mound of winter gear blocked the front door.

On his way home, William had been consumed by thoughts of Donna and their surprising connection over Scottie's oddball behaviour. He had watched her leave the field with Frankie, Randy, and Dean. If only I were older, William wished. He walked along the hallway past the kitchen toward the bathroom. He could hear indistinct voices issuing from the living room and the smell of chicken thighs covered with Campbell's mushroom soup baking in the oven—his dad's favourite Friday night dinner. The house seemed strangely quiet despite the TV noises.

"Me home!" Timmy announced. No reply. He called out a second time, "Mum?" He felt a spark of apprehension, "Mum…ya here?" He followed the voices into the living room. His mother was standing next to the ironing board, iron in hand, dressed in her usual laundry day garb. A royal blue ankle-length dress, a starched white apron cinched tightly at her waist, and a baby blue sweater, which she had knitted many years ago, covered her shoulders. Vivan was neither ironing nor watching her second-favourite soap opera of the day. Instead, she was lost in thought, oblivious to her surroundings, her shoulders trembling under the sweater as she stared blankly through the bay window. Sensing a presence in the room, she slowly turned toward a frightened Timmy.

*   *   *

"Cut it out…stop bangin' on the door," William barked. He flushed the toilet, ran his hands under cold water, slid his wet palms down his corduroy trousers, then opened the door. Timmy stood in the doorway, tears streaming down his cheeks.

He could no longer contain himself; he wailed, "Mum's watchin' TV, cryin'—she cryin' Will'am."

"Sometimes her TV shows make her sad," William offered.

"No…no…" Timmy grabbed his brother's sleeve, "Come!"

William almost tripped over Timmy's leg while exiting the bathroom. Appreciating the concern on Timmy's twisted face, a sense of urgency gripped him. He ran into the living room, followed closely by Timmy. He smelled cotton burning. He glanced around the room. The light streamed through the bay window, casting long shadows across the room.

Vivian had moved to the chesterfield. She sat stiffly by the armrest, arms crossed, head down, and eyes shut; semi-dry tracks of tears were noticeable on her cheeks. Timmy sprang onto the chesterfield next to his mother. He snuggled against her. She quietly hugged her youngest.

William walked swiftly to the ironing board, stood the iron upright, and yanked the electric cord out of the receptacle. He wheeled around to console his mother, but the stilted, despondent voice coming from the TV stopped him in his tracks. He recognized the newsman's voice. His parents habitually watched CBS Nightly News; they liked and trusted this American newscaster. He stepped back toward the chesterfield and listened carefully to the newsman. Vivian shifted slightly toward the TV as a visibly shaken Walter Cronkite sat at his CBS NEWS desk, attempting to explain to the American people what had just transpired in Dallas, Texas.

He held up a photo of the motorcade, looked off camera, removed his glasses, then looked into the camera and said: "President Kennedy died at 1 p.m. Central Mountain Time…one hour and fifty-six minutes ago. Vice President Lyndon B. Johnson will be taking the Oath of Office as the 36th President."

Tears streamed down Vivian's cheeks. Timmy hung tight as her body heaved and swayed. "Wha' wron', Mummy? It ok…it ok."

William stared at his mother, "What happened…who died?"

"The President," she sighed heavily, "…of the United States of America." She swiped her hand across her wet cheeks.

"Did they shoot our President too?" wondered William aloud.

"Oh my…no, no…that will not happen, William," Vivian consoled. She tried to sort through and make sense of the myriad thoughts that gripped her unsettled mind. She needed to say something more to William; she was desperate to ease the concern etched on his face. She drew a deep breath and absently rubbed away more tears. She looked down at the top of Timmy's head and patted his cheek. She wished Pete were home.

She turned to William and mustered a response, "Canada is a much different country than the United States of America. In Canada, we have a Prime Minister, not a President."

Timmy tilted his head up and looked at William.

She hesitated, inhaled and continued, "Oh dear…um, Canadians believe in peace, order, and good government and um…. the politicians, the people that govern our country, do not get shot by bad people."

William and Timmy stared blankly at their mother.

She sighed and went on, "There is no doubt in my mind that our Prime Minister, Lester Pearson, will not be shot today, tomorrow or any day thereafter." She slowly drew in a breath, then, with feigned confidence, she said, "We don't have to worry about such violence because we live in a safe and wonderful country."

William moved to the TV and changed the channel. He tried channel four, then five and continued around the dial. The scheduled programming on all nine channels had been interrupted by the devastating news.

Vivian watched the talking heads on each channel report on the American president's assassination. She eyed William and thought her flimsy answer may have assuaged his concerns. Timmy, on the other hand, remained glued to his mother's side. He had never seen his mum cry, and it profoundly unsettled him.

"You ge' bedder…Mummy," Timmy said.

Vivian felt herself tearing up again. She attempted to mask her emotions by clearing her throat. Her mind reeled—no more self-pity, no more shed tears in front of my boys. My God, he was only 46 years old, and now his poor wife, Jacqueline, is a widow. She hugged Timmy, stood up and looked through the bay window.

She stared across the street in the gloaming as the daylight fled behind the homes. She wondered how a country so advanced, unparalleled in riches and freedoms, a melting pot of cultures, where the American Dream exists for all and yet…some Americans still harbour such hatred that they would assassinate their political leaders, their President.

Meanwhile, William had left the room and returned with a box of tissues. "Thank you, dear. You are very thoughtful." Vivian dabbed at her eyes, then tucked the wet tissues in her apron pocket.

"We now return to our regularly scheduled programming."

Vivian exhaled as the heavy dark cloud began to dissipate. She walked to the TV and turned it off.

William watched the screen's black-and-white image slowly fade to black.

She looked at the boys and said, "Your father should be home from *the* Bell in about twenty minutes, and dinner will be ready in less than an hour. William, please fold the ironing board and put it back in the hall closet. And dear, thank you for acting so quickly and unplugging the iron…that news about President Kennedy hit me like a ton of bricks." Her eyes began tearing up. She fought the impulse and carried on, "Timmy, you need to change out of those wet clothes, and I…I need to peel some potatoes and put them to boil." She picked up one of the two baskets of folded clothes and proceeded to the stairs.

William followed and then noticed the hamper in the hallway filled with clean laundry. His crisp white jockey briefs were folded on top. "Why do you iron and fold my underwear?"

Vivian stopped on the first step, turned and swayed toward the wall. She leaned into the railing and gathered herself. "God forbid…what if you had an accident and we had to take you to the hospital; what would the doctor think if you showed up in wrinkled, dirty underwear!" she said, exasperated. She then noticed William's bare feet. "When you boys came in from outside, did you hang up your wet clothes?"

Timmy threw a sideways glance at his brother. William didn't reply. With the ironing board tucked under his arm, he stared at his toes, as if focused on the toe jam wedged between them.

"All right…I want the pair of you to hang your winter coats in the closet, boots on the floor register—upside down, so the warm air blows into them, and put your mitts and toques on the register in your bedroom."

With the laundry basket supported in both hands, her body exhausted, she pushed on up the stairs. As each stair receded, she enjoyed the refreshing, invigorating scent of clean laundry even as her stamina oozed from every pore. Without the strength to look back, Vivian summoned her brusque voice, "I will be very cross if I find wet socks buried in the bottoms of your boots."

The rugged, unsinkable Boston Whaler equipped with a 60-HP outboard motor skimmed across the muddy, tranquil water. Will steered the boat toward a tower located on an artificial island. The skeleton tower, an open iron framework with four legs, was built to withstand the harshest storms. He zipped up the green government-issue winter jacket. Although it was late May, there was still a chill in the air, especially while in an open boat in the middle of a lake.

The deckhand, Jeremy, was sitting behind Will, a lifejacket acting as a cushion. "Hey man," he yelled over the wind whipping around and through them, "thanks, I don't know why, but heights scare the livin' bejesus out of me."

"Don't sweat it," Will yelled while imagining his own irrational fear of spiders. He squinted, looked out across the extensive shoal area, reduced speed, then shifted to neutral to allow the boat to coast toward the stony shoreline of the postage-stamp island.

Suddenly, before his eyes, the island transformed into a misshapen, grey, cancerous mole surrounded by a vast sea of reddish-brown, undulating skin.

The hydrographer, Chris, sat on the port side, fiddling with a folded navigation chart. He had told Will earlier that they needed to record a distance from a known geographic position on the southern shore of the St. Lawrence River to the peak of the eighty-two-foot tower erected on Platform I-437, the official designation for the engineered island.

Will cut the engine. Jeremy jumped into the shallow water, bow line in hand, and pulled the Boston Whaler several feet up onto the rocks.

Will stepped carefully on the uneven boulders by the base of the tower. He knelt, retied his shoelaces, stood up and tucked the portable two-way radio into one of the jacket's deep pockets. He reached for the nearest rung of the ladder, raised his head, and scanned the skeleton tower. The sky was a pristine blue. The air was still—dead calm. An ideal day for sightseeing, he thought. He turned to signal the guys in the boat, but to his surprise, he was alone. He began his ascent of the tower.

He cast his eyes skyward, then downward and estimated he was sixty feet above the island. He leaned against the ladder and wrapped an arm around a rung, removed the two-way radio and scanned the horizon for the Boston Whaler. He looked east and west, surely, he thought there would be ONE laker transiting the shipping lane. He keyed the push-to-talk button. The two-way radio squawked, then was silent. He shook the radio, hoping to wake it up. It squirted out of his hand. Instinctively, he lunged, grasped at it and missed. The exertion almost caused him to tumble from the ladder. The ground beckoned as he wrestled to keep his arm locked around the rung. He grabbed the side rail and clung to the ladder. He exhaled loudly and yelled, "Fuck me…that was way too close." A dark corner of his mind interrupted, *nearly took the express route to the rocks below.*

A dense mist encompassed the island.

Will reached for the next rung. He counted each step as he slowly scaled the ladder. He stopped, tilted back his head and eyed the large antenna, ten feet above him, perched atop the tower. His eyes were drawn to the horizon.

Tsunami waves of turbulent fog loomed. Beneath him, the skeleton tower vanished into a swirling dark mass that heaved and bubbled up the iron framework.

A voice whispered from below.

The temperature dropped precipitously. He shivered, wished he had worn a jacket, and then wondered why his feet were bare, given he was climbing an eighty-two-foot tower. As he reached for the next rung, his hand dissolved in the heavy fog.

A cold breeze lapped against his neck, carrying silent voices.

"Hang on, Will'am."

Tremulous voices brushed by his face then faded into the grey nothingness.

"Hang on, Will'am."

"Timmy?"

Will tried to see through the blinding fog, "Timmy…where are you?"

Shrill voices erupted from above, "He can't hold on much longer."

"Hang on, Will'am...don't let go."

"He's slipping," they whispered.

Will ran a hand through his wet, matted hair, then stared at his sticky hand covered with warm blood.

Veronica leaned over Ellie's bed and whispered, "Hey, hon…wake up." She gently shook Will's shoulder. Father and daughter were both sound asleep, snoring lightly. A Dr. Seuss book lay open on the floor beside the bed. Across the bedroom, Adam rolled over, kicked the sheets off the bed and began mumbling incoherently while grinding his teeth. Veronica moved over, pulled up the bed covers, then kissed him on the cheek. Adam grinned lopsidedly. She returned to Ellie's bed, put her hand on Will's shoulder again, leaned in next to his ear and whispered, "Wake up, handsome."

"Timmy! Where are you, don't let go…" he barked in a gruff, concerned voice.

"Will, wake up, you're dreaming."

"Huh…" He bolted upright, narrowly missing her face. Bleary-eyed, he looked around, rubbed his eyes and stared blankly at Veronica.

"It's me, your wonderful wife," she grinned. "Let's get out of the kids' room before we…you, wake them."

Will sighed, "It was just a nightmare…" he mumbled to himself. He again surveyed his surroundings, swiped at the drool on the edge of his mouth, rubbed his face vigorously with both hands, then slipped out of the bedroom seconds after Veronica. He made his way to the bathroom, relieved himself and then splashed water on his face.

"God damn, what a nightmare," he slurred while staring at himself in the mirror. This has been one hell of a strange day, he thought. He tried to puzzle together the day's events, beginning with Adam launching himself onto their bed and ending with him waking from a nightmare in the kids' bedroom. He squinted at his tired reflection in the bathroom mirror and felt strangely unbalanced. The alarm bells erupted. He rubbed his temples as he wrestled to recall the day's events. Just brain fatigue, he tried to reassure himself; an uneasiness gripped him. He leaned forward, his nose almost touching the mirror, and studied his reflection—looking for an answer. Could it be a brain tumour? He considered the odds.

Will rounded the corner and stepped into the kitchen. Veronica stood with her back to him, busy washing and drying the supper dishes. Chinook padded into the kitchen, observed the two most important people in her life, dropped down, curled up under the table and saluted them with a single tail wag.

Standing beside the counter, Will sucked in a deep breath while he admired his wife's shapely figure tucked into tight jeans and a floral print blouse. To complete her ensemble, she wore her tattered yellow latex gloves. She had pulled her hair up in a messy bun, pinned to the back of her head. She looked stunning from his vantage point. He smiled as his negative thoughts decided to take a powder.

*　　*　　*

At the age of nineteen, Veronica landed a job with a large corporation, Ivy Investments, Assets and Properties. IIAP had office locations throughout North America. Pacerville (pop. 3,800) would be the company's first venture outside a major metropolis. An empty, run-down three-story building in the town centre was bought and repurposed to meet the corporation's requirements. A secretarial staff of thirty-six technical typists, women, aged 18 to 71, were hired to manage the document workload for fifty-three companies.

Thirty-six desks were crammed onto the second floor. Socializing and milling amongst the desks was prohibited. Moreover, according to IIAP regulations, each typist was allowed to place one framed picture on the work desk. To personalize the sterile office space and to demonstrate noncompliance, many typists placed numerous knick-knacks on the desktops.

Light fixtures hanging from the ceiling ran counter to the desks. Always careful to ensure the supervisor was out of earshot, the women would grumble that they needed sunglasses to tame the lights' intensity. On the east side of the office, a small glassed-in lunchroom housed a table, surrounded by six plastic chairs. One end of the table provided space for a leaky coffee machine, an oversized stapler, and office paraphernalia. Six additional chairs were stacked next to the table, gathering dust. On the opposite lunchroom wall, a clanging and gurgling refrigerator competed with the women's conversations during their lunch and coffee breaks. A note stuck to the refrigerator read: *Fridge must be cleaned first Monday of each month. Do NOT abuse this privilege.*

On many a Friday night, a group of women from Ivy Investments would meet at the only pub and dancing establishment in town. The Tiltin' Tavern began life as a two-story clapboard home. In the mid-sixties, after multiple additions, the home was converted into a rooming house and tavern. Success, however, was fleeting, and by the early seventies, the sprawling multi-roomed building shuttered its doors.

Three years later, the old rooming house was refurbished and, with the addition of a large neon sign overhanging the street, The Tiltin' Tavern threw open its doors to the public. There were rooms designated for patrons interested in more sedentary activities, such as dining and drinking, as well as rooms reserved for Poker, Bridge, and board games. For those patrons looking for something extra, the Venue room accommodated a regular influx of Rock and Roll bands and exotic dancers that worked the corridor from Windsor to Toronto and along Lake Ontario to Montreal. The TNT, as it became known, was much more than just a drinking establishment; it indulged many different passions.

∗   ∗   ∗

The Tiltin' Tavern's house lights had been turned down as the boisterous crowd drank and waited for the band to begin. Will and three colleagues sat near the back wall, close to the exit and watched the three-person band from Toronto fine-tune their instruments. A roadie hidden offstage assessed the overhead stage lights. Beams of light danced across the stage, bounced off the drums and cymbals, and sprayed light across the rack holding both acoustic and electric guitars. One shaft of light circled the stacked keyboard and synthesizer. A pea-souper device, hidden from sight, discharged fog that billowed across the stage floor, surrounded the instruments and climbed the artists' legs.

Will finished his beer and watched as two roadies raced around the stage, kicking up fog as they completed last-minute adjustments to the equipment. "I'm gonna grab a beer before the band starts bringing down the walls. Any takers?" Will asked as he looked around the table.

He walked toward the crowded bar and noticed an attractive woman leaning against the bar wearing a tan leather jacket and snug jeans. As he closed in on the bar, the lantern lights behind the counter illuminated her shapely silhouette. Will's thoughts of beer vanished. He stopped and waited for an opportunity to approach the counter. After a moment, he turned sideways and squeezed in next to the woman. Her back was now to him. After a minute, he caught the bartender's attention, held up four fingers and mouthed *Labatt 50*. The woman in the tan leather jacket took a sip of her mixed drink, then leisurely turned her head. Their eyes met. Will's stomach rolled. He gazed upon the face of the woman with whom he would spend the rest of his days.

*   *   *

Veronica turned to see Will staring at her. "What are you grinning about?" She asked and peeled off the latex gloves.

He stepped out of his reverie, "Funny you'd ask. I was thinking about the first time we met at that charming dump of an establishment, The Tiltin' Tavern. Who could've guessed that RUSH was playing live on their stage?"

Veronica smiled, "Really! I haven't thought about TNT in ages. Too bad you didn't get Geddy Lee's autograph." She snorted derisively.

"In my defence, they were just a local rock band."

Veronica nodded, then raised an eyebrow: "What gives? You wake up in the kids' bedroom, very confused and then you cry out to *Timmy*." She eyed him, "I have never heard you call your brother anything other than Tim and…let's not forget about this morning and the breakfast spider! And now you're in a mood to reminisce—what gives?"

Will pulled out a chair, parked himself at the table, crossed his arms and said, "Well, Ronnie…I have been tripping down memory lane…" He raised his eyes to her and attempted to smile. He then sighed heavily, "It seems…well, it's like every time I fall asleep, I am transported back to Gilwood School Drive, the date is November 1963, and I am *inhabiting* eight-year-old William."

He shook his head, "What's more, the dreams are, well, they are so ordinary…but, also so unconventional. It's difficult to explain. There's an intense realism, and strangely, the dreams unfold in chronological order. Bizarre, right?"

He exhaled and raked a hand through his hair. "And, not to be dramatic, but when I wake up, I experience this persistent, inexplicable sensation that I wasn't dreaming!" He shook his head, breathed in deeply and waited for Veronica to add her two cents.

"Hon, please lower your voice. You don't want to wake the kids." She hung the wet latex gloves over the faucet, walked to his side, rested a hand on his forehead and said, "You don't feel warm. No fever." She pulled a chair out and sat next to him. "I can certainly understand how your dreams may leave you feeling disoriented and puzzled. Have you considered that at least they are just dreams of your childhood and not of something so disturbing that it keeps you awake at night?"

Her eyebrow reached for her hairline. "Well…don't you agree? Besides, you would be the first to argue that dreams are only imaginary narratives played out as we sleep." Veronica smiled reassuringly. "So, don't sweat it…dreamer."

Will nodded and dropped his head in thought.

"Tell me…is it a recurring dream. Like one of those dreams where you are in school surrounded by laughing students, staring and pointing fingers at you, and with teeth chattering, you look down at your shivering, bare-naked pink flesh and to your horror, there's no way to hide your goosebumps." She giggled mischievously.

Will's smirk morphed into a smile, "Very funny, Ronnie." He suddenly perked up and asked, "Hey, want to hear about them?"

With a resigned shrug, she said, "I'd love to hear about your *unconventional* dreams."

Will launched into an account of his dreams before Veronica could change her mind. "I dreamt I was in my house on Gilwood Drive. It was 1963, and U.S. President John F. Kennedy had just been shot," he said, dropping a hand onto his twitching leg. Chinook stirred under the table and plopped her head heavily onto his lap. He absently rubbed behind her ears.

Suddenly, a surprised look crossed his face. He pursed his lips and, with a renewed sense of enthusiasm, said, "Ronnie, a few days ago…I read a couple of newspaper articles about the conspiracy theories still circulating about Kennedy's assassination. You know, questions about the infamous grassy knoll, the Cuban connection, and even the possibility of CIA involvement. I wonder, did reading those articles trigger my dreams?"

He exhaled and went on, "Anyway, once I finished the articles, I then leaned heavily on our set of Encyclopedia Britannica." He paused and stared at her for a moment. "As you are fully aware, I do tend to be a wee bit obsessive."

He cleared his throat, "Coincidentally, it just so happened that I slid down the Britannica rabbit hole, skimming, scanning and reading about the social upheaval of western society during the sixties and seventies."

He was about to wink and thought better of it. "It is amazing, all that information at our fingertips, like having our own library right at home. I predict twenty years from now our pristine set of leather-bound Britannica books will be worth thousands." He eyed Veronica. "I must say, it was an exceptional gift from your parents."

"I have no intention of selling my folks' generous gift of knowledge."

"Of course not," he said too quickly.

"Ronnie, we inherited a much different world than the one our parents and grandparents occupied," Will said incredulously. "First off, I learned beaucoup societal changes occurred in our own little country almost thirty years ago. I do question, though, why I wasn't taught about the Quiet Revolution—a seismic political shift in opinion and values during the sixties that set the stage for the separation of church and state, thus altering Quebec's economic and social fabric." He inhaled deeply and went on, "The Quebec government enacted legislation to guide and assist in building a modern, more equal and just society and in doing so, the Catholic Church's influence took a huge hit, especially among young people, as control over education and healthcare was assumed by the province." He paused to breathe, then smiled, "Interesting, huh?" He narrowed his eyes and tried to gauge her mood. "Heady stuff, right?"

"Hmmm, is it possible you were absent or daydreaming during those school lessons on Quebec?" She covered a yawn, crossed her arms and said, "I know you find this stuff interesting…and I do too, within limits, but my attention span is slipping fast, going the way of the dodo bird." She yawned again. "Look, hon, do me a solid and just give me the skinny on how our world changed."

Will was deep in thought and scarcely heeded his wife's grumbling. He was in the moment. He was cooking with gas. He went on, "Societal change just didn't happen in Quebec.

Not a chance. In 1960, the birth control pill was approved by our neighbours to the south, and soon after, it was introduced in Canada. We can only imagine how that changed the dynamics in the bedroom and eventually the boardroom."

He stood, reached for the ceiling, then settled back on the chair. "In addition, during the sixties, the American civil rights movement, through nonviolent protest, aimed to achieve social justice and equal rights for all Americans under the law."

Veronica smiled inwardly. She admired his perseverance. He would research and exhaust all avenues of inquiry on a particular subject of interest, then close the book and move on to another topic that immediately required his full attention. She secretly enjoyed watching and listening to his animated discourse. She sighed and thought her husband missed his calling.

"…and then also gaining traction in the late sixties and into the seventies, the women's liberation movement redefined women's role in society."

Veronica gave him the side-eye.

"Well, obviously, you have firsthand knowledge of being treated as a second-class citizen. And finally, Ronnie, we can't forget about the sexual revolution." Will attempted to wink.

Chinook shifted under the table, raised her head and forced her snout under his arm. He pressed on, "Western civilization's perception of *normal* was being challenged by a growing segment of society that took exception to traditional relationships, sexual attitudes and behaviours."

Veronica masked a yawn.

Will took a leisurely breath and ruffled the fur around the dog's ears. "Anyway, you will be thrilled to know that concludes my presentation…stay tuned." He stood up, curtsied and said, "I want to thank you for your patronage and indulging my quest for knowledge."

"You are such a clown."

He hesitated. "Ronnie, seriously though, in my opinion, Homo sapiens are still on the bottom rung of the evolutionary step ladder! Shit, we are just hairless apes swinging among the trees."

Veronica nodded.

Will heard a rustling from the hallway. He glanced at his watch: 8:26 p.m. "I'll go." He held out a hand, "Chinook…stay, girl." He walked along the hallway into the children's bedroom. Adam had tossed his covers and was precariously close to the edge of the bed. Will picked him up and whispered, "All right, Champ, let's take a trip to the bathroom."

NINE

Will walked into the kitchen, bent over and pecked his wife on the lips. He retreated to a chair and said, "Adam had a wiz. Fingers crossed his bladder holds out until the morning."

"Is that Supertramp?" Veronica asked.

"Oui. Still one of my favourite prog rock groups. This song is 'Give a Little Bit' from the *Even in the Quietest Moments* album. And don't worry, I closed the kids' door." Will closed his eyes and listened to the music.

"Hey, just thinkin', Ronnie," he said offhandedly.

"Uh-huh."

"Growing up through the sixties and seventies, at least in my household, any show of affection or intimacy between adults was strictly frowned upon. And sex—forget it!" Will laughed. "If a couple kissed on TV, Dad would demand we change the channel, or sometimes he would just grumble and leave the room." He smirked and shook his head. "My folks…never, ever mentioned sex or money! Two taboo subjects, at least when kids were around."

"You got thirty seconds, then I'm off to the shower." Veronica stretched her arms over her head and yawned.

He gently brushed aside the interruption and said, "I remember Dad had two magazine subscriptions: *Popular Mechanics* and *National Geographic*. Besides comic books, *National Geographic* was my magazine of choice. I could hardly wait to read the stories each month!" With noticeable effort, he winked at her. "Seriously, though, it seemed that most issues had an abundance of glossy photos of African women going about their daily routine topless." He emphasized *topless*.

Will tilted his head and went on, "And then, there was the lingerie section of the *Eaton's Spring and Summer* catalogue. Page after page of half-naked women in lingerie." He looked expectantly at her. Veronica stared at him like a poker player. He couldn't decide whether she held a pair or a full house. "It was the sixties, Ronnie, and seeing bare skin was a valued distraction for a boy on the steps of puberty."

Veronica silently rehashed their conversation and then said, "Something for you to consider." She crossed her arms. "I bet my bottom dollar that those topless women photographed in *that* magazine did not give their permission. For that matter, did they have any idea what was happening? I'd call that exploitation!" She stated emphatically.

Will paused, "I, hmmm…I never thought of it that way."

Supertramp's "Downstream," with its melodic vocals and piano, faded away.

"Be right back," Will said. "I'm going to flip the album. I have a *hankering* to hear 'Fool's Overture.'" Moments later, he flopped down on a kitchen chair as the energetic tempo of "Babaji" followed in his wake.

Will crossed his arms as his thoughts returned to his unsettling dreams. His gaze fixed on a point beyond Veronica, through the kitchen to his uncertain, murky past. Now that she knew about his dreams, he reckoned it was time to come clean and share his health concerns.

Veronica stared intently at him. "Is everything alright, Will? You look like you've seen a ghost."

He smiled thinly and focused his attention on her. "Look, Ronnie, um…in addition to my bizarre dreams, there's something else I've neglected to share with you, and frankly, it's been weighing on me." He ran a hand through his hair and went on, "I'm considering a visit to the doc might be the right call and, well, you know how I feel about going to the doctor's office."

"Will, stop. What is it…what is the problem?"

He exhaled. "In a nutshell, I've had a few episodes of light-headedness and a bit of a muddled brain. It passes quickly, although my memory is, well…spotty; even now, I'm finding it a challenge to recall recent events." He eyed her for a moment, "For instance, my memory of what we did today is, to put it mildly, underwhelming. Truthfully, it has me kinda freaked out." There, I told her, and it's out in the open now, he thought. He grinned lopsidedly. His eyes, however, remained concerned.

Veronica leaned into the table and said, "First thing, next week you need to call Doctor Pierce's office and schedule a physical, a full checkup. I'm sure it's nothing, but you don't want to take any chances with your health." Then, exasperated, she said, "Why did you put off telling me until now. Why Will?" She stared fixedly at him.

He sucked in a deep breath and said, "I don't want you to worry, especially if it's nothing." He ran a hand through his hair again, then admitted, "And, you know how it is when you spill your guts, divulge your inner feelings…it may embolden, energize those negative thoughts and then what had been imagined, suddenly becomes something tangible, has substance and consequences!"

He looked down at the dog sleeping under the table. He inhaled and pushed out his bottom lip, "I guess it's easier to keep my head buried in the sand and ignore all the brain chatter. Anyway, as we speak, I'm trying to piece together what we did today."

Veronica continued to study him. "Do you remember replacing the oil in the car or taking the kids over to the park?"

"I…I guess so. I'm sure it's nothing, working too hard, not getting enough sleep…fighting an infection," he suggested to reassure Veronica and himself.

"We both know that you tend to overthink things, especially health-related and let's face it, Will, you are a bit of a hypochondriac," she said sympathetically. A niggling uneasiness settled in her stomach as she contemplated his memory lapses.

He passively eyed her.

Veronica cupped her hands and rested them on her lap. "Do you have any numbness or weakness in your arms or legs? How's your vision? Any loss of balance?" she asked.

"Physically, I feel great. Ninety-eight percent."

"An hour ago, you were on the couch with the kids watching *The Littlest Mermaid*."

Will tried to imagine himself and the kids watching the animated movie.

Veronica stood up and reached for the bottle of wine on the counter, "Do you remember buying this earlier…"

Will's eyes searched the kitchen while his mind foraged through sparse memories to sort and retrieve his most recent. Flashes of cartoon fish swam around his barnacle-encrusted grey matter. He continued to search, then triumphantly said, "I do remember, Ronnie. I almost bought a Chianti, but it was too expensive." He exhaled audibly. A sense of relief washed over him, "And…midway through the movie, Ellie dropped to the floor to cuddle with the dog, Adam fell asleep, and you carried him to the bedroom." He exhaled as the heaviness began to slip from his shoulders.

Veronica nodded, placed the wine back on the counter and said, "You still need to call the doctor's office Monday morning."

Will heard a Supertramp song begin its march down the hallway. The determined, steady voice of Winston Churchill reached the kitchen as a snippet of his famous June 4, 1940, speech, '…we shall fight on the seas and oceans…whatever the cost…we shall never surrender…' echoed around the kitchen.

He closed his eyes and whispered, "'Fools Overture' always sends goose bumps down my spine." He peeked at Veronica and whispered, "It's an eleven-minute masterpiece, listen…first the orchestra…now the piano and flute, building to a crescendo and wait for it…Big Ben chimes and, finally, Roger Hodgson's distinctive high tenor vocals bring—"

"Shhh…please."

*   *   *

Five minutes later, Will slipped the album into its dust jacket. Feeling a spring in his step, he re-entered the kitchen, determined the moment was right to change the subject and lighten the mood. As he resumed his seat, he smiled, "Ronnie, did I ever tell you about the time I had an *encounter* with Barbie?"

Veronica's eyebrow crept upward. "I do not believe so…Barbie who?" She attempted but failed to stifle a yawn.

"Well, it's not Barbie *who,* it's *the* Barbie created by the good people at Mattel," he said, trying to glean her reaction.

No response.

She should be a Poker player, he marvelled. "Yup," he chuckled, "not one of the proudest moments of my youth." He waited for her to react, to say something, anything. He waited, then sighed, and with both hands, mimicked tuning radio knobs. He went on, "Back in the day, I reckoned that firsthand touching, so to speak, would help when it came to the real McCoy." He smiled and again waited for a reaction.

Veronica crossed her arms and studied him. "So…you're telling me that you had a thing for Barbie's enormous plastic boobs? I don't know if I should laugh or be disappointed in your choice of companionship."

"Very funny."

"But really, Will, a Barbie doll?" Veronica opened her mouth to speak, then hesitated... "Anyway, it has been a long day, and I am feeling a wee bit knackered." She looked at him earnestly, "Maybe, for the rest of the night, we put Barbie and your repressed childhood to bed." Then, in a lighter tone, she said, "What do you say, Sigmund Freud? Is it time to enjoy the present and move beyond the old days, dream analysis and random doll stories?"

Will grinned and said, "You are surely onto something, my dear. I agree wholeheartedly." He glanced at the wine bottle. "How's this sound for a plan. You pour us each a big glass of red while I'm letting Nook out back for her last run of the night. We can then relax, sip our wine and watch the movie."

Veronica's head snapped up. "You remember renting a movie for tonight?" she exclaimed with a renewed sense that all might be well in the world.

Will grinned. "Damn tootin'…Indeed, I do." Through playful eyes, he said, *"The Dead Poets…*a gory blood fest of brain-eating, eyeball-sucking zombie poets."

"Close enough," Veronica sighed. She picked up the wine bottle and chirped, "A screw cap, cheap date night, I see. Well, before indulging in a glass of this fine wine, I'm going to enjoy a nice warm shower. Oh, and before I forget…" she reached for her oversized purse, removed a nondescript paper bag and dropped it on the table, "while I'm in the shower, please take care of this?"

Will eyeballed the bag and said, "You picked up rubbers?"

"No, silly, that type of purchase falls under your domain; condoms are your responsibility."

"You do know…times, they are a-changin as we discussed, and enlightened women are buying rubbers."

Unveiling an amused expression, a glint in her eye and a bewitching lilt to her voice, she said, "That may well be true, but I prefer the man in this relationship to purchase the protection."

"A riddle for you Ronnie, why does a thirty-something, married guy with two kids walk into a pharmacy to buy *one* product—rubbers, but, for some unknown reason this guy methodically canvasses every aisle and when he eventually does exit the store, he has a newspaper tucked under his arm and a Shopper's Mart bag filled with gum, breath mints, assorted sundries and lastly, rubbers."

"Hmmm…interesting, and so very sad for you."

Will opened the paper bag and discovered a nightlight shaped like Disney's Pluto. He raised an eyebrow.

"I thought a nightlight might help Ellie stay in bed and, just maybe," she crossed her fingers, "Adam will call out if he needs to tinkle during the night."

Will nodded.

Veronica stood, pushed the chair against the table, turned and in her best sultry voice, echoing Kathleen Turner in *Body Heat,* said, "After the movie, if you're in the mood, you could demonstrate your Barbie moves."

"Most definitely. I would love to show you my nifty moves, although…why wait? We could watch the movie *later* tonight?" Will said in his most persuasive voice, reminiscent of Kermit the frog gargling Listerine.

Veronica stealthily tiptoed down the hallway past the children's bedroom, looked back and whispered, "Don't forget to let the dog out." She winked and slipped into the bathroom.

CHAPTER

TEN

The late-November Arctic front had slipped south, blanketing the province with an early blast of wintry weather. Vivian leaned against the house near the kitchen side door. The cold air quickly penetrated her wool knit sweater. Rather than running upstairs to retrieve her winter coat, she had settled for wearing the heavy sweater. She regretted her choice and wondered when she would get used to Canadian winters.

Nonetheless, warm or cold, Vivian was content; she was ahead of schedule. The family's Sunday Roast beef dinner was well in hand. The roast was prepped; the potatoes were peeled, and the Yorkshire pudding batter would take all of two minutes to prepare.

She reached into her sweater pocket and withdrew a pack of cigarettes and a lighter. She removed a cigarette, thumbed the lighter and inhaled deeply as the cigarette began to burn. She exhaled slowly and read aloud the slogan written on the Pall Mall cigarette pack: "Wherever Particular People

Congregate." She smiled, inhaled slowly and again wished she had worn warmer clothes.

As Vivian exhaled, she considered that *this Particular* person was not congregating but rather sidled up against the house, intentionally making it difficult for neighbours to see her indulging in this small pleasure. On the far side of the driveway, a cedar hedge ran the length of the driveway to the ditch adjacent to the street. The hedge conveniently kept her hidden from the neighbours on the opposite side. She assumed that her neighbour, Hillary Tuttle, would be exasperated, irate, knowing that she, a mother of five, enjoyed the occasional cigarette. She stared into the hedge and inhaled slowly, enjoying the smoothness of the Pall Mall.

*   *   *

Vivian thoroughly enjoyed Sunday dinners. It was a family ritual, dating back to her childhood in East London. Each Sunday, the Greene family gathered around the table to enjoy a wonderful dinner, then finished with a discussion of the people and events that touched their lives that week. She brought the cigarette to her mouth, breathed in and thought for the umpteenth time that she should quit smoking. That is, as soon as she finished this pack of Pall Malls, she told herself.

She studied the burning cigarette and appreciated that her Sunday family dinners would not last forever. It was fast becoming a habit for her three daughters to miss dinners. Caroline, her firstborn, was in her second year at Dunford Nursing College, sharing a dorm room with two girls. Because the college was eighty miles away, commuting every day was not feasible. And now that Susan had her beginner's license, she would confiscate their only vehicle every waking minute if she were permitted. Mary Lynn, at the tender age of twelve, was quite independent, juggling friends, gymnastics, dance, and *free* piano lessons courtesy of their next-door neighbour, Hillary Tuttle. Free lessons, mind you, if you don't count the fruit pies and squares she baked for Hillary and her kids.

Surprised by Ernie's unexpected visit, Vivian thought this Sunday dinner would be lovely, albeit hectic. She decided to take one of the apple pies out of the freezer for dessert. She knew Pete would be exhausted when he arrived home from his Bell Telephone colleague's funeral. However, she would still ask him to run to the store for vanilla ice cream. He would grumble, but she would insist.

What's more, Ernie had been smitten with her apple pie the first time she had offered him a slice, topped with ice cream, and she knew Pete would not want to disappoint his father. She inhaled and noticed the cigarette had burned to within an inch of the filter. She bent over and poked the cherry end into the snow. This will be my last pack of cigarettes, she concluded.

Vivian stepped inside and closed the kitchen door, walked to the sink, and ran a few drops of water over the cigarette's burnt end. Better safe than sorry, she thought. She opened the cupboard below the sink and dropped the cigarette butt into the garbage pail. She then stood on the chair beside the counter and opened the cupboard above the fridge. She dropped the cigarette pack and lighter into the ornate, two-handled sugar bowl. A wedding gift that had survived her trip to Canada, still intact and unchipped after almost two decades.

She replaced the lid, pushed it to the back and closed the cupboard. She stepped down and pushed the chair back to the table.

Still feeling chilled, she left the sweater on, surveyed the kitchen and walked out into the hallway. She did not hear Ernie moving around, and he was not in the living room. She assumed he was still resting upstairs.

It was mid-afternoon. She had one hour to herself. At four o'clock, she would put the blade roast in the oven. Delighted, she settled into the chesterfield and plucked the *Reader's Digest* magazine from the side table.

When her monthly *Reader's Digest* subscription arrived, she would peruse the Table of Contents, evaluate the thirty articles, and, time permitting, read the articles that interested her most. She would then move on to "Humour in Uniform," followed by "Increase Your Word Power." Inevitably, she saved the feature story "Drama in Real Life" for last. The stories were often based on the perseverance and resilience of vulnerable people facing demanding situations. The latest month's "Drama in Real Life" was about a family attempting to escape from behind the Iron Curtain. Vivian savoured the family-based stories that focused on courage and determination under harsh, perilous conditions. The stories reminded her of London during World War II.

The phone *dinged* twice just as she was mid-way through the story. She exhaled, dog-eared the page, then dropped the magazine on the chesterfield. She scurried along the hallway into the kitchen and answered the phone on its fifth *ding-ding.*

"Hello, Greene residence, Vivian speaking." She listened to the scratchy sound emanating through the telephone line. She waited. Talking on a party line took patience and tolerance. "Hello…" The crackling noise diminished. "Oh, hello, dear. I thought by now you would be on your way home?" Vivian eased into the kitchen chair closest to the wall-mounted phone. "Are you all right, dear? Is there a problem at school? I hope there are no issues with your friends or instructors?"

Vivian lowered her head and eyed the red kitchen tabletop. She wondered why she ever listened to Pete. He was so gassed about the kitchen dinette set in Maxwell's Furniture store with its race car red tabletop, Pete's description of the red Arborite surface, and matching chairs that when the salesman offered to lower the price of the display model by a whopping ten percent…well, he could never turn down a deal.

"Yes, dear, sorry, I'm still here." Vivian pulled herself back to the conversation. "Caroline, I'm glad to hear all is well. I wish you had told me yesterday that you would not be joining us for dinner. Your grandfather dropped by unannounced earlier today, and now that you won't be home, I suppose we will have enough elbow room around the dinner table. Still, though, I would much rather you were home, and we could all be together, crowded around the table."

Vivian looked up as a refreshed Ernie walked into the kitchen. She smiled. His white hair was neatly parted on the left, accenting his well-groomed white goatee. It was obvious where Pete got his good looks. He wore beige slacks, a matching vest, shirt cuffs folded to his elbows, and a thin fabric belt with a bronze oval buckle. She watched him and wondered how on earth he could wake from a nap, and his clothes appeared freshly starched with not a wrinkle in sight!

"Just a minute, Caroline, your granddad just walked into the kitchen."

Ernie sauntered over to the counter, picked up a mug from the sink and filled it with tap water. He raised his voice, "Hey, number one granddaughter, hope to see you soon."

"Caroline says hello."

"I didn't know that I had to *announce* to the entire neighbourhood every time I decided to visit my family," Ernie said with feigned annoyance.

"Dad, that mug was in the sink because it is dirty. I will make a fresh pot of coffee if you like."

Ernie smiled and said, "Viv, don't go to any bother on my account—although if you are going to brew a pot for when Peter gets home, then by all means I'd enjoy a cup o' Jo…on second thought, let's get that coffee brewed soon, all right. If I have my coffee too late in the afternoon, I will never sleep tonight." With a mug in hand, Ernie winked at Vivian and sauntered out of the kitchen.

She straightened her back and stared at him as he moved down the hallway. "Sorry again, dear. You know, your grandfather has a way of getting under my skin." She listened. "I know…he enjoys getting me riled up, and I should be stronger. Anyway, enough about that. How did you do on your last two assignments?" A second later, she heard a click on the line.

"Hello…hello," a distant tinny voice echoed along the telephone line.

Vivian recognized her neighbour's voice from three doors down. "Hello, Alice. It's Vivian Greene, your neighbour," she said, then listened and counted slowly to five—no response. She raised her voice, struggled to enunciate each word, and said again. "Alice, it's your neighbour, Vivian. Please hang up so that I may complete my telephone call."

"Oh, hello, Vivian. My error. I am getting so hard of hearing, and I swear these connections are getting worse by the day. I picked up the telephone to make a call, but I did not know the line was already in use. How are you, dear?" Alice said, forgetting that Vivian was in conversation with another person.

"I'm fine, thank you. Alice, I must get back to my conversation."

"Yes, of course, dear. Wasn't it a shame about poor President Kennedy? Such a crime."

"My heart goes out to his family and the whole country for their loss. Now, I must get back to my daughter before we lose our connection. Goodbye, Alice."

"Yes, of course…enjoy your evening. Please say hello to Pete. Goodbye, dear."

"Caroline, are you still on the line?" Vivian asked.

"She is eighty and doing quite well for a person her age, but, to your question, she could definitely take advantage of a hearing aid." She glanced at the wall clock. She felt pressed for time. "Listen, Caroline, the boys will be home any minute, and your father should be home soon, and I need to start dinner." She sighed. "I am relieved everything is grand, and you're in good spirits…I miss you too, dear. And Caroline, if you want to talk next weekend, please call. One extra long-distance call will not put us in the poorhouse." She had a sudden urge to smoke a cigarette.

Vivian replaced the receiver in its cradle and turned the oven on to preheat. She had 15 minutes before it was time to slide the blade roast into the oven so that dinner would be ready promptly at 6:00 p.m. She glanced again at the clock, reassured.

She returned to the living room, determined to finish the *Reader's Digest* story. As she sat down on the chesterfield, Mildred loped down the stairs, padded into the living room and dropped her head on Vivian's lap, then looked her in the eye. She sighed heavily, dropped the magazine and escorted the dog to the back door. Mildred watched the door open, lowered her snout to the ground, and plodded toward the back of the yard.

Vivian prayed there would be no more interruptions for the next ten minutes. She quickly retraced her steps to the living room, nestled into the chesterfield and opened the magazine to the dog-eared page.

"Mum, we're home," William said as he and Timmy stormed through the front door.

She shook her head, disappointed that the *Reader's Digest* feature story would have to wait. She dropped the magazine on the end table and met the boys at the front door. "Oh, hello, Jimmy," she said, taken aback.

Jimmy Henderson stood at the door wearing an old, snug-fitting winter coat, zipped up to his chin. The coat's sleeves were several inches too short, exposing his wrists to the elements. He looked comical.

"Can Jimmy stay for a while?" William asked as he removed his winter gear.

"Of course, dear."

"Hello, Mrs. Greene."

"So nice to see you, Jimmy. How's your mum? I haven't seen her outside in weeks." Vivian watched him struggle with the zipper. She was quite fond of Jimmy and was pleased that he and William were such good friends.

Jimmy glanced at her, then lowered his eyes and said, "She has been under the weather for a few weeks, Mrs. Greene."

Vivian put a reassuring hand on his shoulder and said, "I am sorry to hear that, Jimmy. I'm sure your mum will be feeling much better very soon. After all, it is cold and flu season." She watched him for a moment and suspected he was holding something back, or at least keeping his feelings bottled up. She exhaled, "…well then, I must get back to the kitchen."

She glanced at William, then said, "Jimmy, would you like to stay for dinner? We're having a lovely roast beef. I can set up the card table in the living room, and you boys can eat out there."

Jimmy struggled to make eye contact, "No, thank you, Mrs. Greene. My sister, Karen, is leaving town tomorrow. I should go home soon." He yielded and dropped his eyes to a clump of dog fur trapped under the floor register.

"Oh, she's leaving town. Is Karen going to another school or college?"

Jimmy quietly said, "Yes, that's what mom said."

Vivian nodded, but she was confused. She decided not to push. He is a slightly odd, solemn young man, she thought. She stared at his pleasant, round face and suspected that the poor boy had put on more weight. She then wondered if he was receiving the kind of support best suited for a child with his exceptional gift. At least Mrs. Thorpe, through her tutelage, is trying to address his needs.

She worried that his high IQ was in some manner a detriment to his well-being. According to Susan, the Henderson household is not a happy one. Lord knows. She then wondered why he wasn't wearing a winter hat or mitts and made a mental note to instruct William to send him home with some of Pete's old winter gear.

"Why isn't Caroline coming home for supper?" William asked.

Still absorbed in her own thoughts, Vivian didn't hear the question.

"Mum, Alice said Caroline isn't coming home for supper," William repeated.

She turned and considered his question. "Her name is Miss Brenner—not Alice. You show respect for your elders, young man, by addressing them by their last name." Vivian clenched her jaw, pursed her lips, and concluded that Alice, that nosy so-and-so, did not ring off. That burns my britches!

William debated for a moment, then said, "She tol' me to call her Alice and to call her daughter Jean."

"Is that so?"

"We were almost home, and they were leaving the house, and Miss Brenner said that…"

"If she told you to call her Alice, then who am I to argue?"

William stared at his mother, hesitated, then went on, "She told us Caroline wasn't coming home today. I tol' Jimmy that you would never let me or Timmy—"

"Timmy or me." She corrected and then added, "Jean is not Alice's daughter, she's…ah, her friend. Alice is quite a fortunate woman to have a close friend like Jean to help her around the house."

A faint scratching noise drifted from the back door into the hallway, accompanied by a shrill bark. Mildred had heard the boys in the house and was eager to greet them.

"You boys skedaddle upstairs to your bedroom. Dinner will be at six." She smiled at Jimmy. "If you change your mind, you're more than welcome to stay for dinner." Another piercing bark echoed through the hallway. She threw up her arms and announced to the walls, "I'm coming, I'm coming…hold your horses."

The three boys ran up the stairs.

Ernie met the boys on the stairs as he trudged down one careful step at a time. In a raspy voice, he said, "Good afternoon, gentlemen. Keeping your powder dry, I trust." He coughed and cleared his throat.

The three boys barely registered his presence as they squeezed by.

Following the scent of the boys, Mildred dashed down the hallway, sliding by the stairs. She dropped her rear end, scooted along the floor, made a course correction and then catapulted up the stairs.

Ernie grasped the handrail and twisted sideways just as the dog sprinted by. "God damn dog. Never understood why people allow animals in their homes," he murmured under his breath.

CHAPTER

ELEVEN

Will opened the front door and said, "Ronnie, I'll be in the car waiting." It had been two hours since the sun had dropped below the horizon, based on the cloudless night and low humidity, he knew it was an ideal evening for stargazing. He lingered on the front lawn, breathed in the crisp evening air and scanned the heavens for Jupiter and Saturn. Check. His gaze travelled north and south as he identified both the Andromeda and Pisces constellations. Check and check.

Veronica cracked open the door and said, "Be one more minute, hon."

Will leisurely walked toward the car. Midway to the driveway, his mind again reached skyward as his thoughts turned to space travel, black holes, and what scientists referred to as Goldilocks planets. He mulled over the possibility of aliens visiting Earth from another star system. As much as he wanted to believe in extraterrestrial life, without physical evidence, it was just too difficult to fathom. Grainy pictures of flying saucers hovering in the clouds were insufficient proof.

On the other hand, he thought, the Milky Way contains more than one hundred billion stars; therefore, how could the Earth be the only planet to sustain sentient life?

While he contemplated the existence of alien life, a shooting star passed overhead. His mind whirled. He conjured a mob of skinny, grey beings, no taller than an eight-year-old with large, unblinking, obsidian-like eyes. From the darkness, three greys effortlessly glided above the ground. He stumbled and shuffled sideways as the lead alien approached. Its neck pulsed and stretched while its dark eyes absorbed the moonlight. One black eye winked at him as it uncurled a long, bony finger. Will then imagined a phlegm-thickened voice say: "ET, go home?"

A raw, bitter wind popped up and slapped him in the face. He stopped abruptly, just as he was about to collide with the driver's side door. That was creepy, he thought. He shook his head to displace the intrusive images.

He was alone. He knew he was alone, but he still had to fight the impulse to look over his shoulder. He squeezed behind the wheel of the Ford Tempo, closed the door and inserted the ignition key. Only then did he turn his head and look out the side window. As suspected, he was alone. Will smirked and said aloud, "ET got confused, thought I was Elliott."

The ponderous beast belched, then growled to life. The engine revved, then dropped to a fast idle. He slid the heater control switch from blue to red, then tapped the gas pedal. He listened to the engine purr as it slowed to a normal idle. To Will's ear, the engine always sounded smoother and less pingy after he replaced the oil. He then fastened the seatbelt and snugged it down across his hips.

Jimmy Henderson crept into his thoughts. Will pictured his childhood friend. Images of their many adventures on Gilwood School Drive flashed and merged before his eyes. How many years had it been since they last got together? Jimmy had made an appearance at their wedding back in 1980. And a year later, he saw Jimmy at Dean's Stag and Doe. Will had attended the function on his own, anticipating that Jimmy would be flying solo, allowing them a chance to catch up.

He was surprised; it had been eight years since he had last seen his friend. Although his memory was fuzzy, he recalled that after attending the University of Toronto, Jimmy spent a couple of years at McGill University in Montreal, then packed up and left the country for an Ivy League university. And now Jimmy was flying in from California. Will reckoned the two buddies had much to discuss.

The passenger door opened, Veronica eased into the seat, leaned over and pecked him on the cheek and said, "I'm so looking forward to dinner, and of course, meeting your friend. You know, Will, we haven't been to a restaurant or on a date in *ages*. And yes, I recognize what an ordeal, what a pain in the rear end it is to get out of the house for a couple of hours, just the two of us. We should really attempt to line up a regular sitter." Veronica looked away and moved on, "Anyway, come to think of it, I only met Jimmy that one time at our wedding."

Will looked admiringly at his wife, "You look very nice tonight. New coat?"

"It's mom's. She let me borrow it." She held out an arm. "Feel it, the leather is so soft and supple. And yes, I know the collar looks like it's fox fur. Mom assured me that it's fake." She looked sideways at him, "I sure hope it's fake. I could not wear a dead fox around my neck. Not on your life…or the foxes for that matter."

She buckled the seatbelt and updated him. "Adam is in bed, and mom and Ellie are watching *ALF,* then the *Cosby Show,* then mom's favourite Tuesday night TV show, *Baywatch.* She is a huge David Hasselhoff fan."

A groupie is more like it, Will thought.

Veronica zipped up the leather coat and went on, "I wrote down the TV channels for her, and she knows Ellie's bedtime is 8 p.m. on a school night. Oh yes, and she has the restaurant phone number—just in case. Will, is the heat on? I'm freezing." Before he could answer, she said, "I'm thrilled Jimmy called you and that we're stepping out for a night on the town with him and his lady friend. You have told me so much about him over the years. I really feel like I know him. It's a shame you guys never stayed in touch."

Will wondered why they had drifted apart. He could speculate. Life gets busy, time ticks by, and people grow apart; they move on. "I'm looking forward to seeing him and meeting his girl…friend," he said.

"I remember at our wedding, he wore an old suit. The jacket was way too tight, and the tie was too thin. Likely one of his dad's old suits. He was overweight but very handsome. The poor fellow did seem out of sorts, and I do recall he struggled to maintain eye contact. On the other hand, he was extremely sweet and thoughtful," Veronica said.

"Huh, just what every guy wants to hear," Will chuckled and glanced at his Sport Timex. "Fuck me, we're gonna be late, Ronnie." He dropped the shifter into Reverse, looked over his shoulder and slowly backed down the driveway onto the street, shifted to Drive and accelerated to the posted speed limit. Without taking his eyes off the road, he said, "Why the hell did we buy this four-wheeled behemoth? I bet this is how it feels to drive a tank."

"You know why, with a monthly car payment of two hundred and fifty-three dollars, it was the only sedan we could afford."

Paul Simon's "Diamonds on the Soles of Her Shoes" filled the cabin with his smooth and effortless singing.

Twenty minutes later and ten minutes behind schedule, Veronica spotted the restaurant. "There it is, the Block and Pestle on your left and look, parking is located behind the restaurant."

Will slowed and entered the lane between two old limestone buildings. He backed into one of the few available spots at the back of the lot.

"I'm glad you took my advice and made reservations last week," she reminded him.

He set the parking brake, exhaled in her direction and said, "I've been thinking, Ronnie, we shouldn't mention Jimmy's family. He never talked much about his parents, but looking back, the poor guy, Dean and their sister Karen harboured some dark family secrets. I don't know what happened behind closed doors…anyway, I'm just saying we don't want to drum up any Henderson family baggage, especially over a nice dinner and not in front of his *friend*." He exhaled, "…unless of course Jimmy does first."

Will casually exited the car while Veronica mulled over his statement. She picked up her emerald purse. Her mind raced—Oh God, what was I thinking—she stuffed the purse under the front seat and exited the car.

"Your purse?"

"I can't have it hanging off my shoulder; it'll clash with mom's leather jacket and my blue dress." She eyed him expectantly, "Don't you say anything," she warned.

"Didn't plan on it, babe. Don't fret, we're going to have a wonderful time." They walked along the uneven cobblestone lane, then turned the corner onto the main street.

"I have been hungry to eat here since it opened two years ago," Veronica said.

"You must be famished!"

She pinched his butt through his Navy-blue corduroy slacks.

He eyed the restaurant's large oak doors, grabbed the oversized brass handle and yanked on the door. It opened effortlessly.

"Good evening, folks," said the young, pretty hostess, "party of two?"

Will stood next to Veronica in the compact lobby and waited a few beats until his eyes adjusted to the dim lighting, then said, "Good evening. How are you? We have reservations for 7:30 p.m., Greene, party of four."

"Just a minute, please," she said, staring at the seating schedule.

To Will's left, through a narrow archway, steps descended to a lounge. He could see a dark mahogany bar with brass trim and, midway along it, beer taps advertising various beer styles. He suddenly felt parched. He turned to Veronica and said, "A cold beer would really hit the spot about now." She smiled while waiting for the hostess to get her act together and escort them to a table. He glanced over her shoulder at a gloomy, cavern-like passageway with a canary yellow floor runner. He assumed the dimly lit corridor led to the dining area.

The hostess finally took her eyes off the seating schedule and said, "Right this way, folks. The other party arrived a few minutes ago." She looked at Will, "Is this your first time at the B & P?"

"Yes, it is."

"Excellent. As we walk to DR3, please watch your step. The restaurant has three dining rooms joined by corridors or catacombs, as I like to call them." She turned and pointed back toward the lobby. "The restrooms are behind you at the far end of the lounge off the lobby where you first entered the establishment."

Will nodded through squinted eyes. Catacombs…that's a little macabre, he thought. A sudden bout of dizziness caused him to stagger. Disoriented, he reached out to steady himself. A surreal sensation of being separated from his body left him momentarily confused. He leaned forward and eased his head against the corridor wall.

The spell passed as quickly as it had overtaken him. He regained his composure, surveyed the corridor in both directions and was satisfied that his stumble had gone unnoticed. He nodded and exhaled. "Yeah…just a bout of low blood sugar," he whispered to himself. He moved quickly to catch the two women.

"Ronnie, do you get the sense we're on a tour to meet the wizard?" he said conspiratorially.

Amused, Veronica clicked her heels together three times, then skipped along the corridor.

A quizzical expression spread across the young hostess's face as she glanced sideways at the odd couple. She then stopped at the entrance to the third dining room and said, "We have arrived at DR3. Please allow me to take your coats. Your server for this evening is Lionel. Enjoy your time at the Block and Pestle." She turned and left with their coats.

TWELVE

A pleasant floral scent met Will and Veronica at the entrance to the softly lit dining room. The couple eyed each other, then scanned the muffled shapes sitting around the tables.

"Ronnie, I think Jimmy would choose a booth. Even in this low light, he would insist on a booth against the wall rather than sitting at a table, feeling like an exposed rooster surrounded by foxes."

As they slowly moved into the dining area, a woman approached from behind. "Oh, excuse me, sir," she said. "I should have zigged instead of zagged."

Will shuffled sideways. "No, no, my mistake, sorry. It's so dark in here, I can barely see my nose in front of my face." He chuckled as he turned and looked at the woman.

She smiled at him and Veronica.

Will observed her as she moved confidently with a graceful self-assurance toward the rear of the dining room. She slid into a booth next to her companion.

Veronica studied her husband, then whispered, "Will…hey, stop ogling her. My God…and wipe the drool off your chin." She poked him firmly in the ribs, then pointed with her chin, "She is lovely. She's gorgeous, and did you see her skin? I would kill for skin like that."

Will thought he noticed something familiar about her companion. He squinted through the dim light and mumbled, "Could it…no, can't be." He turned to Veronica. "I appreciate a certain ambience, but damn it's dark in here. Ronnie, can you see the guy in the booth next to her?"

"I was too busy watching her…and then you, and I must say in this dingy room—"

"Holy fuck, Ronnie. It's Jimmy," he said, dumbfounded.

They stood motionless, eyes squinted, staring toward the booth, tormented by the subdued lighting. The woman's companion raised an arm and waved in their direction.

Jimmy and the woman slid out of the booth while Will and Veronica threaded their way between tables. Jimmy fussed with a leather cord around his neck, then fingered the attached charm that lay hidden under his tailored plaid shirt.

A moment later, the two men stood face-to-face, clownish grins plastered on their faces. They both hesitated, then stepped forward and fiercely hugged and clapped each other on the back. The two women watched with interest as eight years of time and distance melted into the floor.

Jimmy stepped back and said, "It's been too long, bro." He studied Will's face. "You look great, man. Marriage and kids obviously suit you. How are you?"

Will observed Jimmy and was astounded by his physical transformation. He even considered that Jimmy had gained a couple of inches in height—was that even remotely possible?

Veronica nudged him.

Will glanced at her, turned back to Jimmy and said, "I'm good man, no complaints…livin' the dream." He reached out and squeezed Jimmy's upper arm, "Christ, man. I gotta say, you have put on some serious muscle."

Jimmy looked sideways at his companion, chuckled, then said, "I got serious about six years ago when I started hitting the university gym, and once my younger fat-boy version started shedding weight, well, I came to the profound realization that a physical overhaul was possible and necessary." He sighed, "Excuse my rudeness…Veronica, Will, this lovely lady is my companion and constant dinner date, Amahle." (He pronounced her name: Ah-MAH-she).

"Heita, my friends," she said.

Without hesitation, Veronica stepped forward, hugged her, then Jimmy. Will reached out to shake Amahle's hand. She intentionally stepped forward and hugged him as if they were dear old friends. Will felt self-conscious, and not because she was two inches taller.

Jimmy stabbed his hands into the pockets of his stonewashed jeans, turned and said, "How are you, Veronica? You look as beautiful as you did on your wedding day."

"Thank you, you're sweet to say that."

"Dean mentioned that you have two kids?"

Veronica's face beamed in the subdued light. "Yes, we do, two wonderful children. Ellie is five, and Adam is three. You'll have to…" she glanced at Amahle, "you both will have to drop by the house and meet them, and I hope it's before they are teenagers!" Veronica teased.

Jimmy smiled. "Yes, definitely. It's difficult for me to comprehend that Will has two children when so many of my best memories are of a time when we were not much older than your kids."

A shadow crossed Jimmy's face as deep creases formed above his brow. He exhaled, lowered his head, rubbed his neck and tried to focus on his surroundings. He inhaled while attempting to slow the thumping in his chest. The uninvited *guest* was expected; however, Jimmy naively had hoped for a night's reprieve. He wrestled to tame the internal tormentor as it enveloped his thoughts. Amahle saw him struggling and moved to his side, putting an arm around his waist. She whispered in his ear. He always found reassurance in her words, and a moment later, the tormentor loosened its smothering hold.

Jimmy sighed, raised his head and said, "Will, I really didn't plan on this conversation taking place this early in the evening, or tonight for that matter. Nonetheless, I would like to set the record straight, acknowledge my eight-year hiatus and come clean about why I abandoned family and friends." He reached up and absently rubbed the charm hidden under his shirt. He exhaled, "There are aspects of my life that few people are privy to…"

Will and Veronica exchanged confused glances, then stared intently at him. Will placed a reassuring hand on his shoulder and said, "It's all good, Jimmy, we don't need an explanation."

Jimmy hesitated, "I need to get this off my chest." He then went on, "For many years, Will, I was a mess—in a weird headspace dealing with emotional issues that, to be truthful, persisted through my twenties. In retrospect, I should have reached out and…well, straight from the shoulder, I apologize, buddy. I apologize for disappearing for eight years." He smiled regretfully. With supreme effort, he eyed his childhood friend. "Christ, we both know you were my only friend on Gilwood Drive."

Will glanced at Amahle, then shook his head, "There's no need to apologize."

Jimmy dropped his eyes to the table and studied the flowers in the centrepiece. A moment later, he said, "Will, only you and, of course, Mrs. Thorpe, had some knowledge of my fuckin' dysfunctional family."

As Jimmy talked, he sounded amused yet sorrowful. "Early on, while at U of Toronto, I accepted…I believed that to attain academic and personal success, I needed to distance myself from my youth, my years in Millington." He cleared his throat, "I was haunted by childhood memories that would suddenly appear in my feculent rear-view mirror. Over time, I realized that by pressing the academic pedal to the metal, I was able to suppress my worst impulses."

He exhaled, raised his eyes and saw the alarm and worry lines on his dinner companions' faces. He had broken the seal on his innermost thoughts, and now there was no retreat—no going back.

Will was shocked and at a loss for words. He turned and eyed Veronica's knitted brow and wrinkled nose.

Jimmy smiled weakly, "Therefore, to outrun my past, I wrestled to purge or contain my adolescent memories."

"It's all right, you don't need to say any more." Will offered.

"Thanks, man, but…" Jimmy hurried on as he coveted his friend's acceptance, his support, "but, on a lighter note, I have travelled a long road since then, and I now appreciate that I was possessed, so to speak, by a teenager's cluttered, traumatized frame of reference. I suppose you could say I enjoyed an epiphany. I could no longer retreat from or bury my past; I had to accept it, accept all my family's dirty laundry. In an unexpected, even bizarre way—embrace it."

Jimmy sighed, "At times like this, I often defer to Dr. Zaius' iconic line regarding man: 'He must be a warlike creature who gives battle to everything around him, even himself.'"

Will remembered that he and Jimmy had watched *Planet of the Apes* three times over a weekend. He then chastised himself: Christ, here I'm daydreaming about talking apes galloping around on horses, and Jimmy is spilling his guts, baring his soul.

Veronica smiled sheepishly, "We should probably sit before the hostess gives the booth away."

Jimmy glanced at her, smiled, then removed his hands from their prison and said, "Goddamn, I am sorry, folks, we are here to celebrate, not wallow in my self-pity." Amahle embraced him. He put an arm around her and said, "I've learned, life seldom unfolds in the way we envision or desire, even with a detailed blueprint."

Will eyed his friend and, for a moment, was convinced he was staring at twelve-year-old Jimmy explaining the ways of the world to twelve-year-old William.

A low hum from the building's outdated heating system and the ebb and flow of diners' conversations invaded Will's thoughts. He tried to push the intrusion aside as he brooded over Jimmy's *confession*. He tried to recall what Jimmy had just said about his need to escape his childhood memories, his family and Millington. Will frowned. He was confused. In his mind, Jimmy was the kid genius; the kid destined for university who would help transform the world into a better place for the rest of the mere mortals. He exhaled and struggled to accept this mature version of his friend.

The recessed ceiling lights clicked, buzzed, then grew in intensity. Jimmy's disposition brightened as the shadows receded, revealing the majestic dining room's nineteenth-century stone masonry walls, black Mahogany wainscotting, and copper tin ceiling tiles.

Veronica picked up the centrepiece and smelled the fresh-cut white carnations. She turned her head and winked at Will. He gazed at his wife, smiled broadly and cast aside his pessimistic thoughts about his friend. He turned to Jimmy and said, "Christ man, you're being too hard on yourself…look, we just happen to be eight years older, wiser and about to enjoy dinner at an expensive restaurant." He raised an empty water glass, "To friends, family, happiness and aging without dwelling on regrets."

Jimmy chuckled, picked up a glass and said, "Honestly, it is wonderful to be home. Salut!"

Sounds of brass and piano, and the emotive voice of Judy Garland, filled the room.

Will turned to Veronica and raised an eyebrow.

"You read my mind, hon," Veronica said. "That is Dorothy…Judy Garland singing 'Shine On, Harvest Moon.' The restaurant owners must be part of the OZ fan club."

Jimmy chimed in, "Interesting observation." His head swivelled from side to side as he looked at possible hiding spots. "Hmmm…no sign of the Cowardly Lion or Toto," he taunted.

"I'm waiting for the wicked witch of the East, or is it West, to materialize and start casting spells," Will said, amused.

Confused, Amahle asked, "James, what is a…Toto?"

Veronica piped up, "Amahle, have you seen the movie *The Wizard of Oz*? It's my favourite movie of all time, even though it came out in 1939."

Amahle thought for a moment, "Oh my goodness…yes, Dorothy and her ruby red slippers…a delightful movie." She smiled, "When I was young, my parents would take me to the local theatre house to watch old American movies. My daddy adored the Westerns, especially any movie starring his icon, John Wayne."

The server arrived at the booth holding a litre bottle of spring water. In a cheery voice, he said, "Once again, good evening, folks. I will be your server this evening. My name is Lionel." While he filled the water glasses, the house sommelier appeared, cradling a bottle of red wine for Amahle's approval. She eyed the label and nodded. He deftly removed the cork and offered it to her.

"That is not necessary." She pushed her glass forward, looked across the table and said, "One of my absolute favourite red wines, Veronica. It's an extra-dry, well-balanced, medium-bodied Chianti. You may experience flavours of chestnut, red berries and spicy notes. It finishes nicely with a velvety touch on the palate. And incidentally, it pairs exceptionally well with lamb and steak; however, I also enjoy it with seafood."

Veronica listened and watched Amahle's hands move gracefully through the air as she described the wine. "I'm not a wine connoisseur, but it sounds delicious." Veronica moved her glass next to Amahle's, "Yes, please."

The sommelier, eyes glued to the beguiling Amahle, was at a loss for words. Jimmy glanced at Will, winked and smiled knowingly as Amahle exuded an effervescence that enchanted all within her orbit.

The sommelier quickly regained his composure and said, "My, my, Madam, you have captured the very essence of this fine Italian wine. An excellent description. It is also my favourite wine from Tuscany," he offered, displaying a toothy grin. He filled both glasses, wiped the bottle's neck and placed it on the table. "My dear ladies, it has been my pleasure."

Will turned to Lionel and ordered a large House Lager. He then opened a menu, ran his finger down the list of entrées and stopped at the 12-oz T-bone. Veronica turned her head, gently kneed him under the table, sipped her wine and mouthed, "I love you."

Will grinned. "Ditto, " he whispered under his breath, then punctuated his response with an awkward wink.

Veronica smirked and uttered several words that Will missed—nevertheless, he was confident he understood the sentiment.

Amahle set the menu down.

"Amahle…your accent…any chance you are from South Africa?" Will asked.

She looked at him and said, "From your side of the table, I do have an accent." She then smiled and added, "I am indeed South African, born and raised in Johannesburg."

Will wondered if he had offended her. He quickly said, "While listening to your conversation with the wine guy…well, on any given Saturday night, once both kids are asleep…Ronnie and I get wild and crazy and watch a video. Recently, we saw *Lethal Weapon 2*." He peeked at Jimmy; his face was still stuck in the menu. Will forged ahead. "Um…anyway, the bad guys are South Africans dealing in drugs and gold Krugerrands…" He stirred uncomfortably in the booth and glanced over his shoulder at Veronica.

She merely smiled and ignored his plea.

His unease and awkwardness entertained Amahle. She interjected, "Will, please do not be offended…how do you say…I was pulling your finger."

Jimmy looked up from the menu, caught Amahle's eye, smiled and mouthed *leg*. He closed the menu and positioned it by the edge of the table.

Amahle stroked Jimmy's left forearm and said, "The first time James and I went out as a couple," she smiled slyly and air-quoted with her left hand, "some people would call it a date…we went to the theatre house and watched *Lethal*

Weapon. I very much enjoyed the camaraderie between Mel Gibson and Danny Glover." She scrunched up her nose, "However, it was too violent for my liking."

Will nodded and tried to imagine what life must be like in Africa. His knowledge of the continent was woefully limited to Tarzan, Second World War movies depicting American soldiers driving jeeps across North African dunes, battling Nazis and wildlife documentaries. He then wondered why the waiter was taking so long to deliver his beer.

"I have always wanted to visit the pyramids," Veronica said.

Amahle smiled. "Time and again, I am asked if I have explored the pyramids or travelled across the Sahara Desert by camel." She laughed, "I have never straddled a camel, though I have been to the Pyramids of Giza. They are magnificent. Truly a wonder to see." She reached across the table and placed a hand on Veronica's. "You must visit and experience a guided tour of the Veld, the grasslands. It is breathtaking to see the beasts in their natural habitat. And I am pleased to say that conservation practices have been established to protect the flora and fauna. A subject close to my heart."

Veronica glanced over her shoulder at Will. His head was down; she assumed he was mulling over a budding research project, probably related to Africa. She smiled and gently poked him in the ribs.

Jimmy spoke up and said that Amahle earned a PhD in social anthropology from the University of the Witwatersrand before her twenty-third birthday.

"My goodness, that is impressive. You were so young!" Veronica said as she picked up the wine glass by its stem. She enjoyed the wine, and especially the warm feeling spreading outward from her stomach. My goodness, I am a cheap drunk, she thought. She giggled to herself, then asked, "Amahle, what does a social anthropologist do?"

Amahle squeezed closer to Jimmy and said, "A social anthropologist studies the ingredients that contribute to the formation and development of a vibrant and thriving community. We study things like a group's language, their culture and belief system, their ceremonial practices, agriculture and so on." She glanced at Jimmy and went on, "Fundamentally, we ask one simple question: Why do people do what they do? It is a fascinating area of research that elicits questions and answers when we view present-day societies."

Jimmy interjected: "I've seen Amahle's passion in action. I must admit she has that rare ability while discussing her research to invite debate and provoke excitement." He winked at her.

Will and Veronica exchanged crafty glances as they both imagined a passionate Amahle.

"How did you two meet?" Veronica asked.

Amahle looked sideways at Jimmy. "I'll spill the cocoa beans," she said. "We bumped into each other at Wits after an anthropology symposium when our mutual love for chocolate steered us both to the same vending machine."

With her glass almost empty, she reached for the bottle of Chianti. "James, my dear, I'm sure Will would be interested to hear what you have been up to for the last decade. Then we can dissect how a boy from a small Canadian town met his future, pleasant companion from Johannesburg, South Africa." Amahle's eyes glinted as she refilled both wine glasses.

Veronica felt she could be friends with this confident, accomplished woman from South Africa. She wasn't even intimidated by her beauty or intelligence—well, just a wee bit, she mused.

Another soothing Judy Garland tune rained down on them.

Lionel placed the frosty glass of House Lager on the table by Will and said, "Sorry for the wait, sir." He turned toward the women, "Ladies, may I take your order?"

Amahle and Veronica ordered the maple-encrusted salmon. Jimmy settled on a T-bone rare with garlic mash, while Will preferred a well-done T-bone with frites.

Water droplets trickled down the chilled pint glass. Will took a large swig of the amber liquid and then looked expectantly at Jimmy, keen to listen as he recounted the events that had shaped his life throughout the 1980s.

Jimmy picked up the glass of water, sipped twice and with painstaking care, replaced it on the circular water mark left on the tablecloth. He looked up, glanced across the table at Will and then plunged into his story. His vision muddied as he drifted back to early December 1984 and his days in residence at McGill University.

In his mind's eye, he pictured himself in his tiny residence pad, staring out the room's only window, observing the inexhaustible snow as it descended and blanketed the university. He could taste bitter coffee on his tongue as it mingled with the stale odour of cigarette smoke leaking in from the neighbour's pad. Crashes, splats and booming cartoon sounds blasted through from the opposite wall. From across the hall, the sweet aroma of Pongal and Poori bread wafted under the door, causing his empty stomach to growl.

Over the next two days, he watched as the early-December snowstorm forced the university to limit access to and from campus. As the bulk of the storm moved east, Montreal's citizens began to dig out from under two metres of snow.

Jimmy turned, looked at Amahle, then explained that after two days in captivity, staring out his cyclops window, he concluded that his graduate work had also ground to a screeching halt—his focus and productivity, he realized, had abandoned him long before the crippling blizzard.

As the newly fallen powder snow weighed heavily on him, he decided to kick rationality to the curb. A former colleague, now enrolled at Harvard, had offered housing privileges if he ever considered heading south of the border. He packed his clothes, stereo equipment, and a few personal items into his Ford pickup, topped up the vehicle's engine oil, closed out his bank account, and set his sights on America. He traversed the St. Lawrence River via the Champlain Bridge and travelled along Route I-89 South to Boston, Massachusetts, a leisurely seven-hour drive.

Jimmy smiled, "Will, I suspect you have a burning question? It's written on your face."

Will was taken aback, disappointed that Jimmy had made such a rash decision to leave McGill. "What about your dream of a PhD?" he asked. "I'm confused…" he frowned. "You are…were the kid genius that we all knew would go on to excel at university and make our world an even better place," he said, annoyed.

Jimmy looked knowingly at Amahle, then placed his elbows on the table. He looked across the table, smiled tightly and said, "That is a hefty weight to wrap around one person's shoulders." He exhaled, held Will's gaze, then said earnestly,

"Those are just childhood aspirations—a pipe dream. However, I didn't leave McGill empty-handed. I was given the consolation prize—a master's degree."

The smile slipped from his face. "Will…let me explain. I was at a crossroads. I needed to get away, to run, to explore the world beyond my own mental and geographical borders. I rolled the dice, and they landed on Boston."

Jimmy exhaled, crossed his arms and continued, "Life has a funny way of throwing you a curveball when you least expect it and you either swing and miss or you figure out a way to hit it into the outfield. Once in a blue moon, you may even hit it outta the park. As *luck* would have it, shortly after I arrived at Harvard, my pickup died a messy death—I was without a vehicle, broke and in a strange country."

He sipped water, positioned the glass back on the water ring, then wiped his mouth with a napkin. "If I can backpedal for a minute. While at McGill, I worked a part-time job as a bouncer at a Montreal club. The compensation was minimal, but I had unlimited access to the appetizers. To this day, I will no longer eat buffalo chicken wings and celery dipped in blue cheese dressing." He looked around the table and was met with steadfast stares. "Tough audience…" he smirked.

"Another byproduct of my employment was an introduction to Poker. Every Friday night, a game was held in the club. A couple of regulars, seeing an easy mark, invited me to play." He guffawed at his own naiveness. "By the end of the night, I left with an empty wallet. There was, however, something about Poker and gambling that kept me awake at night wanting more. The confrontation between players sitting shoulder to shoulder, the bluffing, eyeing a large pot of money while sweat dripped down the sides of my chest…the co-mingling of cigar and bodily sweat hanging in the air."

Will listened, intrigued. His dad fancied himself a card shark. He, on the other hand, never exhibited the temperament for card games.

"As I became more proficient, I developed the ability to *read* people's body language." Jimmy glanced across the table, "As you well know, Will, a skill I struggled with during my adolescence. Moving on…I discovered most Poker players were lousy at mechanics and at bluffing. I sensed an opportunity. I hoofed it to a nearby used bookstore, bought half a dozen books on the fundamentals of Poker and on the tactics employed by professional players."

Lionel appeared at the table, "Excuse me." He placed a basket of warm sliced bread on the table and then motioned toward the wine bottle, "Ladies?"

Amahle answered for both: "Yes. Thank you. That's wonderful."

He poured the last of the wine into their respective glasses. "Ladies, perhaps another bottle or a glass?"

Veronica raised a hand to her flushed, tingly cheeks, "Oh my, I am quite content with this glass…thank you, no."

Amahle eyed Veronica warmly, "A glass of the Chianti would be lovely."

"Another lager for you, sir?"

"Much appreciated."

"Excellent. And sir, a tea or coffee?"

"I'm good with water," Jimmy said.

Lionel slipped away as quietly as he had appeared. Jimmy eyed his companions, then went on, "As I mentioned, my Ford pickup cashed in its chips four weeks after I arrived in Boston. The next day, Lady Luck intervened. I answered an ad for a position at the Prosaic Mosaic club in Boston. Despite the club's name, it was anything but humdrum. It was a lively, bouncing joint, and the work was similar to my Montreal gig: I checked IDs, hovered over troublemakers, confiscated the odd weapon, and when the need arose, escorted naughty patrons off the premises."

"So, did you rediscover your potential in Boston?" Will asked.

"I suppose I did…for a stretch." He ran a hand through his hair. "I also allowed myself time to pursue other interests. I joined the Harvard Poker Club and routinely entered two games a week, augmenting my modest income."

His mind twisted and turned around thoughts of the *internal tormentor* that constantly tried to fuck with his life. He glanced at Will. "I was making real headway, so to speak, and then…well, once again things went sideways," he said with a measure of self-loathing. "I realized before long that Boston would be relegated to my rearview mirror."

He sighed, "On a lighter note, a famous space traveller in a distant galaxy, Captain James Tiberius Kirk, said: 'To be human is to be complex. You cannot avoid a little ugliness—from within—and from without.'"

Will stared at him for a moment, then said, "'Our species can only survive if we have obstacles to overcome.'"

"'Without them to strengthen us, we will weaken and die,'" Jimmy chuckled. "Another notable quote from the old space opera."

Veronica piped up, "You boys and your Star Wars."

Jimmy smiled at her.

Veronica thought for a moment, then quickly corrected herself, "Humph. It's Star Trek!" Will smiled and acknowledged her with a sidelong glance.

"Amahle, are you a Star Trek fan? Are you a Star Trekker?" Veronica asked.

Amahle replied, "No, not really my cup of tea. Jimmy is a science fiction buff. I will say, though, I do like Mr. Spock and his innate struggle with his human-Vulcan heritage."

Will observed Veronica. She was pleasantly inebriated. "Ronnie, fans are referred to as Trekkies," he said.

After a moment of navel-gazing, Jimmy asked, "Will, do you remember when your dad would drive along the county roads, and we'd forage for wild asparagus?" He dropped his eyes to the shiny dinner knife on the table. "He would give us each an old, rusty knife, and I always imagined I was in an Edgar Rice Burroughs story, ready to test my mettle against a sharp-toothed, big-bellied creature."

Will's eyes lit up as he envisioned Timmy, Mary Lynn, Jimmy, and himself hiking along fences and through waist-high grasses searching for asparagus stalks. He smiled, occupied in thought. "After a morning's harvest, at high noon, Dad would be in the kitchen boiling the asparagus, and then he would pile the spears onto an open-faced sandwich. I have never known anyone more passionate about asparagus." He grinned, "I was always about the hunt." He looked over his shoulder at Veronica. "When Ellie and Adam are a little older, we will have to take them on an asparagus hunt, you know, to carry on the Greene family tradition."

After a moment, Jimmy raised his head and said, "I always thought your dad was one cool dude. I can picture him on speed skates with those extra-long blades, his hands clasped behind his back as he glided across the Bay at least twice as fast as all the other skaters. And then once we were exhausted, frozen to the bone…remember, he would use the butt of his skate blade, chip a hole through the ice into one of the bigger methane bubbles, then light the escaping gas with his trusty Zippo lighter."

"Some of my favourite childhood memories too…sitting on the ice watching the dancing flames. You would think we were around a bonfire on a summer evening," Will said. He then stuck out his chin. "I can honestly say, I never thought of Dad as being cool, though he is still athletic." He shrugged, wondering about his own lack of athletic ability.

Amahle turned her head, gazed at Jimmy and said, "I so rarely hear James's chat about his Canadian childhood. I find it illuminating. I am witnessing another side to this man."

Veronica keenly watched the couple. She delicately held the wine glass by the stem and thought it quite extraordinary that Jimmy rarely spoke about his childhood. She wondered if he had something to hide.

A waitress sidled up beside Jimmy, excused herself and placed a glass of Chianti next to Amahle, then handed Will a pint of beer.

Jimmy patiently waited until the waitress walked away, then removed the charm hanging around his neck. He smiled conspiratorially as if he held in his hand a secret or a puzzle. "Will, what do you think of my *trinket*? Go ahead, have a closer look, inspect it," he said.

Will held the leather cord and studied the charm. He stared intently at the glossy black object. It appeared to wink at him as the light from above reflected off its black fluted surface. He continued to study it, then asked, "Is this black glass object recently rendered to depict a projectile point?"

"No. It is an authentic obsidian projectile point," Jimmy said. "It was a gift from an archaeologist friend, excavated during a dig in the Rocky Mountains of Colorado. In the last grid location, the team uncovered bones, pieces of pottery, similar *trinkets* and a partial mammoth skull and mandible in a sediment layer carbon-14 dated to about 12,500 years ago."

"Man, it's amazing. By its size and shape, I assume it's a spear point?"

Jimmy smiled slyly, "You tell me."

Veronica remarked, "It looks like a big arrowhead with long grooves. It's so black and lustrous, and the way the light shimmers off its surface. It's exquisite."

Will dropped the projectile point onto his palm to gauge its weight. "Hmmm…well, I'd say it's a spear point fashioned from black volcanic glass…igneous rock. What say you, James?"

"Indeed, it is. And culture?"

Will grimaced, "It's too old to be from the Folsom or Dalton prehistoric cultures. The more I look at it, and its characteristic elongated fluted shape…I reckon it must be a Clovis spear point." He leaned forward, eyed Jimmy suspiciously, "Wait…" he said, perplexed, "I have never seen a picture of a Clovis point made of black obsidian. I thought Clovis people made their spearheads out of chert or other common stones."

"I will say that Clovis spear points are named after the city of Clovis, New Mexico, where they were first found in the 1920s," Jimmy offered. "Since then," he went on, "thousands of Clovis points have been unearthed across most of North America. Interestingly, Margaret, the archeologist, proposed that the paleolithic peoples may have utilized obsidian spear points during their rituals as a kind of Talisman to ensure a successful hunt and to hasten the recovery of their sick and injured."

Veronica sipped the last of her wine. She coyly peeked across the table at Amahle and wondered whether she felt threatened by a woman archaeologist gifting Jimmy a semi-precious charm. To her surprise, Amahle's expression remained pleasant and engaged. She then noticed Amahle smiling at her. She hastily concluded that this lovely, sophisticated woman didn't feel threatened by *any* woman.

"Final Jeopardy question: What type of spear point is it?"

Will pursed his lips, handed the *trinket* back to him and said, "I will stick with my original answer: What is a Clovis spear point?"

"We have a winner!" Jimmy chuckled.

"I hope you don't mind me asking, but I'm curious about its value?" Veronica asked.

"Some Clovis points are quite extraordinary and are worth tens of thousands of dollars. This one, I would estimate a street value of…oh, three thousand dollars." Jimmy eyed Veronica, "I would never sell it, however."

She glanced at Amahle, anticipating a reaction. Nothing.

FOURTEEN

The constant chatter, chairs scraping, and cutlery clashing drew Will's attention. He slowly scanned the dining room and the faces at each table. He exhaled as an uneasiness pulled at him; something about the other diners' behaviour was peculiar. Bewildered, he stared at the faces closest to them, and suddenly it occurred to him that it was the four of them out of sync—as if they were *invisible*, as if they didn't…exist!

He shook his head, sighed and silently berated himself for entertaining such ridiculous thoughts. He caught Veronica eyeing him. Was that concern written on her face, he wondered. He winked weakly at her, turned to their company and said, "Jimmy, why don't you tell us about your adventures in California?"

"I thought you'd never ask," Jimmy chuckled. He glanced at Amahle. "Two years ago, we formed a partnership with several Stanford University colleagues entrenched in the Information Technology ecosystem. The relationship opened the door to discussions with five Silicon Valley companies.

These five IT companies, in addition to expanding their software applications and creating new hardware products, are determined to push the envelope on internal workplace relationships, that is, between employer and employee."

Will nodded. His mind was still spinning, locked on the faceless strangers surrounding them. He slowly exhaled and tried to gather his thoughts.

"Then, eighteen months ago, we relocated to Half Moon Bay, a community close to Stanford University and Silicon Valley."

"I think they filmed *The Right Stuff* around Half Moon Bay," Will said.

"It's a beautiful scenic area on the Pacific Ocean," Amahle said.

"Were you able to improve their workplace environment?" Veronica asked.

Amahle shook her head, "We underestimated the tenacious hold of the existing workplace culture."

Jimmy nodded, "Our...*novel* concepts and processes collided with the instituted standard operating procedures that have been the backbone of office and factory floor interactions for decades. In fact, I'd argue all the way back to 1913, when the Ford Motor Company implemented the assembly line."

He glanced at Amahle and went on, "To their credit, the IT companies, in addition to driving profit and progress, are determined to introduce evolutionary workplace changes. They envision a work environment that is collaborative, innovative, and adaptable, while fostering confident and empowered employees." Jimmy frowned, "Great Caesar's ghost! That is quite the word salad."

Veronica smiled warmly and remarked, "Thank you, editor-in-chief Perry White of the Daily Planet."

Jimmy eyed Veronica. "I am impressed you know your comic book characters."

Veronica teased, "Look who I'm sitting beside. Actually, I have been a fan of Superman since I was a little girl, although I didn't own any Superman merchandise—unlike some people." She nudged Will.

Will exhaled, "I mostly collected Superman comics."

Jimmy and Veronica both laughed.

Amahle sipped her wine and observed.

Jimmy waited a moment, then launched into the last of his *sales pitch*. "Eventually, with a measure of deviousness, we convinced four of the five companies to implement our system-wide processes," he crossed his fingers, "which should generate financial opportunities and accelerate social benefits. Finally, we will compare the quarterly data against our projected outcomes…" Jimmy sensed Amahle eyeing him, "My apologies, I'm getting too far into the weeds."

Veronica smiled at Amahle, "It all sounds very exciting."

"I'm on board," said Will. He then asked, "I'm curious, how did you promote your concepts to the Silicon Valley companies?"

"Excuse me," Veronica said. Will shifted and slid out of the booth.

"I will join you," Amahle said, grabbing her Chanel bag.

Jimmy waited until the women left the dining room, then eagerly went on, "Will, we struggled mightily with that question: How do we convince these companies to invest in our paradigm-shifting methods without subjecting the target audience to boring graphs, dry text and sundry information that would surely cause a stampede to the nearest fire exit." He grinned, "Eventually, after many presentations, it was the brilliant Amahle who saved the day."

He eyed Will. "I'm getting ahead of myself. Are you sure you want to hear how we resolved our dilemma?"

"Of course, I do. I'm intrigued."

"All right. Awesome. We took our research, boiled down the pertinent information and created visually striking diagrams and contextual data overlays. We still, however, needed a hook, something to draw in our audience. We settled on a splashy triangle-shaped diagram, labelling its points as People, Profit, and Progress. We then refined our presentation and prepared answers to anticipated questions. We were prepared…we thought." He smirked, "With each presentation, we dropped a smelly steaming turd." He chuckled as Will looked on, surprised.

"Our audiences showed limited interest, no probing questions—we were doomed before we unlocked our briefcases." He exhaled, "Anyway, following each presentation, we would hold a debrief with our colleagues."

A waitress stopped next to the booth and unfolded a tripod serving stand.

Jimmy waited, then pressed on, "Nonetheless, we were lost, out of giddy up, on the precipice, ready to pack our bags and call it a day. Then…late one night, Amahle and I were in our den, listening to the waves breaking on shore, hunched over on the floor, papers and overlays strewn everywhere. We surfed through the presentation material for the umpteenth time, looking for a clue. We were at a loss and exhausted. We took a break. Thirty minutes later, Amahle was devouring a slice of meat-lovers' pizza when the overlay of the Triangular diagram caught her attention. Her excitement bubbled over, and she shrieked, 'Let's flip this mother fuckin' diagram on its head.'" Jimmy put his hands together in the shape of an inverted triangle. "So…that's what we did. We shifted the Profit and Progress labels to each end of the triangle's top line, and at the downward-pointing vertex, we pasted the People label. Therefore, Profit and Progress now visually trumped People."

"She really said mother fuckin'?"

"Fuckin' A."

With an edge of excitement, Jimmy leaned forward and said, "The response to our revised presentation was overwhelmingly positive, just fucking phenomenal. Amahle's genius, coupled with a slice of meat lovers' pizza, and we were sailing the high seas. Four companies immediately jumped on board." He sat back and smiled broadly.

"And now, that the trials are underway, by the end of next quarter, certainly by spring of 1990, we will have enough data to analyze the implementation of our processes against each company's metrics. Will…never underestimate the power of simple drawings."

Will shook his head, impressed with Jimmy's determination and asked, "Are you able to modify your workplace concepts and apply them to companies with different products or services?"

"Absolutely. We are in the process of establishing our consulting firm and finalizing our business model. We still don't have an official company name—"

The two women returned and claimed their seats.

Jimmy leaned forward, put his elbows on the table and said, "Welcome back, ladies. While you were away, we discussed the relevance of the upside-down Triangle and the power of elementary illustrations."

Veronica appeared confused. Amahle smiled knowingly.

Will, meanwhile, was drawn in by Jimmy's Clovis spear point. It pulled on the leather cord about his neck and tantalizingly rocked from side to side, barely clearing the tabletop. Captivated by its movement, unable to turn away, he sensed someone standing next to him; the aroma of steak filled his nostrils. He watched as the black charm shimmered and slowed. A sudden weariness embraced him. He tried to steady his eyes and resist the heaviness of his lids. Somewhere distant, he heard Veronica's voice praising the maple-encrusted salmon. His resistance buckled. His eyes closed, dark shadows surrounded him.

FIFTEEN

As Pete neared the Church's vestibule, he felt lighter now that the funeral service had concluded. From the closet nook, he retrieved his beige trench coat, pulled the bundled mohair scarf from the left sleeve, slipped the trench coat over his charcoal grey Brooks Brothers single-breasted blazer and looped the checkered maroon scarf around his neck.

He turned and eyed Benjamin Jones' son, standing by the double doors, in conversation with the Priest who had presided over the service. Pete quickly considered his options and realized there was no escape; he had to walk past the pair to reach the exit.

Stephen Jones shook hands with Father O'Clery, thanking him for his thoughtful sermon and guidance during the family's time of grief.

Pete approached, extended a hand and said, "Stephen, I worked with your father at *the* Bell." Appearing remarkably composed in a black three-piece suit, Stephen shook hands.

Pete went on, "I am so sorry for your loss. Your father passed away far too soon."

"Thank you for coming to my dad's service. It means a lot to my mom," he said, detached.

"Of course. Your father…was a good man, one of the best, always there to lend a hand and help his colleagues. We will sorely miss him at the office."

Stephen nodded.

Pete fidgeted, waited, then moved to fill the silence. "Your father was one of the finest linemen at *the* Bell. He knew his stuff better than anyone. And when we weren't out in the field repairing downed lines or doing routine maintenance, a number of us would gather in the office, chew the fat and occasionally someone would break out a deck of cards." He smiled, "Benny enjoyed a card game as much as the next guy…incidentally, he was a hell of a good Poker player; he could bluff with the best of them." Pete turned and looked sheepishly at the priest, "Very nice sermon, Padre."

"Thank you. We are pleased you attended." The Priest leaned in, put a hand on Stephen's shoulder, "I will talk to you a little later, Stephen. Presently, I have several tasks requiring my immediate attention." He turned and walked toward a group of mourners milling around the Nave.

"Again, Stephen, my condolences to you and your mum." One of Stephen's cousins, tears streaming down her face, came up and threw her arms around him. Pete stepped back, turned, and quickly exited through the double doors. He squinted and inhaled the cold, wonderful daylight. He looked out across the crammed parking lot and thought Benny would be happy that so many people had attended his send-off. He then spied a telephone booth next to the lot.

*   *   *

Pete left the telephone booth and walked toward the back of the parking lot. He loosened his tie, inhaled deeply, letting the biting, prickly air settle in his lungs while he thought about his own unease attending a funeral or any ritual that honours the deceased. He assumed that others felt the same discomfort. Nevertheless, he hoped the next funeral he attended would be his own. He smirked—at least not until he was an old man in his seventies. He approached the Sapphire Blue 1957 Pontiac Safari station wagon, the perfect car for a family man with five children.

Two months prior, he and Vivian visited the local General Motors dealership on the outskirts of Millington. The salesman recognized Pete from high school and said he would twist the manager's arm to get the best possible price. Moreover, as a war veteran, Pete was assured that the dealership would do right by him. The salesman winked conspiratorially at the couple.

Vivian was enthralled as she viewed the pristine six-year-old station wagon that Pete was considering; it had soft bench seats, air conditioning, power steering and power brakes.

Pete peered under the hood at the large V8 engine and the state-of-the-art, Strato-Flight Hydra-matic transmission. Vivian sidled up next to him and whispered that she adored the car's deep blue colour. The next day, he withdrew $1400 from their vehicle savings account. With new rubber installed on all four wheels due to his negotiating prowess, Pete happily drove the Safari station wagon home, then took the family out to celebrate at the new A&W drive-in restaurant. Home to the Baby, Teen, Mama and Papa Burger Family.

Pete opened the Safari wagon's oversized door, slid onto the soft blue bench seat and closed the door, ensuring the bottom of his trench coat was fully inside the vehicle. He removed the keys from his pocket, then leaned over, opened the glove box, and fished out the Altoids tin container. He flipped the lid, pinched a mint, and smiled. He had persevered and grown accustomed to the taste of the 'Curiously Strong' breath mints. He believed the Altoids masked smoky breath better than the competition.

He picked up speed as he drove away from the Sacred Heart Church located in Millington's business district. Rather than going to the Dominion grocery store to save ten or twenty cents, he decided to buy ice cream at the corner store.

He turned onto County Road 3 and moments later, eyed a four-legged creature, also heading north, trotting along the shoulder of the road. As he got within shooting distance, he recognized the amber fur, long bushy tail and pointed white snout of a red fox. With no other vehicles on the road, he pushed the Safari wagon into the oncoming lane and slowed to a walk. He looked across the hood as the fox turned and eyed the large mechanical beast. It held a small brown animal in its jowls that, on closer inspection, was a groundhog.

Pete eased the Safari wagon by the animal. As the tailgate slid by, the fox picked up its pace and only then maneuvered into the ditch. He watched the fox diminish in the rear-view mirror for as long as he could. He mused, what a beautiful fur collar that would make for some lucky woman. *If only I were a hunter.* He glanced at himself in the rearview mirror—*when pigs fly.* Two miles along the road, he turned onto Gilwood School Drive, then pulled into the McGregor General Store parking lot.

*   *   *

"Good afternoon, Mrs. Yang." Pete closed the door against the cold and walked to the counter.

"Hello, Mr. Greene. Your son William came into the store the other day. He is such a nice, well-mannered boy."

"Thank you, Mrs. Yang. He is a good boy," he said candidly.

Mrs. Yang eyed him. "Are you returning from church? The family in the car?"

"In a manner of speaking. I was at a colleague's funeral. Incredibly sad."

"Oh, I am sorry. My condolences."

Pete promptly shifted the conversation and said, "Mr. Yang left you alone to mind the store?" He stepped over to the magazine rack and noticed the November issue of *Mechanix Illustrated*: "BIG NEWS! In New UHF and Fringe TV Antennas." He tucked a copy under his arm.

"He is upstairs watching TV. My word, when it comes to sports, he is such a fanatic."

"Well, good for him."

"Truthfully," Mrs. Yang smiled, "I so much more enjoy my time as proprietor without his interference. Oh my…please, you must never tell him I just said that. It must be our secret."

Pete chuckled. "Of course. My lips are sealed." He wandered to the rear of the store, where a large chest freezer was tucked against the wall. He opened the lid and removed an ice-covered tub of vanilla ice cream. He walked back, dropped the ice cream and the magazine on the counter next to the cash register and said, "I will also take a pack of Peter Jackson Filter Kings."

Mrs. Yang nodded, ducked below the counter and searched through the rows of cigarette packages.

Thirty seconds later, Pete said, "They are in a black package with two silver stripes."

"Peter Jackson Filter Kings…black package, Jackpot!" She placed the cigarettes on the magazine. "Please bear with me, our old clunky cash register broke down, so now I am forced to use pencil and paper." She smiled at him. "Not to worry, Mr. Greene. My math skills are excellent."

With pencil in hand, she jotted down the prices:

Magazine: 0.25 cents

½ gallon vanilla ice cream: 0.90 cents

Peter Jackson cigarettes: 0.35 cents

"That will be one dollar, fifty. Thank you, kindly."

Pete placed the correct change on the counter, scooped up his purchase, and wished Mrs. Yang a wonderful evening. As he reached the car, he placed the tub of ice cream on the ground beside the driver's door. He opened the door, slid behind the wheel, pulled the door shut and cracked the window open. He dropped the magazine on the seat, pushed in the cigarette lighter, and opened the pack of cigarettes. Moments later, the lighter popped. He filled his lungs, then exhaled through the cracked window.

Mrs. Yang stepped outside and swept away the light blanket of snow that had accumulated at the store's entrance. Pete dragged on the cigarette and thought about a conversation he had had with Mr. Yang the previous summer. On that day, Mr. Yang was in a talkative mood; his wife was visiting family in Vancouver. He was alone; he was happy. After a couple of minutes, the conversation turned to their respective ancestry.

Mr. Yang chatted about his grandfather's voyage on a chartered ship that sailed from Guangdong, a coastal province in South China, to British Columbia in the 1880s. He joined thousands of Chinese labourers hired to finish the western stretch of the Canadian Pacific Railroad from Vancouver to Fraser Canyon. He passionately noted that his grandfather witnessed the hammering in of the Last Spike at Craigellachie, near Eagle Pass, British Columbia, on November 7, 1885, signifying the completion of the greatest engineering project undertaken by the young nation.

Pete recalled seeing a grainy black-and-white photograph of the Last Spike ceremony in a high school history book. He, however, harboured reservations about whether Mr. Yang's grandfather was present at the historical event; regardless, it was an intriguing story. He tossed the cigarette butt and rolled up the window. He pinched two Altoids mints, stuffed the cigarette pack under the bench seat and drove home.

CHAPTER

SIXTEEN

Vivian stood in the living room, looking out the bay window as the Safari wagon turned into the driveway. She admired the car from nose to tail. She was thoroughly satisfied with their purchase of this big safe wagon, even though it was the most money Pete had ever spent on a vehicle. She knew he was not thrilled with the blue colour, but when the dealership agreed to throw in four new tires, well, that cemented the deal. She admired her husband's negotiating skills. She did not possess the means or the desire to barter; whatever the sticker price, that is what she expected to pay.

To her astonishment, Pete slowly reversed the wagon and then lumbered along the street, retracing his route back to County Road 3. She watched the car move down the street, and then the light bulb burned bright—he had forgotten to buy ice cream.

"Everything all right, Viv?" Ernie asked as he peered over the *Reader's Digest* magazine.

"Yes. I suspect your son forgot to buy vanilla ice cream." She turned and observed him sitting on the chesterfield, legs extended, crossed at the ankles. The dog was curled up next to him, her head resting on his feet, snoring lightly. "Mildred sure does seem to have a thing for you," she said, bemused.

"I don't understand it either," Ernie said, eyeing the ninety-pound, snoring black lump of fur. "She is keeping my feet warm, and that's much appreciated." He smiled crookedly.

"How's your coffee? Would you like another cup?"

"Thank you, No. I have had my quota for the day."

"I will be in the kitchen if you need anything...Dad." She walked to the end table, retrieved the empty coffee mug and left him alone to enjoy her *Reader's Digest.*

Ernie nodded and stuck his nose back into the magazine.

On her way to the kitchen, Vivian stopped at the bottom of the stairs and summoned William. She waited, then called again, "William."

"What?"

A flash of anger passed over her face. "In the kitchen, now!" she said. Rustling noises filtered down from the second floor. As she entered the kitchen, William jogged in behind her.

"Did you go into my bedroom closet and dig out your father's old hats and mitts for Jimmy?"

William thought for a moment, then said, "Jimmy has mitts at home." He looked up at his mother, "Jimmy went home. He wanted to see his sister before she goes away tomorrow."

Vivian was doubly disappointed. She was certain he could use the winter gear. She had also expected he would stay and enjoy a lovely home-cooked roast beef dinner. Only the Lord knows when the poor boy last had a decent meal.

She shook her head. She had heard many hurtful rumours concerning the Henderson household. Moreover, on several occasions, she had witnessed Jimmy's mum displaying behaviour unbecoming of a mother. She exhaled and rebuked herself for such thoughts.

"I am so sorry Jimmy had to leave before dinner," Vivian said. She took her apron from the back of the chair and tied it snugly around her waist. "William, I want you to run up to my bedroom, and at the back of the closet, you will find your father's moccasin slippers. Please retrieve…grab the slippers and take them to Granddad. I know if I try to give him the slippers, he will deny that his feet are cold."

William's brow furrowed.

Vivian locked eyes with her son. "It's a male thing. Promise me when you grow up, you won't be a stubborn old codger."

He didn't understand but nodded anyway. He turned and jogged out of the kitchen.

While rummaging through his parents' closet, he discovered his father's World War II ration tin. Hearing a commotion, Timmy left his bedroom, wandered the hallway and poked his head in his parents' bedroom. He spotted William on his knees, clambering around in their closet. He opened his mouth to speak, had second thoughts and quietly retreated down the hallway. Timmy was learning.

The green ration tin was the size of a child's shoe box. William held it in one hand, the slippers in his other and jogged out of the bedroom.

*   *   *

"Slippers, Grandpa. Mum said you might want these for your cold feet." William handed him the soft leather slippers, then sat down beside his grandfather.

"Thanks, Sam. My feet aren't cold, but these moccasins are the cat's meow!" Ernie slowly leaned forward and managed to slip on one moccasin. "Hey Sam, how about a hand?" William leapt off the chesterfield, assisted his grandfather with the second moccasin, then returned to his seat and held up the green tin for a closer inspection.

Ernie noticed the ration tin and said, "See, during the war each soldier was given a ration tin, like this one, and it contained items like biscuits, chocolate and concentrated meals—meals that just required water and a wee bit of mixing."

"I know. Dad told me that a lot of the food he ate in the army looked like powder, and he would have to add water."

"That's exactly right, Sam." Ernie took hold of the ration tin and pried open the lid. "Let's see what treasures we have hidden inside here?"

Grandfather and grandson leaned in and peered into the ration tin.

*   *   *

Dressed in a heavy parka and carrying a knapsack, Susan walked into the house, followed by Mary Lynn wearing a turtleneck sweater.

"You're both home. Good. Dinner will be ready in an hour," Vivian echoed from the kitchen doorway. She wiped her hands on the apron as she walked along the hallway toward the girls, "Mary Lynn, how was your piano lesson?"

"It was a bummer. Mrs. Tuttle…she was surprised to see me and left me alone in the piano room. I guess because yesterday Mr. Tuttle got home from Iceland or Greenland—from one of those frozen countries."

"Oh my. I am sorry, dear. Hilary mentioned that David's six-month overseas tour was almost complete. I was under the impression he was due home next weekend."

"Yeah, well, she told me to practice my piano scales and chords, and she left me all alone in the room for the whole hour!" Mary Lynn whined. She squeezed by her mother and traipsed along the hallway to the living room. "Hi, Grandpa," she said. William looked up at his sister. She glared at him. Mildred lifted her head, slowly wagged her tail, then dragged her body along the chesterfield and settled in a thin ribbon of receding sunlight.

Mary Lynn turned back toward the stairs. She eyed her mum standing by the kitchen entrance and said, "At least the piano lessons are free, right, Mum?" Vivian held her tongue as she watched her daughter trudge up the stairs.

Meanwhile, Susan had hung her parka in the front closet. She barked, "Hello, Granddad." With her knapsack slung over her shoulder, she beelined it past the living room to the basement stairs.

"Did you and Trudy get much accomplished on your school assignment?" Vivian asked. She admired her second daughter's gumption and obsession with academic excellence. On her eighth birthday, she told her mum she wanted to be a doctor, one who performs surgery. Vivian encouraged Susan to pursue her dream, even though she assumed her daughter's passion would fade with time. However, now that she was in grade 12, her motivation to gain acceptance into medical school had not withered; in fact, it had blossomed along with her beauty.

Susan halted at the stairs to the basement and said, "We're wrapping the summary and will be ready for the class presentation on Wednesday. Mum, please keep everybody off the telephone tonight from 6:30 p.m. to 7:00 p.m. Trudy will be calling."

"I will do my best, dear. You are sure it's not a boy calling?" she needled.

*   *   *

Ernie reached into the ration tin and fished out Pete's military medals. They dangled from an assortment of wide, vertically striped ribbons, dyed in multiple colours. He held two out for William to inspect and said, "Your father earned these medals during World War II when he was overseas fighting the Nazis."

"Wow, those are neat, Grandpa." William quickly moved on, reached into the ration tin, and pulled out a handful of smooth grey coins, then dropped them on a seat cushion. The coins were of contrasting shapes and sizes; two looked like small doughnuts with holes in the middle. He held one up and read: "Neder…Neder…lands."

"That is a coin from the Netherlands," Ernie said, then pointed out a couple of coppers, a few half pennies, farthings, and a couple of half crowns. The other coins scattered on the cushion were from various European countries. Ernie picked up a small red book and held it in his palm. The English-Dutch dictionary was the size of a matchbox. In faded black ink on the inside cover, his son had printed: Peter Greene. "Look at this miniature book, Sam. Your father would have used this dictionary to help him understand people who did not speak English." Ernie set the dictionary back in the ration tin, then removed a folded rectangular piece of cardboard. He carefully separated the cardboard to reveal two 4-inch strips of red-and-gold embroidered cloth. "Ah, these are the Shoulder Titles that were stitched to the shoulder area of your father's military uniform, identifying him as a member of the Princess Patricia Canadian Light Infantry."

Ernie lifted his head at the rumble of a car. He looked out the bay window. "Oh, wonderful, your father just pulled in the driveway." He carefully deposited the Shoulder Titles in their cardboard pouch. "For your father's sake, I do hope he remembered to pick up some ice cream." He winked at William.

*　　*　　*

Vivian held the kitchen side door open as Pete stepped across the threshold and handed her the ice cream. He removed his trench coat and lazily threw it over the back of a kitchen chair. He bent over, unzipped and slipped off his cumbersome galoshes, then dropped them on a folded newspaper beside the door.

Vivian waited patiently and then pounced. "You forgot, didn't you? I only asked you to pick up one thing—ice cream for *your* father's pie, and it slips your mind. I swear you never listen to me," Vivian said, exasperated.

"Sorry, what did you say?" Pete asked through a crooked smile. He regarded his wife for a moment and said, "Yes, I forgot to buy ice cream. Does a confession make it better?" He had been relieved when he returned to the store and spied the bin of vanilla ice cream where he had left it in the parking lot.

Vivian mulled over her husband's forgetfulness as she watched him remove his blazer. Then again, he did telephone home after the service. As Susan would say, *I should cut him some slack*. He did have a lot on his plate today, what with the funeral and his father's unexpected visit. Her fingers tingled from holding the ice cream. She walked to the refrigerator and put the ice cream in the freezer. She turned and faced him. Her resolve softened. "How did Benjamin's family hold up?" she asked.

"They held up better than I thought they would," Pete said as he leaned over and gave her a quick peck on the lips. "I had a chat with Benny's son, Stephen and with the padre." He shook his head in disappointment, "I never know what to say to a man of the cloth." He shook his head again and said, "Anyway, I am done with funerals. I know…it is not about me, but in my lifetime…I have witnessed too much mayhem and too many mourners suffering the loss of loved ones. Mark my words: I am through with funerals," he exclaimed.

Vivian quietly accepted Pete's angry tirade and said, "When you change, please put your blazer and slacks over the bedroom chair. I have no time tonight, but tomorrow, I will hang your clothes on the line to air out and then run the iron over your slacks." She smiled and eyed her husband. "Then my dear, you will be all set for your next…um, occasion." She quickly went on, "I have left the empty box for your dress shoes by the bed."

Timmy, hearing his dad's voice, wandered into the kitchen.

"Hey, big fella." Pete reached out and mussed his hair. "The girls are home?"

"Susan and Mary Lynn are home," she replied, then added, "Caroline called and said she couldn't make it home for dinner." She then whispered, "I wonder if the reason she stayed at school has something to do with a boy?" They locked eyes; neither wanted to address such a charged question.

After a moment of silence and inward contemplation, Vivian said, "Your father is in the living room with William. They are on a mission to explore your war memorabilia."

Pete nodded, tucked the magazine under his arm and put a hand on Timmy's back. "Let's go see what granddad and your brother are up to."

*   *   *

Ernie scooped up the loose coins on the seat cushion and returned them to the ration tin. He slid his hand between the seat cushions, fishing for coins. He withdrew his hand, and a tiny black stiletto shoe was pinched between two fingers. He raised his hand to see what he had caught.

William eyed Barbie's shoe. He shrank into the chesterfield and immediately dropped his eyes as if looking for coins hidden in the carpet.

"How old is your sister…Eleven?" Ernie asked.

"Mary Lynn's twelve," William mumbled.

"I thought by now she would have outgrown her desire to play with dolls. Twelve, you say!" Ernie held out his hand, "Here, give your sister this toy shoe."

William, relieved, quickly tucked Barbie's shoe deep in his pants pocket.

Ernie eyed a grey dime-sized metal pin shaped like a small skull held up by two crossed long bones.

Timmy ran into the living room, followed by his father.

"Hey, Dad. Nice of you to join us for dinner. I hope you are planning to spend the night. We have a spare bed in the basement. It's not the Taj Mahal, but the mattress is firm," Pete said as he offered the magazine to his father. "It's the November issue of *Mechanix Illustrated.*"

Ernie looked at the cover, then placed the magazine on the armrest and said, "Good afternoon, son. I may take you up on your offer of a firm mattress." He studied his son, "A good turnout at the funeral?"

"Yes. A full house." Pete surveyed the room. A sleepy Mildred lay snuggled against Ernie's legs. She stirred and peered up at him. He looked at the dog. "Grandpa visits and *you* abandon me—didn't even greet me when I walked through the door," he said, perturbed. Mildred eyed him as if it were a two-way conversation, yawned and weakly wagged her tail. "Too late, Dred," he said.

Ernie turned on the lamp atop the end table. William jumped up and switched on the corner floor lamp.

"You have a wonderful family, son, and a nice, comfortable home."

"Well, thanks, Dad." Pete eyed his father suspiciously, "Something amiss?"

"Me? No, no. No complaints." Ernie shifted the direction of the conversation. "What do you make of the shocking news from our neighbours to the south. What's your take on it?"

"Well, it really is hard to fathom that JFK is dead—assassinated. He was a good man and a good president," he said sincerely. Pete studied his father for a moment. "A terrible blot on the American way of life. And let's be clear, the world takes notice and pays particular attention to the USA and its political establishment. I bet my bottom dollar there will be global repercussions. Right? Don't you agree?" Pete waited a moment, then went on, "We depend on the stability of the United States government, and this shooting is certainly a stain on the American landscape." He sighed, "Anyway, a real blow for the American people and devastating for the Kennedy clan." He shook his head in disbelief and added, "Vivian took it especially hard."

"Yes, we discussed the Kennedys at length. Whilst the Americans investigate his assassination, I have wondered these last couple of days whether his faith played a part in the killer's motive. He was, after all, the country's first Roman Catholic president."

Pete considered his father's theory, "I imagine we'll find out soon enough."

Ernie then noticed he still held the grey skull-shaped pin in his hand. "What do we have here, son?" he asked.

Pete squinted at the object and said, "That is a Totenkopf lapel pin. The German SS officers wore those pins on their uniforms. In German, it translates to Death's head. It symbolizes death and the German soldier's defiance of death." He glanced at William and said, "One of many disturbing symbols from that period of the world's history."

Pete stood in front of the chesterfield, his back to the bay window. The sky's orange and yellow hues were dissipating into shades of brown and rust as the moon solidified in the distance. "William, there should be a blue jewellery box in my ration tin," he said.

William spied the small blue box and passed it to his dad. Pete removed the lid and inspected the nickel-sized, blue pendant protected in a bed of cotton. He appraised the pendant, then held the box at an angle so Ernie and the boys could view the contents.

Ernie watched Pete and instantly recognized the distant look on his son's face and said, "You should tell the boys the story of how this pendant came to be in your possession."

Pete nodded, turned toward the bay window and moved to the well-used leather armchair situated in the corner. He dropped heavily onto the chair, looked across the room at his father, the boys sitting next to him, and Mildred curled up by

Ernie's feet. He then looked intently at the Windmill painting hanging above the boys' heads.

His mind drifted back to the autumn of 1944 as he imagined the Dutch town of Arnhem. He set his story in motion: "The Germans had blockaded the Dutch railways and cut off food and fuel shipments. During the long winter that followed, thousands of Dutch people died from malnutrition and sickness."

He hesitated, studied the pendant for a moment, then went on, "By the spring of 1945, we had liberated the southern Netherlands and were preparing for a push to the north across the Maas River to the more populated western provinces. It was the first week of April when we received our marching orders…our objective was to force the Germans back to the Grebbe Line. The 1st Canadian Infantry Division and the 5th Canadian Armoured Division prepared for the impending assault. After advancing north for seven days, we halted and set up camp next to a forested area within striking distance of the town of Arnhem. We then waited for resupply trucks.

"As we settled in, the boys set up a secure perimeter while I ran power cords, connecting each soldier's pup tent to a generator. Starting with the majors on down through the ranking officers to the enlisted men, I wired each tent with one light bulb."

Pete visualized himself in a pup tent, under the warm glow of a light bulb, reading one of Vivian's letters. He would often reread her letters even though he could recite them from memory.

He returned to the present, smiled, and said, "That simple light source was great for morale. Anyway, I kept busy servicing and repairing the backpack radios, the jeep and truck radio equipment, and the communication systems in the heavily armoured vehicles like the tanks."

William's head jerked up when he heard *tanks*. He wanted to ask about swinging the turret and firing the big gun, but as he observed his dad sitting stiffly in the armchair, he swallowed the question.

"While travelling through the Netherlands, I had been assigned an army green Norton 16C motorcycle. It was a heavy, 490cc brute of an engine, with a spring-loaded suspension seat." He smiled. "My knees constantly banged against the fuel tank, and I am sure I shook several teeth loose riding that thing. Anyway, while we waited to be resupplied, I motored around on the Norton, scouring the countryside for any materials useful around base camp.

"On the third day, I was rumbling along the narrow, hard-packed roads, not a cloud in the sky, five or six miles from camp, when I noticed a man and his daughter walking along a foot trail. He waved me over as his daughter kneeled and retrieved something from the ground. I pulled over, and we exchanged guarded pleasantries.

"In broken English, Hendrik explained that he and his daughter followed the same trails daily in search of edible plants. Fortunately, for both of us, his daughter spoke English. Hendrik and his daughter were talkative and friendly and had obviously struggled to survive the long, harsh winter. He mentioned that his wife rarely stepped outside the farmhouse and relied heavily on their fifteen-year-old son's assistance during the long hours he and his daughter spent foraging for food."

Pete ran his hand through his thinning hair and went on, "The three of us stood on the trail exchanging war stories. Once the sun was low on the horizon, I set my sights on the easterly ride back to the encampment. Hendrik gestured, raised his voice over the rumbling motorcycle and invited me to share a meal with the family. At first, I begged off the invitation; however, he was very insistent.

"The next evening, I arrived at their home, which was in severe disrepair. They greeted me outside. I reached into the Norton's jerry-rigged duffel bags and handed Hendrik's wife a large can of Spam and four bars of chocolate to their son. Hendrik devoured the pork product with his eyes, saying they had not tasted meat for months. He then put a hand on my shoulder, extended his other hand and swept it 180 degrees along the horizon as he expressed regret for the disrepair of his homestead. He continued to point toward the distant horizon and their once fertile fields, now overgrown and indiscernible from the rest of the countryside. He motioned toward the broken-down fences and commented on the crumbling barn that was slowly being turned into firewood. Gaping holes, large enough for a jeep to drive through, allowed the elements to stoke the rotting fir planks and the timber frame holding the rickety roof aloft.

"We entered the sparsely furnished home and sat at a small rectangular table near the centrally located wood stove. We drank black tea and discussed the war effort and their tenuous hold on the farm. Their passion and intensity were awe-inspiring and heartwarming, fueled by their belief that one day the Germans would be defeated, and the family would again work the bountiful soil and rejoice in a life of happiness and tranquillity." Pete exhaled heavily.

"Hendrik's wife busied herself at the wood stove and in the kitchen nook. As she prepared the meal, Adelaide—Aletta, as her parents called her, dragged me outside to help her fill a leather pouch with meadow grasses. She explained that her mother would mix the grass in with their boiled potatoes, and this simple addition to their nightly meal would help ward off illness and keep their family strong."

Ernie smiled inwardly. He never tired of listening to his son's accounts of his time overseas. He dearly valued his wartime stories as they said so much about the human condition during challenging times.

"Once we finished the evening meal, we talked well into the night. It was profoundly disturbing to learn of the suffering and sacrifices the Dutch civilians had endured during the years, struggling to shield their bodies and souls from the ravages of war. As the evening light scattered and the shadows stretched, I promised Hendrik that I would scrounge up replacement parts for their broken radio.

"Two days later, loaded with vacuum tubes and assorted parts, I managed to repair their beautiful mahogany Tombstone radio. The family was ecstatic when we found a local underground station on the radio dial. Soon after, we picked up BBC radio and Radio Orange, the exiled Dutch government's broadcast. Hendrik let me know that for the past five years, local and foreign radio broadcasts had been forbidden. He whispered that when the Germans were out on patrol, the family would scramble to hide the Tombstone radio along with their few precious belongings in a hole hidden beneath a camouflaged door in the floor of the barn."

Pete again ran his hand through his hair and tried to wrest his eyes from the Windmill painting. He crossed his arms and said, "The day before we were scheduled to advance on our first objective, I borrowed a jeep and arrived at the farmhouse with two weeks' supply of food and fuel. We sat next to the warm stove and drank strong black tea and…"

Ernie glanced over at his two fidgety grandsons and appreciated that one day they would understand.

Pete cleared his throat, "and finally, with the evening meal approaching, we said our goodbyes. As I walked to the jeep, Aletta ran out of the house. She slipped the pendant around my neck, fastened the clasp and said, 'Saint Christopher, the patron saint of travellers, will protect and guide you on your journey through the Netherlands.' She kissed me on the cheek, turned and vanished through the open door. That was the last time I saw Aletta and her family." He looked up and smiled at his father.

"And the Saint Christopher pendant…it remained around my neck until I was safely back home in Canada. And now the pendant is tucked away in my ration tin, awaiting the day when someone else needs protection." He glanced at the boys. "Anyway, the next day we began the assault on Arnhem. Three days later, we were on the steps of Apeldoorn, and by April 17th, we had liberated the city. The Infantry and Armoured

Divisions then continued north into the heart of the Dutch countryside."

"Was she your girlfriend, Dad?" William asked.

Ernie looked soberly at the boys and said, "Over seven thousand Canadian soldiers died liberating the Netherlands from the German occupation."

Vivian walked into the living room and observed the three generations of Greene men; she was overcome with a deep sense of contentment. When she left the kitchen, she had suspected Pete was reminiscing about the war years.

William noticed his mum and announced, "Dad had a girlfriend during the war."

"Oh my...I would say your father was a very fortunate man." She then looked across the room at Pete and said, "Dinner will be ready in twenty minutes." She turned and set her gaze on William, "I would like you to set the table for dinner."

William stuck his neck out, eyeballed his mum and whined, "Why me? Why not Timmy? Why not Mary Lynn?"

Vivian glanced at Ernie and then, summoning a calm voice, said, "Because...I asked you." She turned and marched her 125-pound frame back to the kitchen. Timmy and William jumped off the chesterfield. Mildred raised her head at the commotion and pulled herself upright as the boys sprinted from the room.

Ernie replaced the lid on the ration tin, crossed his arms and said, "You know, son, I don't believe I ever shared with you the challenges we, the country, faced during the 1930s. It was a decade of extreme hardship across our land. By the grace of

God, we stumbled but endured the economic calamity that was the Great Depression." Ernie stared through the bay window at another place and time.

Pete leaned forward and eyed his father as the dog loped after the boys.

Ernie exhaled, "By the mid-thirties, there was growing optimism that we had weathered the worst of the economic and social upheaval. Unfortunately, the enthusiasm was short-lived. Once the dust settled, it was apparent that unemployment remained rampant—a persistent riddle the government could not solve, droughts and dust storms persisted across the prairie provinces, crops continued to fail, and the banks' impotence to loan money led to additional hardship and more families abandoning their homes."

He fell silent for a moment and thought, 1936, that was the year we had our own reckoning. He looked across the room at Pete and said, "During the spring of 1936, we experienced our own loss: with no funds, overdue bills, bank loans denied, unable to buy seed, equipment and whatnot…well, son, those starch collared bastards at the Toronto bank stepped in and foreclosed on our farm. The bank's manager, Chester Parker, to his credit, went out on a limb and convinced the Toronto Bigwigs to lease the farm back to us. Three years later, however, a buyer stepped in—we had thirty days to vacate."

"Christ, Dad, I had no idea you and Mum were in such financial straits! I thought you sold the farm because you were too old to work the land." Pete said sheepishly. "I always wondered why we moved in with Aunt May."

"Your Great Aunt May kindly offered to put us up while we got back on our feet. I don't believe for a second any of us thought it would be for two years. I tell you, she was quite the broad, spinster May. She sure enjoyed life." Ernie volunteered.

"I remember living under her roof, and for about six months we shared a bedroom," Pete said.

"That's right. We all had to make sacrifices. I converted May's sewing area into a bedroom for your mother."

"I am dumbfounded. Why did you keep it a secret?"

Ernie, in a matter-of-fact voice, said, "I suppose it was the times such information was, frankly, not shared with children."

Pete nodded at his father's candour and said, "It certainly doesn't feel like it was almost twenty-five years ago—it could be yesterday. I remember many a night sitting by the fire discussing the events unfolding in Europe, our own national affairs and my reasons for enlisting."

Pete's eyes crinkled as he smiled. "I can still see you conducting your nightly ritual, sitting on the edge of your bed, hunched over, an open bag of tobacco on your lap. You would roll three cigarettes, then carefully place them on the nightstand. And every morning when I woke, the smell of burnt tobacco lingered in the room, and the cigarettes would be gone."

He exhaled heavily, "Dad, do you remember December 22, 1939, my last morning at Aunt May's? You were up before me and had breakfast on the table."

"Oatmeal, back bacon, three eggs, toast with mother's strawberry jam and black coffee," Ernie answered.

"It is strange how time has a way of compressing in on itself. Honestly, I can almost smell the bacon and taste Mum's strawberry jam."

Both men fell silent.

A moment later, Pete broke the silence. "And…I had to scarf down my breakfast because Walter Hughes, the other active service member, had arrived at Aunt May's thirty minutes early. I remember Mum dashed into the kitchen wearing that God-awful robe I bought her the previous Christmas—we hugged, and she sternly reminded me to write home every week. I grabbed my duffel bag, suitcase and scrambled to the front door." Pete eyed his father, "You were a step behind—"

William swung around the corner into the living room and said, "Mum says you need to cut the roast meat." He turned and ran out.

Pete brushed aside the interruption and went on, "I threw my gear in the bed of the pickup, you came over, placed your hands on my shoulders, and said: 'Fear God and keep your bowels clear.'"

Ernie stared sombrely at his son, "I remember."

"Then, in the truck as Walter drove down the laneway, I looked through the rear window just as a dusting of snow swirled around Aunt May's house. You were standing outside the front door, stoic and resolute, arms crossed, wearing only your pajamas and house shoes, watching as the vehicle slowly moved away and out of sight."

EIGHTEEN

Standing in the parking lot behind the Block and Pestle restaurant, Will gazed up at the stars in the moonlit sky. His head felt thick. He felt disoriented. The chilly air, though, slowly scraped away the murkiness that had jammed his senses. He pulled his shoulders back, inhaled the autumn air and held it for a count of seven, then exhaled. He turned and watched Jimmy slide his hand along the back seat fold of the rental sedan.

"There you are, my little pick-me-up," Jimmy said. He straightened up, closed the door, and held the clear bag up to the moonlight. Will eyed two joints dancing inside as Jimmy shook the bag and smiled, "A little gift of grass from Dean." He turned to Will, "I'm not used to this cold Canadian climate," he half-joked, then added, "You copacetic if we jump in the car while I have a couple tokes on one of these bad boys?" Jimmy held the bag close, eyed the joints, and said, "Brother Dean has an innate talent when it comes to rolling a big fatty."

"No problem, I got a chill on myself." Will then considered, "We should have thought to grab our jackets before heading outside. Anyway, let's crack the windows open. I don't want to reek of pot when we walk back into the restaurant."

"You bet, buddy. I'll start the car too. Dean did say it's a skunky indica, very smelly and very potent." He walked around to the driver's door and slid in while Will occupied the passenger side. They lowered the windows just enough to allow fresh air to circulate. Jimmy started the car, tapped the heat control button, then pushed in the car's lighter. He placed one joint on the dashboard and rolled the bag snugly around the remaining joint. He swivelled his upper body, stretched and pushed the bag into the rear seat fold. The joint was once again hidden from prying eyes.

Will watched a little amused, "What if you got pulled over and the car was searched?"

"A lawyer friend in California told me that when transporting your grass, it's best to tuck it in the rear seat fold, then if you're pulled over and the stash is discovered, the gendarmes cannot prove possession as the driver could argue it belonged to a hitchhiker," Jimmy said as he turned back and resumed his seat. He smiled. "Nervous?"

"No, just curious."

The lighter popped; Jimmy jerked it out and eyed the fiery orange coil. He scooped the joint off the dash and held the hot coil against the twisted end. He inhaled as the rolling paper ignited and the flower began to burn. After a few seconds, he exhaled through the gap in the window. He pushed the lighter back into the socket, took another deep drag, then exhaled. He studied the joint pinched between his thumb and index finger and said, "Hmmm…good stuff, smooth too." He glanced at Will, "It helps tame the nasty demons that gnaw at my grey matter." He held out the joint. "You in for a toke? No pressure though, buddy."

Will eyed the joint, reached out and slowly pinched it just as Jimmy had demonstrated. He remembered the one time he tried pot was at a party when he was twenty or so. He didn't like it then.

"Don't gulp, just inhale slowly and steadily for two or three seconds," he coached.

Will began to count silently as he inhaled. *One…two…*his lungs revolted, he barked and snorted like a rabid pig, gagged and coughed. "Damn Jimmy…here, take it," he rasped between coughs. He rubbed his dry, irritated eyes. "Goddamn, my chest feels like I just spit up a lung, and my eyes…are burning."

Jimmy grinned as he dragged on the joint, held and exhaled through the window. He then chuckled and explained, "Sorry, buddy. A little too harsh for your virgin lungs. Don't fret, give it a couple of minutes and they'll settle."

Will stuck his face by the open window and breathed in the frosty night air. He turned to Jimmy and grinned, "Give me some slack, this is only the second time I've tried pot. First time was at Gerald's wild house party."

"Oh, really. You know what *they* say—round two, you are now addicted and officially a pot head!" Smoke escaped through Jimmy's mouth. "That was some wild and crazy party at his parents' colossal home, while they were out of town.

And if memory serves, Gerald's twenty-first birthday party launched on May 27, 1977, one week after my twenty-first birthday." Jimmy smiled, eyed the joint, inhaled deeply and mumbled through his teeth, "…the first and only time I had a drink of alcohol!"

"…twelve years ago!" Will said, then coughed. He leaned against the window and breathed in the fresh, chilly air. He glanced at Jimmy, weighed his options and said, "Oh hell, pass it here." He held out his hand, index finger and thumb ready to receive the joint.

"You sure?"

"Lay it on me." He put the joint to his lips and inhaled. A moment passed, his eyes grew wide, he cranked his head toward the door and violently coughed, spraying spittle across the window. "Oh, Shit, sorry, man," he chirped.

Jimmy plucked the joint, took two long drags and sent the roach out the window. He turned his head and said sincerely, "Hey man, just want you to know, over dinner, I appreciate you steering clear and not asking about my family's…difficulties during the old days on Gilwood Drive."

Will nodded and wiped his mouth with his shirt sleeve.

Suddenly, it occurred to Jimmy that it was an opportune time to come clean and set the record straight, before he and Amahle jetted back to California. He suffered from a nagging belief that he had betrayed his friend. His *only* childhood friend, he reminded himself. He looked sideways as eight-year-old William wiped his sleeve across his mouth.

Jimmy clutched the steering wheel with both hands and peered through the dirty windshield. His knuckles quickly turned white. He agonized over his hesitancy. He glanced at Will and wondered if the grass was prompting him to talk, to confess. He shrugged. Then, in a subdued voice, he said, "Will, do you remember…way back in November 1963, I was hanging with you and Timmy· at your house, and your mom invited me to join the family for Sunday supper? As I recall, your granddad was visiting, and your oldest sister didn't make it home for the weekend because she had met a guy at school."

Will lifted his head, rubbed his eyes and said, "I see your memory is still razor-sharp." He smiled and said, "Now, this might sound bizarre, right out of Twilight Zone, but recently I've had many dreams about that November weekend!" He exhaled, "And to answer your question, before the Sunday dinner, you raced home to spend the evening with Karen because the following morning she was jumping a bus for Tilbury and you didn't know when you'd see your big sister again."

Surprised, Jimmy could only nod in agreement.

Will went on, "And it was the only time Mum invited you for one of her Sunday night roast beef specials, and you dared to bolt before dinner." He laughed.

Jimmy's face crinkled in bewilderment. "It was never my intention to insult your mom. Truthfully, I was always envious of your Sunday night family dinners," he smiled fleetingly.

"No, no, buddy…she was just sad you couldn't join us. Nothing more." Will then noticed Jimmy's troubled expression and his unyielding grip on the steering wheel. "Why are you asking me about a day that occurred twenty-six years ago?"

Jimmy sighed, dropped his head and said, "That Sunday afternoon, I raced home and stood at the side door, paralyzed by a foreboding sense of dread. I finally found some courage and went through the door—Mom was in the kitchen crying, reeking of stale booze. I hurriedly looked around the house. We were alone. Through her drunken stupor, I learned that the old man couldn't stomach looking at his daughter any longer, told her to gather her stuff, and then he drove her to the depot so she could board the four o'clock bus to Tilbury. He then disappeared for five days."

Will could hear the venom in Jimmy's voice.

He went on, "I felt hopeless and pissed off. The old man had thwarted my plan to spend the evening with my sister." He dropped his aching hands to his lap, turned and eyeballed Will. "Three years later, Karen returned to Millington for a quick visit along with my niece. I was in the dark, had no clue that she had a daughter, and I was an uncle."

Jimmy exhaled loudly, "Their marriage expired that Sunday. Financially, neither could survive on their own, so the old man moved into the basement. For the next ten years, they remained under the same roof, leading separate lives."

Jimmy shook his head and said, "Mom, the clever and disciplined alcoholic would wait for the clock to strike four before indulging." He smirked, "However, she didn't even fool the dog. By 6 p.m., Brandy would retreat to her kennel to avoid the raucous, inebriated woman. Some years later, even though she would put on a brave face, she had changed into a timid, despondent drunk. On the other hand, the old man morphed into a basement dweller, rarely left the house, and only at night. His hermit stage, Dean dubbed it. And predictably, when he was three sheets to the wind, he would stagger up the basement stairs, angry and in a confrontational mood."

He eyed Will and went on, "I never wanted to speak about what happened behind closed doors…just made it all…too real. Only one person, Mrs. Thorpe, knew about our dysfunctional family and even with her, I was guarded in our discussions." He breathed in slowly through his nose, employing a relaxation technique.

"I had no idea…" Will trailed off. He reached out and put a hand on Jimmy's shoulder, "Fuckin' hell…I am so sorry, man." Will exhaled, "Christ…did he hit you and Dean?"

"Sometimes he would drag Dean out to the shed where he kept an old leather belt." He smiled tightly, "Dean is one tough hombre."

Lost in thought, Jimmy stared through the windshield at the line of trees silhouetted against the sky. He glanced sideways at Will, turned back and said, "All through secondary school, the old man shut me out and not once did he drag me out to sample the inside of the shed. Of course, any rational person would agree that would be a good thing. However, as the years passed, I was saddled with immense guilt. He would unleash his wrath on Dean and treat me as if I didn't exist— I got off scot-free! Then, when I was thirteen, during one of his drunken rages, he told me I was no longer his son. I knew he was an asshole, but it still left an indelible mark." He crossed his arms against his chest.

Will watched him, scarcely believing what he was hearing. He found it difficult to fathom that his best friend lived in such an abusive household and kept it secret…for decades.

Jimmy pushed on, "I'm nervous. I'm going to meet the old man tomorrow. Mom did mention that he has clocked seven years sober and still goes to monthly meetings. Apparently, he's a different person than the basement-dwelling ogre from my past. To his credit, he's been employed with the same automotive parts company for the past six years. I guess…there's hope for him…and for me."

"Jimmy. Tomorrow, if you want company—"

"Thanks, man. I appreciate the offer. I had this conversation with Amahle, and I asked her to hang out at the motel. This is something that…that, I feel compelled to do solo. One-on-one, on my terms. I told him I would meet him for coffee at a Tim Hortons."

Will nodded, then asked, "Tell me, how is Karen?" He detected a glimmer in Jimmy's eyes as his disposition noticeably lightened.

"Thank God, the best thing he ever did was to send Karen north to Tilbury. A year later, she met her future husband, Andrew. They were both employed at the local A&W Restaurant. Today, her daughter, Evelyn, is attending UBC in Vancouver, pursuing her master's degree in social work. And Andrew is a great guy, a straight shooter, and devoted to Karen. He worked his way up to manager, bided his time and bought out the owners when they retired. Then, three years ago, they purchased a second A&W franchise, managed by Karen. She has done extremely well…a true success story."

"That's great, man. So, you are an uncle…uncle Jimmy."

"Evelyn calls me, Uncle Jim-shorts. I assume based on her early memories of me wearing shorts all the time."

"That's great, your niece has a sense of humour. And how is Dean?"

Jimmy chuckled. "Dean is also doing extraordinarily well. He is the top auto sales representative at the Chevrolet dealership. The one on the corner of Nixon and Elm. He has been the Salesman of the Year for seven of the last nine years. And the fix was in on the other two, because the awards went to the owner's son. That was the scuttlebutt around the watercooler, according to Dean."

He shrugged and went on, "His marriage to Lucy, well, it only lasted two years. Today, he and Cheryl, his girlfriend, have been dancing together for four years. Yesterday, I spent a couple of hours with Mom, and then we walked the three blocks to Dean's place. In his den, he has a massive, solid walnut desk where he has his Salesman of the Year plaques on display."

Jimmy chuckled. "Dean says there's room on the desk for plaques eight through fifteen. He certainly has the salesman's gift! Hell, he could sell his skid-stained skivvies and turn a profit."

Will laughed. "I suppose we should get back to the restaurant. The girls must be wondering what happened to us. We've been out here for…thirty…forty minutes," he estimated.

Jimmy looked at his watch and smiled, "It's 9:38 p.m. It's only been ten minutes."

NINETEEN

Surprised, Will said, "Really…just ten minutes. Well then, in that case, I'm wondering if I can run something by you. I have a…a bit of a conundrum, a quandary, an enigma dressed up as a puzzle!" He attempted to smile.

Jimmy reached across the seat, squeezed his shoulder with a friendly Vulcan nerve pinch and said, "Of course, Will. I have been running my mouth off long enough. Fire away."

"Great. Just so we're clear, I am asking your opinion because you are number two on my list of smartest people. As this is more of a personal matter, I don't feel comfortable approaching Amahle and picking her brain." Will grinned, showing a mouthful of teeth.

"Huh, fuck you too, buddy." Jimmy chuckled and said, "She's not just brainy, she's all that and a bag of chips."

"That she is," Will said. He tilted his head from side to side, attempting to ease the sudden tension in his neck. He counted four crumpled chocolate bar wrappers on the dashboard, then eyed the wiper blade streaks on the windshield. He inhaled deeply and reckoned he had stalled long enough.

"Where to begin. Alright…well, this sounds extreme, but I have experienced frequent short-term blackouts and several…I would describe them as out-of-body experiences." He sighed heavily and went on, "I'm trying to determine whether there's a trigger, something that prompts these…episodes. Any thoughts or counsel?" He continued to stare through the grimy windshield into the darkness.

Jimmy watched as the anxiety played out across Will's forehead. He considered his friend's dilemma. With such limited information, he attempted to offer a sensible explanation. "Will, a dissociation from one's body is not that uncommon and may result from any number of factors: trauma, drugs, environmental conditions, even everyday stressors."

"I considered stress. The other things you mentioned don't apply." He frowned, "Some days, I feel like John Hurt in—"

"*The Elephant Man!*" Jimmy said to buoy his mood.

"A great movie, too bad it was filmed in black and white." He then said cryptically, "You know the movie…John Hurt played Kain, one of the crew members on the doomed spaceship Nostromo."

"I should have known it was *Alien*. You concerned a creature is going to burst through your ribcage?" he asked with an attempt at levity.

"No, not really," Will said, not taking the bait. "It's just that Hurt's character wakes up after his traumatic encounter with the face hugger and then devours his *last* meal, none the wiser that he has become an incubator for the xenomorph." He smirked, "I've seen *Alien* so many times, it's inevitable the movie will slip into my consciousness. In any case, I have this persistent churning in my gut that I have a…a disease that is patiently biding its time waiting to pounce." He glanced over his shoulder at Jimmy. "I'm just being irrational, right?"

Jimmy thought for a moment, then tried to offer some reassurance. "Honestly, you would have other consequential health-related symptoms. Granted, the short-term blackouts are concerning. See your doc, get a physical. Tell me, any other symptoms you haven't mentioned?"

"Hmmm…well, I keep having these ultra-realistic dreams and annoying phantom smells."

"Ultra-realistic dreams. Explain?"

"I can't remember exactly when these vivid dreams started, but there is a surreal flow, a continuity to them. What I mean is…it's always November 1963, and I am experiencing different moments of…well, William's young life. What's more, I am cognizant of the sights, sounds, smells, and so many mundane details. It is like the…my ah, I suppose my internal processes that generate typical dreams are damaged…" Will shook his head, "I know, sounds fuckin' looney tunes." He shrugged his shoulders.

"Have you spoken with Veronica about your concerns?"

"Briefly. I don't want her to worry for no reason. I worry enough for the two of us." Will caught himself looking for patterns in the streaks on the windshield.

"One scenario that has fucked with my head is whether my dreams are just a figment of my imagination. In other words, have I invented a childhood and subconsciously masked my real past!" He felt numb except for the chill that crept down his spine. He inhaled, then muttered under his breath, "If I have no past to draw on, how then do I recognize and comprehend the person I am when awake?" Will threw the question into the darkness, not expecting an answer.

"Goddamn…that is a disturbing thought. Listen carefully, buddy. What you are describing is confabulation. As my only friend on Gilwood Drive, I can verify that you have not constructed false memories of your childhood. Alright? So, bury that fuckin' notion."

Will sighed, shifted his weight on the seat and said, "Thanks…thanks, man. That helps, helps immensely. You know, I do have a habit of leaning into worst-case scenarios."

Jimmy raised a knowing eyebrow and then raised his hand toward the ceiling and made a circling motion with his index finger. "Have you considered that—all this is a dream?" He smiled.

Will turned away from the windshield. His eyes bulged and pulled against their sockets as he scanned the car's interior.

"I'm just pulling your *finger*."

Will exhaled. "Oh…oh, right. Asshole!" Will laughed as he truly recognized his childhood buddy.

"Movin' on. What's this about phantom smells?"

Will rubbed his nose impulsively as he considered the question. A moment later, he said, "During the dreams, I sometimes experience phantom odours; they come and go. At times, I'm surrounded by sharp, ammonia-like scents, while at other moments, I'm swamped by rancid, rotting smells. Even after I wake up, the scent seems to linger." He sighed heavily.

Jimmy detected the agitation in his voice. "Have you experienced any metallic odours, like after a rain shower?"

Will pursed his lips and shook his head.

"And of course, no smell of burnt toast?"

Will smiled and shook his head. He turned to Jimmy and said, "Lionel, the server, was wearing Stetson aftershave."

Jimmy cocked his head and waited for the punchline.

"I smell cologne, Stetson cologne, in some of the dreams. I wonder why that cologne?…is there a connection with the server or the restaurant?"

"Not to make light of your olfactory *condition*, but that's some weird and wild shit." Jimmy exhaled and said emphatically, "See your doctor."

"It's on the list."

Will stared through the windshield at the blurry moon. "Hey, reminds me…I watched a documentary about the space program, and one of the questions posed to the astronauts on the panel—by the way they're now called mission specialists— was whether the Milky Way galaxy has an odour? One astronaut had an interesting reply. He revealed that after a space walk on re-entry into the airlock, the spacesuit smells like burnt meat and old coins." Will grimaced. "I never would have guessed that the galaxy smells, and it is foul," he marvelled.

Jimmy cringed, "Just imagine you didn't have your space legs, your mind and gut are still adapting to weightlessness, and those pungent smells settle on your skin, invade your nose."

He gave Will a sidelong glance. "Moving on, let's think through your out-of-body predicament and see if we can rationalize how you are shifting between two timelines—separated by a distance of twenty-six years. I have two improbable theories. Number one: due to an unknown source, mechanism or by some alternative method, you have breached the space-time continuum?" He smiled.

Will tipped his head to the side, like a dog trying to understand his owner's commands and said, "That's way out in left field, Mr. Spock. But as you know, I am a champion of any story that contemplates a rift in the space-time continuum. Proceed."

Jimmy reached over and took a road map out of the glove box. He held up the unfolded map and signalled that one end represented 1963, the other 1989. "All that is required for a temporal distortion to occur is to influence the warping of space and time," he said nonchalantly. He folded the map in half so that the top and bottom edges met. "As simple as Einstein's Theory of Relativity." He said, amused.

"Now, we release one end of the map, and the timeline flattens out and reverts to its previous space and time." The map hung flat and inverted, separating driver from passenger.

Will observed the map presentation. "And how does one create a temporal distortion?"

"An excellent question. Quantum physics may hold the answer—string theory. The scientific community aint there yet and won't be in our lifetime. So, with that said, let us move on to theory number two: parallel universes or as the comic book aficionado would say, the multiverse."

As a car exited the parking lot, its brake lights reflected in the rearview mirror. Jimmy's eyes glowed red.

"Now, let's say for shits and giggles, that during these dream sequences, physically or perhaps just your essence, is transported to a parallel or alternate universe. Think of it like diving into a lake, which causes near-infinite concentric ripples spreading out in incalculable directions across time and space. In effect, you may be skipping from one parallel universe to another along a skewed or altered timeline. This theory, however, poses countless obstacles."

Jimmy rubbed his eyes and went on, "Foremost, what comes to mind is that each time you travel or are carried away on a ripple to a parallel universe, you are in a loop, and to return to the same universe at the identical spatial and temporal axis implies that your travels must be buffered or controlled. Hence, there must be a mechanism or governor controlling your *jump* as well as your return passage from these alternate destinations—universes."

A wry smile crossed his face as he looked at Will. "For that answer, and how to build a time travel accelerator, we would need to speak with Dr. Sam Beckett," he chuckled.

"All right…so, we are to speculate that Scott Bakula is a Quantum Mechanics genius who solved the time travel conundrum and poses as a TV actor," Will said, mirroring Jimmy's smile. "Bakula is good, but my money is on Admiral Al Calavicci. Dean Stockwell is the backbone of the TV show. Without him, it's just another low-budget, sci-fi show filmed on a soundstage."

"I will give you that," Jimmy said and kicked open the door. "You must admit, though, space-time, temporal anomalies…it's thought-provoking, fascinating stuff." He glanced at his watch, "We should bounce and get back to the girls."

"So, you are saying that I am a traveller of space and time."

"Hmmm, more like a hypothesis."

Jimmy ran a hand through his hair and said, "Dean was bang-on-the-money, his grass sure packs a heck of a wallop." He got out, ducked and looked back in the car. "Will, in all seriousness, next time you dream or *jump,* be observant, look for changes, discrepancies…any deviation from previous dreams. And buddy, get in to see your doc for a check-up, tout de suite. Perhaps consider discussing your symptoms with an alternative health professional."

Will spied the Clovis point dangling from the leather cord about Jimmy's neck. The charm winked at him as the moonlight sampled its black, fluted surface.

*   *   *

Will slid out, closed the door and moved around the back of the car. The two men walked along the cobblestone laneway, shoulder to shoulder. They walked in silence, hands in pockets to fend off the cold, while each reflected on how they reached this point in their lives. They rounded the corner and moved briskly toward the large oak doors of the Block and Pestle. Jimmy reached for one of the brass handles.

"Fuck. I came out here to get my wallet from the car, and of course, it's still in the glove box." Will sighed and shook his head.

"Don't sweat it, man. I've got to make a pit stop at the Men's room, so I'll see you back at the table." Jimmy walked through the doors into the lobby.

CHAPTER

TWENTY

Jimmy smiled at the hostess and explained that he had just stepped out for a smoke. He moved to his left and descended the three steps to the lounge. He looked around the lower level. On his right, he admired the brass-accented mahogany bar that stretched the length of the lounge. Neon signs: Jill and Jack, hung from the ceiling by the back wall. Behind the bar, a wall of glass panels supported shelves crammed with bottles offering a wide selection of spirits.

The crowd had thinned considerably. Five patrons sat at the bar enjoying a nightcap. On the opposite wall, only two of twelve pub tables were occupied. A busser, sleeves rolled to his elbows, held a tray tucked under his arm while he methodically wiped down a table. As he moved along the bar, he eyed the intricate assembly of polished brass pipes and valves connected to multiple beer taps, showcasing an assortment of lagers, ales and pilsners.

The bartender, apron around his waist, wiped down the counter while he dispensed beer into a chilled glass. He nodded and said, "What is your pleasure, sir?"

Jimmy eyed the beer taps and said, "All good, my friend."

The bartender nodded again, topped off the glass and moved along the bar toward the lobby, frosty beer in hand.

Jimmy quietly sang along to Queen's "Under Pressure." He was drawn to his left as a man helped a woman with her coat. He edged closer to the bar to allow the couple space to pass, then, in mid-step, his leg hit an immovable object. Surprised, he turned and looked down at the obstruction. A thirtyish-year-old guy, wearing a ball cap and sunglasses, was sitting on a stool leaning back against the mahogany bar, elbows on the bar, his right leg extended out like a parking gate blocking his passage. Jimmy noted the guy's black military boot, then detected the glint of a knife protruding from the top.

The guy grabbed his left forearm and, in a voice slurred by too much liquor, said, "You a big boy, aint ya. I bet you plays pro football for one of them teams up here."

Jimmy eyed the guy and, in a measured tone, said, "I am asking you to remove your hand from my arm."

The guy held tight. "I'm a Navy SEAL, three tours…SEALs don' takes orders from civvies," he grunted.

"I'm just on my way to the crapper, friend," Jimmy said good-naturedly, trying to defuse the situation.

"…to the crapper," the Navy SEAL mocked.

*   *   *

Meanwhile, Will wandered through the parking lot looking for the Tempo. He finally spied the car. He walked over to the passenger door, then crossed his arms against the cold, invigorating breeze and tilted his head skyward. As always, he was amazed by the number of twinkling stars puncturing the blackness of space. He eyeballed the waning crescent moon, casting an orange glow across the hoods of the parked cars.

One day, he theorized, a colony of Earthers or Earthlings will be stationed on Tranquillity Base in recognition of the first two humans to land on the moon. He tried to imagine what went through Armstrong and Aldrin's minds as they stepped onto the Moon and looked back at the blue planet from 380,000 kilometres away.

*　　*　　*

He had a white-knuckled grip on Jimmy's forearm. His sunglasses had slipped from the bridge of his nose. Through watery eyes, he glared up at him. "They grows them big up here…I seen you come through the door back there, and I says to myself, Zeno, look at that big fucker…thinks he's tough. Well…you tough boy?" he sputtered as spit flew from his mouth.

A man in a leather bomber jacket exited the restroom, took two steps, and then noticed his cousin involved in an altercation.

"Hey…Danny, my boy, we gots are-self a sit-iation here."

Danny halted. He momentarily eyed Jimmy and then said, "Ah…man, what are you doin'?" He attempted to take control of the situation, "Zeno, come on, man, let go of his arm. It's late, time we blow up the joint… 'sides I gotta be at work for 6 a.m."

Zeno flashed a lopsided toothy grin, then drawled, "Don' be a shit-heel now…Cuz."

Jimmy thought that while Zeno remained planted on the stool, his best course of action was to *stick around* and hope for a non-combative conclusion to this perplexing dilemma.

Jimmy glanced to his right along the length of the bar. The bartender, towel draped over his shoulder, was at the far end, leaning across the bar, chatting with one of the waitresses. He then looked over his left shoulder and quickly decided Cousin Danny was not a threat. He was a big man, certainly not as inebriated as Zeno, and so far, not interested in dancing. On the other hand, he may just be biding his time waiting for an opportunity to strike.

Zeno watched his movements, and as their eyes met, he grinned and pressed his fingers deeper into his flesh. Jimmy winced as blood began to stream down his forearm. Zeno then turned his head and looked along the bar. He grinned broadly, showing a mouthful of teeth. He shouted, "Well, where ta fuck ya bin, Reggie, bet ya bin talkin' up the waitress…huh." His eyes flashed a new awareness and confidence.

A tingling sensation, a warning sign, wormed its way up the side of Jimmy's neck. He followed Zeno's eyes, looked to his right and tried to gauge the third guy's intent.

*   *   *

As Will stood by the passenger door of the Tempo, he exhaled and contemplated his situation. He wondered how long he had been standing among the parked cars, without a coat on, speaking to himself and shivering in the frosty night air, mesmerized by the twinkling stars. He then uttered, "Fuck, could it be…" He quickly looked around the parking lot, "shit, maybe I'm stoned?" He sighed, relieved no one had witnessed his boneheaded foolishness. He opened the door, reached into the glovebox and was surprised to see his Timex Sport watch on his wrist. He wondered how he could forget he was wearing a watch. He shook his head, weary from being absent-minded, then pocketed his wallet, slammed the car door and hurried back to the restaurant.

He stepped through the large oak doors and rubbed his hands together. A hostess appeared, "Good evening, sir—"

"I forgot my wallet in the car," Will smiled sheepishly. He looked past the hostess into the near-empty lounge. He squinted, his teeth clenched. At the far end of the bar, a big guy sitting on a stool, his face hidden under a ball cap, ominously held Jimmy's arm. Another guy wearing a black puffer coat was striding purposefully toward the two men.

Will scanned the premises; only the bartender was in sight. He rushed toward the lounge, vaulted the three steps, landed heavily, grimaced, then called out to the bartender, "Hey, might need some help." He pointed to the back of the lounge.

*   *   *

The air was charged with stale cigarette smoke, the scent of deep-fried food and spilled beer.

Jimmy watched Reggie approach, noting his bald head with a five o'clock shadow and a neck as thick as a linebacker's.

Zeno, meanwhile, was thrilled with the unfolding situation.

Reggie was weighing his own options and silently cursed Zeno—even though he didn't know what was happening, he had his suspicions.

Jimmy assumed that Zeno planned to provoke him into action. However, it was now readily apparent that it was a stalling tactic, biding time until Reggie joined the party. He glanced to his left, satisfied that Cousin Danny had decided to maintain his distance. For now, anyway. Jimmy pulled back, testing Zeno's grip.

He grinned and held fast.

Jimmy stopped resisting and promptly raised his other arm, ready to defend or strike against the oncoming threat.

Reggie glimpsed his defensive posture, slowed and came to a halt; his breathing laboured as he eyed the stranger. His puffer coat hung open, exposing his large belly.

Jimmy eyed the revitalized Zeno and the panting Reggie. He inhaled deeply; he sensed the presence of his own internal tormenter. His focus sharpened. The *thing* pulsing in his head was quickly ticking off the seconds to zero.

The ticking stopped.

His burning red eyes narrowed, veins throbbed and squirmed across his forehead, and his lips pulled back, baring his teeth. His inner tormentor gnawed away at his gut, clawing to escape, screaming profanities. It begged to be released—to *wander*. Jimmy exhaled, glowered at Reggie and demanded he stand down.

Reggie, shocked and speechless, stared open-mouthed at the transformed stranger. He didn't have a choice. His facade penetrated, his survival instincts surfaced. He retreated.

A moment later, Will appeared, stepped sideways against the bar, raised his arms in a defensive posture and eyed Reggie. He quickly contemplated his situation and wondered whether he was the substitute side of beef like the one depicted in the movie *Rocky*. Under different circumstances, he might have laughed at the thought. He inhaled deeply as the pulsating behind his eyes distorted Reggie's sweaty face.

Jimmy watched as Will put himself in harm's way. He leaned back and again attempted to dislodge his left arm from the Navy SEAL's ruthless grip. Zeno reacted, held fast and leaned back against the bar. Jimmy pounced—thrusting his body forward, he slammed the stool, knocking Zeno off balance. He wrapped his left hand firmly around his neck, forcibly pressing his thumb into the jugular notch midway between his clavicles.

Zeno recoiled and flailed away on the stool. His legs shot toward the ceiling; his sunglasses hurtled through the air. Jimmy shifted and caught Zeno's right leg under his arm as he forced his thumb deeper into his neck.

Zeno gasped and gagged. His mouth opened and closed like a Largemouth Bass, hooked and thrashing on a sandy riverbank. His eyeballs bulged, and his crimson face distorted as his lungs burned for oxygen. Spittle dribbled down his chin, dripping on the back of Jimmy's hand. A barking noise erupted from his throat; his grip loosened. A moment later, and his hand fell away. He continued to struggle and claw at the air with his other hand. Seconds later, his eyes rolled back in his head.

Jimmy kept his thumb pressed against his throat. In one swift move, he confiscated the knife protruding from his polished black boot and slid it into his own back pocket. He then glanced over Will's shoulder. Reggie, eyes wide, mouth still hanging open, had decided to sit this one out.

Zeno's arms fell to his sides as he lost consciousness. Jimmy glanced to his left; Cousin Danny had fallen back a step. He looked down at Zeno, pulled him off the stool and dropped his limp body. He collapsed on the floor in an awkward sitting position. His head slumped forward over his legs as he vented a wet gurgling sound. Snot and frothy saliva leaked on his jeans.

Bowie singing "Starman" interrupted the commotion in the lounge.

Four servers, led by Lionel, ran up and surveyed the scene. The few patrons left in the lounge were aghast, speechless and heading for the exit. Zeno's stool lay upended on the floor; nearby, a puddle of blood was seeping through the plank floorboards.

Reggie looked at Will and said, "I'm going to check on him." He stepped back, walked around Will and past Jimmy. He knelt just as Zeno retched and vomited on the floor.

Will turned, looked at Jimmy's forearm and said, "Christ, man, he did a number on your arm." He looked at Jimmy's red, pained face, "Does it hurt much?"

"Not too bad…it's basically numb now," he answered as he looked down at his damaged arm.

Will couldn't believe what he had just witnessed. "You're like a fuckin' superhero. That move you put on him and that choking maneuver," he said excitedly, "you didn't even break a sweat." He swiped at the sweat beading on his own damp forehead.

With the threat eliminated, Jimmy said, "Thanks for having my back, buddy."

Will laughed. "Any time. Although I was worried the buzz cut guy with the linebacker neck was going to pummel me senseless. Luckily, my guy wasn't in a fighting mood." An intense sense of relief washed over him. His legs and arms suddenly weighed a ton while his heart pounded rapidly in his chest.

Jimmy held his left arm against his chest and smiled, "Glad it didn't come to that."

The bartender circled the bar, walked up and said, "Hey, your arm is bleeding all over the place. I've got a first aid kit behind the bar. Come on, follow me to the bar sink. We'll get you fixed up." He led Jimmy around to the back of the bar and to the sink next to the beer taps. Jimmy positioned his bleeding arm over the sink. The bartender produced a first-aid kit and then inspected his forearm, "Gosh, he got you good. I think you'll need some stitches to close those deep punctures."

Two young waitresses suddenly appeared and said they would minister to Jimmy's arm.

The bartender relented, stepped back and said, "How 'bout a drink. You earned it, boss. On the house."

"A glass of cold water would be appreciated."

"You got it. We have chilled Perrier." He moved past the two waitresses on his way to the refrigerator.

Jimmy kept his arm extended above the sink as the waitresses fawned over his forearm, fussed with the antiseptic and fought with the butterfly-strip bandages. He raised his other hand to his neck and was relieved as he touched the Clovis point still hanging from the leather cord.

Cousin Danny rounded the bar and approached. He held his hands up, eyed Jimmy and stopped two arms' lengths from the man who had just defeated his Navy SEAL cousin. "I just want ta talk," he said.

Jimmy stared at him, "Well?"

He lowered his arms and maintained eye contact, "Look, man, three months ago my cousin got home from an overseas tour, and he's, well…he's bin strugglin'. We hoped a trip north might help shake things up…do 'im some good, get 'im back on the straight an' arrow. So, anyways…I seen you confiscate his blade."

"You tell him it's illegal to carry a concealed weapon in Canada."

"I will, man. I will tell him. But here's the thing. That blade means a whole lot to 'im; it has real sentimental worth. It's like a…a family heirloom."

The two young waitresses listened intently as one applied the sixth and final butterfly bandage. They eyeballed their handiwork and were satisfied—they had stanched the bleeding.

Jimmy glanced at his arm and said, "Thank you, ladies." The young waitresses smiled, shared a look, and then waited for this new drama to unfold.

Cousin Danny waited for Jimmy to reply. After several uncomfortable seconds, he pleaded, "He has a ticket for a flight home next Saturday. So…look, man, I will keep the blade and return it to 'im that morning."

Jimmy suspected that Cousin Danny was being sincere. Moreover, he did attempt to defuse the situation. He reached into his back pocket, produced the knife and handed it to him.

"Hey man, for whatever it's worth, thanks." Cousin Danny slipped the knife into his own back pocket. He turned and walked around the bar to a pub table near the back wall where Reggie was standing, sipping coffee.

The bartender returned with a cold bottle of Perrier. Jimmy thanked him and the two waitresses. He removed the bottle cap and took a long swig of the sparkling water. He looked at the end of the bar where Zeno was recuperating on a stool. Someone had placed a folded towel on the bar for his comfort. His head was down, resting on crossed arms. A hot cup of black coffee was next to him.

The bartender, hoping to keep the two men separated, asked Jimmy to exit by the lobby. Jimmy ignored the offer. He slid his hand along the bar top, humming Queen's "Under Pressure." He stepped from behind the bar into the lounge area. All evidence of vomit and blood had been mopped and erased from the old plank floorboards. He moved over and placed a hand firmly on Zeno's upper back, leaned in and whispered in his ear. Seconds later, he removed his hand and walked away.

Zeno lifted his head slightly, looked sideways at Jimmy, and in a raspy voice said, "You are all right, Jesse James." He laughed pitifully.

Will eyed Jimmy's bandaged forearm, then gestured toward Zeno, "What was that about?"

"I informed him that if he ever decides to venture north of the border again, to remember, up here in the frigid north, we not only hunt seals—we club them to death!"

Will was taken aback. "I don't see the connection."

Jimmy grinned unexpectedly, "He claimed he's a Navy SEAL." Blood began to seep around the bandages and trickle down his arm.

CHAPTER

TWENTY-ONE

Timmy jogged down the stairs holding a folded tablecloth in his outstretched hands. He sped into the kitchen, slammed on the brakes and presented the offering to his mother.

"Thanks, dear," Vivian said. She unfolded the pastel sky-blue tablecloth and spread it across the kitchen table, covering the unsightly red tabletop. She smoothed the creases with her hand, trying to make them less noticeable. Ironing the tablecloth was out of the question; it was too close to dinner. She exhaled loudly.

William walked in holding a folded chair. He unfolded it and placed it beside the chair he had just brought up from the basement. Timmy, meanwhile, had crawled under the table and rested his head on Mildred's rising and falling chest. She was curled up in a ball with her tail tucked and her nose resting on her hindquarters.

Vivian listened to the rhythmic snoring of the dog, then said, "Timmy, please come out from under the table. I could use your help to stir the gravy." He excitedly accepted the task. He popped up beside the table as Mildred weakly wagged her tail at the disturbance.

Vivian had stacked the fine China dinner plates on the kitchen counter next to the silverware. She looked at William and said, "I am trusting you to set the table with my very special dinnerware."

He nodded. He understood the gravity of her request.

"On second thought, before setting the table, I want you to *walk* to the living room and remind your father that he needs to slice the roast."

Timmy slowly stirred the gravy with the oversized wooden spoon as his brother jogged out of the kitchen. Mildred snored peacefully under the table.

*   *   *

William entered the room, "Mum wants you in the kitchen."

Pete stood up. "I'm on my way as soon as I change out of these clothes." Ernie handed the ration tin to his son. As Pete reached the stairs, Vivian appeared in the kitchen doorway, hands on her hips, apron cinched tight around her waist. She scrutinized him. Pete smiled; she had applied some makeup, he noticed. He raised his hand, showing five fingers and mouthed "five minutes." She looked perturbed, he thought.

Her countenance softened, "You look very handsome, very *debonair* in your suit." She glanced over her shoulder at Chef Timmy and decided he needed a break.

*   *   *

William studied his grandfather. He reminded him of his own dad; although Ernie was much older, there was a strong physical resemblance. When they talked, they even sounded alike. Ernie shifted his body sideways on the chesterfield. It allowed him to look at his grandson without straining his neck. The light from the table lamp reflected off Ernie's bronze belt buckle. The buckle drew William's attention.

Ernie smiled. "An old friend gave me this belt buckle. What do you think, Sam, is the buckle hip, or do you kids say, boss? It's challenging for me to keep up with the changing lingo," he chuckled.

"I say, boss. What is that shirt called, Grandpa?" William asked.

Ernie laid a hand on his shirt sleeve, looked at William and said, "It is a button-down shirt."

"The brown shirt, Grandpa, with no arms, with the yellow chain hanging out of the pocket."

"Oh, you are interested in my vest," Ernie said. "It is a five-button vest, and see, it matches the beige colour of my slacks. A gentleman wearing a vest looks very dapper." He winked at his grandson. "The ladies like a man in a vest."

William studied the shiny vest and decided he liked this old, wrinkled man with white hair on his head and chin. He also liked how he dressed. "Grandpa, what's on the end of the yellow chain?"

Ernie wrapped the chain around his index finger and withdrew the gold-plated double hunter watch from his vest pocket. He opened the back lid to show William the intricate clockwork, powered by interlocking gears, springs, and escapements. He then turned the watch over and opened the front lid. The simple watch face featured Roman numerals and two moving hands. He then explained, "I have to hand-wind the watch every single day, or else it stops keeping time."

He looked at William and continued, "This watch has been handed down from my grandfather to the eldest sons of our family, and one day it will be yours. You will inherit it."

William stared at the watch. He was unsure how to reply. He quickly concluded that if the pocket watch was in his possession, his father was…gone.

Ernie sensed his conundrum. "Sam, you will be a father with your own children long before you get this watch." He hesitated for a moment, "I have a photograph of my grandfather and grandmother on their wedding day, taken in 1864 while they were living in India. He worked as a boat captain for the British East India Company. In the photograph, you can see this very pocket watch sticking out of his vest pocket. Now, that is *boss*." He closed the front lid.

*   *   *

Pete walked down the stairs, dressed comfortably in grey slacks, a button-down shirt and a forest green cable cardigan. His favourite chunky-knit sweater. He walked into the kitchen as Vivian stood at the stove stirring the gravy.

Perturbed, she said, "I asked William to set the table after he fetched you." She glanced at the empty table, then moved toward the hallway.

"He's in the living room with his granddad. They're discussing the family heirloom, Dad's pocket watch. Don't worry, dear, I'll carve the roast then set the table," Pete said and added, "I'm happy the two of them enjoy each other's company. Where's Timmy?"

Vivian rolled her eyes. "He's back under the table, cuddling with Mildred." She wiped both hands on her apron and sat at the table. She exhaled, "I just need to rest for a minute and catch my breath."

Hearing her name, Mildred pulled herself upright, ambled over to Pete and got a pat on the head for her effort. He looked under the tablecloth. "Timmy, come on out, son…and take Dred down the hall and let her out for a run."

Timmy crawled out, yawned and said, "Come on, girl." Mildred obediently followed him along the hallway to the back door.

*　　*　　*

Ernie handed the pocket watch to William and said, "This watch has its own rich history; it has travelled from Geneva, Switzerland, to London, England, sailed on a passenger ship to India, and after the Greene family immigrated to Canada, the watch was present at a battle on the Canadian Prairies."

"If only this watch could talk rather than tick!" Ernie smiled and eyed the watch. "When you reach high school, you will learn about the rich history of Canada, about Confederation in 1867, and the events that in 1870, led to the establishment of Manitoba as our fifth province. You will also learn about the Métis leader Louis Riel, who, in 1869, was involved in the Red River Rebellion."

"That sounds…boss, Grandpa. What happened to Louis, the leader?"

"Well, after the Rebellion, Louis Reil went into hiding because he knew the government was looking to detain him. Years later, though, he was selected to be one of the leaders of the 1885 North-West Rebellion." Ernie motioned for the pocket watch. "I'm telling you about this sliver of our early history because my Uncle Frederick, in a small way, helped to suppress the North-West Rebellion."

William placed the pocket watch back in his grandfather's hand.

"Many years after father inherited the watch, his younger brother, Frederick, joined an Ontario volunteer militia group. Little did Frederick know that in 1885, he and about two thousand volunteers would be directed to board the recently built transcontinental railway for Batoche, Saskatchewan, under orders to bust up the Metis and Indian resistance movement."

Ernie glanced at William and said, "You see, Sam, years of disputes left unresolved with the government made it difficult for the people of the Prairies to safeguard their traditions, including their French language and Roman Catholic roots." Ernie's eyes drifted to the watch, its weight noticeable in his palm.

"Frederick told the family that he was moved by a sense of duty, embarking on a grand patriotic adventure to help settle the West. The day before he was scheduled to board the train, father proffered the Greene family heirloom to his younger brother. After riding the rails for six days, the volunteer militia units, accompanied by five hundred soldiers, arrived in Saskatchewan to reclaim the town of Batoche and the parish church. The Battle of Batoche lasted for four days."

Ernie inhaled and chewed over his uncle's story. "Well...according to Father, two months later, Frederick returned to the farm, a broken man." He lowered his head and exhaled, "He went to his resting place, never to discuss the Rebellion or his part in it."

Ernie wistfully slid the watch back into his vest pocket and secured the chain. He tapped his vest pocket and said, "Well, Sam, Louis Riel surrendered after the battle and months later, in a Regina courtroom, he was found guilty of High Treason and sent to the gallows. The poor fellow was hanged in a public square."

He glanced at William, "History continues to judge Riel's contribution to our nation's growth. On the one hand, he is seen as a defender of his people, while on the other hand, a traitor. We must, however, always keep it top of mind that when it comes to the subject of history, it is recorded and promulgated, er, told, through the narrow lens of the conqueror…the usurper. Do you understand?"

William stared vacantly at his grandfather.

Ernie looked at his grandson, "Well, you are a smart lad, one day you will. Consider this your first history lesson courtesy of granddad." He grinned and said, "My formal education ended at grade six because in those days, an education was secondary to working the farm, helping to support one's family. You, though, young man, need to stay in school, study, complete grade twelve, and use your diploma to land a good-paying job—the local steel plant is always hiring secondary school graduates."

TWENTY-TWO

Timmy opened the back door. Mildred dashed into the house, sat on her haunches and waited. He closed the door, patted the dog's head, turned and scampered along the hallway toward the kitchen. Hearing Ernie's voice, Mildred followed it to the living room. She padded into the room, rubbed her body along the chesterfield and flopped down on the carpet encircling his moccasin-slipper-clad feet.

*   *   *

Ernie watched Mildred settle at his feet and thought he could get to like this animal. He turned and said, "How old are you, William?"

William looked away from the dog, glanced at his grandfather and said, "I'm eight, Grandpa." It was not lost on William that his grandfather had referred to him by his Christian name.

Ernie studied him and said, "I believe I will share a personal story with you. A short story before we sit down to supper." William perked up and eyed his grandfather.

"A long time ago, when I was about your age, eight or nine, father needed supplies for the spring planting season, and he asked me to accompany him to town. The next morning, before first light, I followed him into the barn where he showed me how to hitch Belle, our ol' nag, to the buggy."

Ernie grinned, "No cars in those days. As the sun crested the horizon, we set out in the buggy. Father had brought a blanket, which he threw over our legs. He taught me that it required only a light touch on the reins to communicate with smart ol' Belle, as she was familiar with the route to town.

"The morning chill in the air left us feeling invigorated. Along the way, we enjoyed the splendour of the surrounding countryside, we whistled along with the birds, and we watched the white clouds rolling in from the west. We inhaled the fragrant breeze and listened to the clip-clop of Belle's hooves on the hardpan. Sitting next to father…I will never forget his distinctive body odour."

William twisted his face into a grimace.

"No, no, he didn't smell disagreeable. After all these years, I have learned that some smells often yield long-forgotten memories. With that in mind, during that morning ride in the buggy, father's characteristic scent…well, it reminded me of the earth, the soil, and as I recall, it was comforting to your nine-year-old granddad." He paused. "See…in those days we did not have the luxury of indoor plumbing, hot water flowing from a faucet or the wherewithal to enjoy a weekly bath." He raised his eyebrows and shrugged.

Ernie reached over and patted William on the head and said, "Father was a man of few words. He would toil in the fields, and at dusk, drag his tired body home, where mother would have supper waiting. He would eat, then listen to the radio or read a book with nary a word said. However, riding in the buggy on that fine spring morning, I learned that he was much more than a husband and father. He talked about many, many things, and when we reached town, he looked down and said to me that it was an ideal time to share his own father's insights—words of wisdom passed down from father to son. Father coined them, the three rules to a content and gratifying life."

Ernie then shared that he lived his life to the fullest by practising the family philosophy. He stared at William for a moment before acknowledging that his wish was for his grandchildren to embrace the rules, to build meaningful lives, to experience peace and happiness.

"Befitting the occasion, I believe it is high time you learn about the family philosophy," Ernie said devoutly.

Timmy appeared in the doorway and said, "Will'am, time ta wash you hands. Time ta eat." He then ran along the hallway to the basement door, opened it and repeated the message to Susan, only louder.

"We will continue this conversation later. You be sure to remind me. Your granddad's memory is not what it used to be," he instructed.

"I will, Grandpa," he said earnestly.

Ernie disengaged his feet from Mildred. He leaned forward, stuck an arm out and said, "Now, lend us a hand. We do not want to keep your mother waiting."

William jumped up and pulled as his grandfather extricated himself from the chesterfield. Mildred stretched and dragged her back legs along the broadloom, yawned and waited for Ernie to leave the living room.

CHAPTER

TWENTY-THREE

Will opened the passenger side door. Veronica eased into the Tempo, bent forward and grabbed her purse from under the seat. He closed the door, puttered around the front of the car, opened the door and slid in behind the wheel. A thin layer of ice had formed on the windows. He closed the door, fired up the engine, and turned on the window defroster.

A car horn beeped twice as it moved through the parking lot heading for the main street exit. He looked through the frosty windshield. Jimmy was sitting on the passenger side of the rental vehicle, waving his undamaged arm. Will flicked on the windshield wipers, waved and flashed the headlights for good measure. He turned to Veronica, noticed the purse on her lap and said, "Oh shit, Ronnie. I forgot to pay for dinner. With everything that went down in the lounge, it completely slipped my mind."

Veronica looked over at him and said, "It's all right. After thirty minutes and two coffees, we got tired of waiting. Amahle paid the tab. We owe $42 for our portion. She insisted that the wine was on them. She is such a lovely person."

"Forty-two dollars! Christ. That's why we don't go out for dinner. That's a pile of rental movies and buttered popcorn." The frost on the windshield melted, leaving it almost clear. He flicked off the wipers.

Veronica sighed, then urged, "Let's go home. I'm ready to check in on the kids." She then asked, "Tell me, what the hell happened in the lounge?"

Will began to drive slowly through the parking lot. The car twitched and bucked, and the rear brakes squealed.

Veronica condescendingly said, "Will, the parking brake is still on…that's why I never use it!"

He exhaled loudly, released the brake, then eased the car between the two buildings and turned right onto the main street. There were no other cars on the eastbound lane. Will looked off into the distance, and the traffic lights at each intersection glowed green.

"So…what happened?"

Will kept his eyes on the road and said, "I am not sure. Three buddies were out drinking, and one of them decided he needed to prove something by challenging Jimmy to a fight. I'll find out more tomorrow. He will call after he meets his dad for a coffee."

He glanced at Veronica, quickly refocused on the road and then went on, "Whatever Bruce Lee move he put on that guy was…it was amazing. I know he's a genius, but the way he handled that guy was fuckin' brilliant." Will then decided he would not tell her about the knife, for now, anyway.

"I'm disappointed and upset that the scuffle happened. It was such a lovely evening, and then for that to happen after our dinner. It makes me angry. I wonder what Amahle must think of our country. I find the whole mess…disturbing." Veronica looked down and shook her head, "I don't want to talk about it anymore."

She mulled it over and decided the incident would not spoil the rest of her night. She abruptly changed the subject, "Amahle and I had a wonderful chat while you boys were outside. Did Jimmy mention that they are looking to buy a parcel of land around Long Point on Lake Erie or on the St. Lawrence River near the Thousand Islands?"

Will's head wobbled as he stared straight ahead. Moments later, the town limits were in the rear-view mirror.

Veronica waited for him to answer. She exhaled loudly then continued, "Assuming everything goes as planned in California, next year they will relocate to Ontario. Jimmy is eager to move back to Canada and believes he can operate his new consulting firm from anywhere in North America. And Amahle has already reached out to several universities in southern Ontario regarding faculty collaborations and research resources." Veronica then swore him to secrecy and revealed Amahle's interest in starting a family. "After all, they are both in their thirties," she reminded him.

A broad swath of clouds moved slowly across the sky, concealing the moon, shrouding the narrow country road in complete darkness. Will was suddenly aware that it was exceedingly difficult to juggle so many activities—maintain his focus, listen to Veronica and keep the car out of the ditch. His eyes burned as he watched for deer galloping along the shoulder of the road.

"So, did Jimmy talk about his relationship with Amahle?"

Will hesitated, "No…no, not really."

"So, what did you guys talk about?" she asked.

He didn't hear the question. While the countryside passed by outside—inside, Will was primed to swerve for any creature that might scurry into the two beams of light.

Veronica sighed and said, "Amahle was thrilled that Jimmy confided in you about his past. She said he still has nights when he wakes up screaming. Not as many as when they first met, but it still happens. The poor fellow…"

Bewildered, she turned and eyed him, "Will, are you okay? What is up with you? I'm trying to have a conversation, and you're not saying a thing. Did I say or do something? Is it Jimmy?" She leaned over and eyed the speedometer. "Is the car acting up? It's eighty kilometres per hour, and you are hardly pushing fifty."

Will slowly dropped his eyes to the speedometer, signalled, slowed and steered the car onto the gravel shoulder. He released the steering wheel, flexed his stiff, aching hands, then slumped into the seatback. He slowly turned his head and looked blankly at her through bloodshot eyes and said, "Ronnie, when Jimmy and I were outside after dinner, I had a couple puffs on his marijuana cigarette and…I must be stoned."

"Oh my…so that's why you've been so quiet and acting out of sorts." Veronica stared shrewdly at him, "You fucking silly bugger. Slide over, I'll drive." She threw open the passenger door. Her eyes crinkled as a smile spread across her face.

TWENTY-FOUR

The kitchen table had been pulled away from the wall to allow just enough space to accommodate two chairs. Pete would sit at one end, Ernie at the other, and Vivian and the two girls would sit facing the wall, across from the boys.

Vivian kept an eye on the boiling turnip while stirring the gravy. She then seasoned the corn and carrots, turned to Pete and said, "Be a dear and put the butter and horseradish on the table."

He nodded as he sampled the sliced roast beef.

Timmy and Mildred burst into the kitchen. Vivian pointed to a chair next to the wall. Timmy fell to his knees and crawled under the table. He popped up beside the chair and asked, "Mum…I hungry, milk p'ease?"

Pete had built a small pile of beef trimmings while slicing the roast. He reached over to the counter, grabbed two large chunks and said, "Here, Dred." Mildred rushed over and sat on her haunches; her tail swept back and forth across the floor.

She gently took the scraps from his hand, padded across the floor and settled under the table.

Vivian patted her face with a tissue, then put it in her apron pocket.

"It is warm in here," Pete said. Using the back of his hand, he wiped the sheen from his forehead.

She nodded, "Dear, you should remove your cardigan."

Pete agreed, then moved to the window and slid it open. "I'll also open a window in the living room…get some air movement, some cross ventilation," he said and slipped out of the kitchen.

Susan walked through the doorway, told her mum she was working on her assignment and preferred to eat in her room. Vivian refused her request and insisted that she join the family for dinner. She offered Susan a compromise of sorts. After dinner, she did not have to help with the cleanup. Susan accepted, then stuck her finger in the pot of gravy.

"Use a spoon, not your finger," Vivian frowned.

"Mum, don't flip your wig. We're all family here."

Vivian ignored the sarcasm and said, "Susan, a little help…please put the Yorkshire puddings on a plate and drop the potatoes in a bowl. Tonight, everyone will serve themselves. We'll leave the puddings and the vegetables on the counter." She moved to the sink, drained the water from the cooked turnip and picked up the potato masher. She then reached up and began opening and closing kitchen cupboards.

Susan arranged the plated puddings and vegetables on the counter next to the stacked dinner plates. She turned, "Mum, what on earth are you looking for?"

"Now, what have I done with the butter?" she asked, flustered.

Susan moved to the table and picked up the butter dish. She smirked, "Here it is, hiding in plain sight."

"Oh my, I'd lose my head if it wasn't screwed on," she laughed wearily. "I feel like I have been run off my feet all day." She added two dollops of butter to the bowl and started mashing the turnip.

Mary Lynn walked into the kitchen, still drowsy from a much-needed nap following her strenuous piano lesson. She yawned, "When is supper gonna be ready?" she asked. "I'm starved."

"Mum, it's no biggie. It's just the butter. I'm sure, based on your gravy, dinner will be delish," Susan volunteered. "Besides, Sunday dinners are always the best."

"Yeah, don't sweat it, Mum," Mary Lynn offered, unaware of their conversation.

"I know. I know. I just want your granddad to enjoy dinner with his family."

Mary Lynn stuck her nose in the bowl of turnips, "Mum! You know I don't like turnip."

Vivian assessed the consistency of the mashed turnip. Satisfied, she said, "It's your granddad's favourite vegetable." She glanced at Mary Lynn, "For tonight, I don't mind; you don't have to eat any turnip."

Timmy decided he had waited long enough and said, "Milk p'ease," then added, "Me don' wan' yucky tur…nip."

*   *   *

William wanted to look dapper like his grandfather. After digging through two boxes of clothes, he left his bedroom wearing his brown, blue and yellow paisley shirt with stretched cuffs and a wide collar. He ran down the stairs two at a time, jumped to the floor from the third step, then stuck his head in the living room. He hoped to show his grandfather his fancy shirt. "Grandpa?"

His dad sat low in the chesterfield, legs outstretched, hands behind his head, watching the six o'clock news. He looked over at William and said, "Your granddad is upstairs." Pete stood up, strolled over to the TV and shut it off. "Come on, let's go, it must be dinner time. It's past six."

William fell in behind his dad, and as they approached the kitchen, he stopped and asked, "Why does Grandpa call me Sam?"

Pete turned around and addressed his son. "William, I don't know why. As far back as I can remember, your granddad called everybody *Sam*." He laughed, ruffled his son's hair and went on, "He called me *Sam* until I was well into my thirties, then one day out of left field I graduated from *Sam* to *Son*. Anyway, I overheard Granddad telling you about his pocket watch—his tick-talk story," he smiled. "Your granddad is quite the history buff."

"Grandpa said one day the watch will be mine," William asserted.

"Yes, I suppose that is true," Pete replied, then commented, "That's a heck of a psychedelic shirt you are wearing. Very spiffy." He turned back and stepped into the warm kitchen, trailed by a swaggering William. Pete removed his cardigan, placed it over the chair and then noticed the closed window.

"Pete, the cold breeze bothers my neck," Vivian said.

"I'm only sliding it open a couple of inches. It feels like a sauna in here."

Resigned to his argument, she exhaled, pointed at a chair and said, "William, go around the table and sit next to Timmy." She then saw his shirt. "I see you ransacked the boxes that were under your bed. When I go upstairs, there better not be clothes scattered all over your bedroom." She rubbed both hands on her apron.

Mary Lynn looked at her brother, shielded her eyes and laughed, "I need sunglasses." She watched as William squeezed between the wall and the table. "Hey, you little *drip*, do me a solid and put a sweater on before we all go blind!" She guffawed.

William plopped down on the chair next to Timmy, looked at Mary Lynn across the table and said, "Just mellow out…sissy." He puffed out his chest, "My shirt is outta sight." He glanced sideways at Timmy, and then at Mary Lynn, "'sides, my clothes don't have cooties like yours."

"That is quite enough," Vivian said.

Ernie sauntered into the kitchen, nose to the ceiling, "Smells wonderful, Viv."

She smiled, "Ernie, you're sitting at the other end of the table."

He nodded, moved around the table behind Susan and Mary Lynn, then eased into a chair. Vivian moved to the refrigerator, removed her apron and hung it from the fridge hook. She picked up the gravy boat and placed it on the table next to the roast beef, then took her place at the table beside Mary Lynn and to Ernie's right. Pete sat down opposite his father. Vivian then informed the family that their Sunday dinner would be a wee bit outside the norm; everyone would serve themselves, cafeteria-style.

She leaned to her right and said, "Susan, Mary Lynn, the plates are on the counter. Please help yourself to the vegetables and take two Yorkshire puddings."

Susan stepped to the counter, offered a plate to Mary Lynn, took another off the stack for herself and reached for the puddings.

William slid off his chair, walked around the table and watched as Mary Lynn moved along the counter, filling her plate. He waited, eyeing the mouthwatering Yorkshire puddings.

Susan offered him a plate and said, "Be careful, you don't want to break Mum's good China." She reconsidered, pulled the plate back and held it against her chest. "On second thought, you go back to your seat, and I'll dish up your dinner."

William shook his head.

She hesitated, then released the plate, "I warned you." She glanced over at her mother.

Meanwhile, Timmy had slipped off his chair, crawled under the table past Mildred, around his father's legs and jumped up near the refrigerator. He opened the fridge door and reached for the milk jug.

"Timmy," Vivian said. She stood up and moved toward him, "What are you doing in the refrigerator?"

"Nuthin." He looked at his annoyed mother, "…me wan' milk."

She pointed at the empty chair, "Back to your seat, young man." She exhaled, "From now on, all you must do is ask. All right, dear." She closed the fridge door and said, "You eat your dinner, then we will see about a big glass of milk."

"But, but…." If Timmy had been older, he would have looked perplexed; instead, he dropped to his knees, scooted under the table and crawled toward the chair.

"Timmy…up, get up off the floor…we walk around the table," Vivian said, exasperated. Too late. Like a prairie dog, his head popped up from beneath the table, next to the wall. She looked over her shoulder and noticed Ernie was still seated. "Dad, I would be happy to dish you up a plateful," she offered.

Ernie fidgeted as he slid the chair back. He placed his hands on the table, ready to stand and said, "Oh, that's not necessary, Viv."

"It's not a problem." She held out her hand, "I insist, please stay in your chair."

Ernie settled and pulled the chair closer to the table.

Susan sat down and helped herself to the roast beef. Mary Lynn resumed her seat, leaned forward, stabbed two slices of meat and snatched the gravy boat.

With both hands held high, William cradled the expensive China plate loaded with potatoes, two puddings and a small hill of corn. He hustled past his sisters, eyed his grandpa and then paused at the wall.

Susan had watched the young prey as he rounded the table.

He slid onto the chair and cautiously deposited the plate on the table. Success. Satisfied, he looked across the table at Susan. She was busy pouring gravy on her potatoes.

Pete returned to the table with a plate mounded high with vegetables and his allotment of two puddings. He sat down, picked up his napkin and unwittingly looked up into Vivian's imploring eyes.

With plate in hand, she glanced at Ernie and then motioned toward Timmy.

Pete exhaled and placed his napkin on the table. He quickly filled Timmy's plate with a helping of potatoes, carrots, corn, and two puddings. He then scooped up a small serving of turnip.

"No, no tur…nip Daddy."

Pete's brow furrowed; he looked at Timmy.

Vivian, meanwhile, was working her way along the counter, loading up Ernie's plate. She nudged Pete and whispered, "It's all right. I may have inadvertently caused this—"

"Viv, I'll have the lad's helping of turnip," Ernie announced.

Pete scraped the turnip off the plate, grabbed a slice of beef and positioned the non-China plate in front of Timmy. He resumed his seat and, with no more distractions, tucked the napkin between shirt buttons.

Vivian forked two slices of beef, walked around the table and handed the plate to Ernie. "Would you like gravy?" she asked.

"Yes. Thank you," Ernie reached for the salt and pepper shakers and said, "Pass the butter."

"Dad says we can only have gravy OR butter on our potatoes," William said, hoping to enlighten his grandfather.

Vivian swiftly filled her own plate and then took her seat at the table. She looked at each member of her precious family and felt exceptionally blessed. Her emotions always bubbled to the surface during Sunday dinners. She glanced at Pete. He smiled at her. Only he knew how special, how personal these weekly dinners were to his bride.

Concerned their dinner would get cold, she turned to Mary Lynn, "Please say grace, dear."

"Oh…Mum, why me?"

Vivian serenely eyed her youngest daughter.

From across the table, William was delighted with his sister's luck. His face lit up, rivalling his psychedelic shirt.

Mary Lynn scanned her audience; every head around the table was bowed in anticipation, even Timmy had dropped his head, fascinated by the creases in the blue tablecloth, except for William. Their eyes met. She mouthed *booger breath,* smirked, then lowered her head,

"For what we are about to receive,

We are truly grateful,

Give us, Lord, our daily bread, Amen."

"Amens," whispered around the table.

"That was lovely, dear. Please, everyone, eat," Vivian said.

TWENTY-FIVE

Vivian slid the apple pie into the warm oven and closed the door.

"Mum, why didn't you take any Yorkshire puddings?" Mary Lynn asked.

"I am trying to lose a couple of pounds…watching what I eat." She smiled, then glanced at Pete.

"You don't look fat," said Mary Lynn.

"Ding, ding."

Pete bristled at the intrusion. He turned his head and looked at the telephone. "Now, who would be calling at dinner time?" he asked, perturbed.

Susan glanced at the clock, 6:33 p.m., "It's for me," she announced. She looked over her shoulder at her mother, raised an eyebrow and said, "It's no biggie, just my friend Trudy." She pushed back the chair and beelined it for the telephone.

Vivian eyed Pete and nodded. She remembered that Susan was expecting a call from her school friend.

Pete shuffled on the chair and mumbled something about telephone calls during the dinner hour. He looked across the table at his father.

Vivian followed his gaze and was pleased to see Ernie savouring his dinner. "More gravy, Dad?" she asked.

Ernie lifted his head and said, "That would be splendid. Just a lovely dinner, Viv. You have outdone yourself."

"Well, thank you. I am delighted someone enjoys a home-cooked meal. Would you like more meat or potatoes—I cooked plenty."

"Oh…My goodness." He put a hand on his stomach. "I need to save room for a slice of your delicious apple pie…and ice cream." He winked.

"Trudy will be over in fifteen minutes," said Susan. She then cast doubt on Vivian's statement: "That's not fair, Mum. We all look forward to your Sunday dinners." She nudged Mary Lynn, then looked across the table at the boys.

Mary Lynn, in mid-chew, bobbed her head in agreement.

William was busy watching his grandfather pour gravy over potatoes. With fork and knife in hand, Timmy was scraping the plate, fighting a slab of beef.

"Timmy," Vivian said louder than anticipated.

Startled, he dropped his knife.

"That's not the way to hold a fork."

He looked down at his hand, confused.

"The proper way is to hold it with your left hand…" She watched him, then said, "Your other hand, dear…now place your index finger on the back of the handle near the base of the fork tines and let the handle rest in your palm…" She held up her fork and demonstrated.

Pete chimed in, "What your mother is missing, Timmy, is that by holding a fork in your fist, if the meat on your plate suddenly sprouts feet and tries to escape, you are ready to fork it—to stab it." He smiled.

Timmy dropped his head and eyed the slice of beef on his plate.

"Oh my God, Dad!" Susan said.

"Stab it, Timmy, before it runs away." Mary Lynn laughed.

Vivian ignored the frivolous cross-table talk. She kept an eye on Timmy as he fumbled and dropped the fork. She raised an eyebrow at Pete and said, "Proper table etiquette dictates there is only one way to hold a fork."

Pete exhaled. He removed the napkin tucked in his shirt, wiped his mouth, leaned over and picked up Timmy's utensils. Holding the fork in his left hand, tines down, he cut the meat into bite-sized pieces. He ruffled Timmy's hair, "Now eat."

Meanwhile, William quietly showed his proficiency, cutting the meat with both utensils. His eyes roamed the table. Surely someone had witnessed his masterful display of etiquette.

"William. Be mindful, as you cut your food, keep your arms tucked by your sides. You do not want to poke someone in the eye with an elbow," Vivian said.

Mary Lynn peered across the table at him and smirked.

*　　*　　*

Vivian sighed and pursed her lips. "I am quite disappointed that Jimmy had to leave before dinner. I hope he knows that he is always welcome in our home." She glanced at Pete. "I worry about the poor boy."

"The Henderson boy?" he asked.

Meanwhile, William tried to keep his arms tucked, elbows tight to his sides. Offhandedly, he said, "Jimmy went home to see his sister Karen 'cause she goes away to school tomorrow."

Mary Lynn stared at William and said, "What are you doing with your arms...you weirdo."

Susan glanced at the clock, then stared hard at her mother and said, "Karen's not leaving home to go to school. She's being sent to Tilbury to stay with a foster family until her...she's preg..." Susan reconsidered her choice of words, "She is expecting around the end of March."

"What's she expecting?" William asked, confused.

Mary Lynn perked up, "Is she old enough?"

Vivian lowered her head and put her utensils on the table.

Pete turned his head and stared through the kitchen window into the night. He would occasionally run into Jimmy's father while walking Mildred after dinner, and they would shoot the breeze for a few minutes. He seemed like an amiable enough fellow, Pete thought. He turned back, cast his eyes at Vivian and wondered—what would possess a father to abandon his daughter!

Ernie used what was left of his Yorkshire pudding to mop up the gravy on his plate. He then slipped the knife through the fork's tines, set the joined utensils on the plate and said, "That is incredibly sad for the whole family. I suspect sending away an unwed daughter who is in the family way is more prevalent than we imagine."

Mildred scurried out from under the table, stood at the kitchen doorway, hackles raised from neck to tail. A muffled knock at the front door reached the kitchen. Mildred answered with a piercing bark.

"Mildred, that's enough." The dog wheeled around, took a step and dropped her head on Pete's lap. He stroked the fur standing up along her neck.

Timmy repeated, "Mil'red nuff."

Susan pushed the chair back and eyed her mother.

"You're excused, dear," she said.

Susan picked up her plate, put it in the sink and walked quickly to the front door.

Pete watched her leave the kitchen. He kept his thoughts to himself. He put his utensils on the empty plate and crossed his arms. Mildred nudged his arm twice. Resigned, she collapsed on the floor, dragging her hind end back under the table.

William pushed his plate ahead and said, "Can I have pie now?"

Timmy eyed William's empty plate and said, "Me dun."

"Timmy. You have hardly touched your dinner…three more pieces of meat and some potatoes." Vivian held up three fingers.

"Mary Lynn. If you are done, please put your utensils on the plate."

"Oh, Mum. Who cares?"

Vivian sighed, "One day, you will thank me." She then fixed her eyes on Pete, anticipating his support. He was staring off into the distance, arms crossed. "Pete, what are you thinking about?" she asked.

"I was just thinking about Benny." He sighed. "Benny started his career at *the* Bell at nineteen. In the early days, we worked on the same crew. A good man. A decent man. He was a devoted husband and father, a genuine family man. His poor wife was so distraught during the service. I hope Diedre and his son Stephen have family...."

"How young a man?" Ernie asked.

"Forty-two," Pete replied. He looked at Ernie, "Jack Johnson found him in his truck in the driver's seat, thought he was napping. He had his climbing boots on, and his harness was on the seat beside him. They say it was the exertion from climbing the telephone pole. His heart gave out." Pete glanced at Mary Lynn, then at the boys.

"Oh my, much too young to...how dreadful for his poor family," Vivian said, shaking her head. "His wife must be devastated."

William stared down at his empty plate and said, "Your friend is dead?" He raised his eyes, "Was he shot with a gun?"

Pete eyed William, "He died from a defective..." he reconsidered, "he died because of a climbing accident."

Ernie said comfortingly, "He is in Heaven now."

Vivian sighed, "Sadly, he will be terribly missed by his wife and son." She picked up Mary Lynn's plate, stacked it on top of her own and then placed both sets of utensils on the plate. "How old is his son...Stephen?" she asked.

Pete momentarily gazed at the ceiling. "Benny was such an avid fisherman. He always had a fishing tale or two to share...he was telling me just a couple of weeks ago about his plan to buy a small aluminum boat and trailer. He dreamed of fishing on Lake Erie and Georgian Bay." He inhaled and said, "Stephen is eighteen."

Timmy slid off his chair and disappeared under the table while Mary Lynn fidgeted in the chair.

Pete went on, "I presume Diedre took some solace in the number of mourners present. The church was at capacity. The Joneses are members of the congregation, and during the priest's sermon, it was clear his words were personal and comforting. And when he invited Stephen to the lectern to deliver the eulogy, the silence from each pew was deafening."

William sensed a sadness emanating from his father. He peered around the table, then stared at his dad, listening attentively to his every word.

"I watched Stephen step up to the lectern, turn and face the mourners, his hands pinned behind his back. The young man paid tribute to his father and shared cherished family memories. Even a story about the fish that got away." Pete met his father's gaze, "I was so impressed by this eighteen-year-old's demeanour. Throughout the eulogy, he held his head high, spoke with a quiet confidence, and all the while controlled his emotions." Pete's eyes darted around the table. "Benny would have been extremely proud of his son." Pete smiled, but the sorrow was etched on his face.

"I am sure Deidre and Stephen were comforted that you, a work colleague and friend, attended his funeral," Vivian said.

"Yes, I suppose so." Pete brushed his hair back off his forehead, then placed his hands on the table. "Timmy left the table?" he enquired.

"He's here on the floor with the dog," Ernie said.

"Mildred is by your side?" Pete asked. Mildred had snubbed him since he got home, he thought. Dad obviously enjoys the dog's attention, although he would never fess up—he would argue animals should never be permitted in the home.

Vivian said, "Timmy, please leave Mildred alone and take your seat. We are about to have dessert."

Ernie said, "She has been my companion all day. I may grow fond of this animal."

Pete stirred in his seat and looked a tad perturbed, Vivian thought. She turned to Mary Lynn and asked her to help clear the dinner dishes and to pour three glasses of milk.

Timmy popped up beside his chair.

Vivian shadowed Mary Lynn, helping her clear the dinner dishes. She then moved to the oven, removed the warm apple pie and placed it on the counter. She turned and put her hands on Pete's shoulders.

TWENTY-SIX

Vivian cheerfully asked, "Well…how was everyone's week at school?"

"You wouldn't believe it," Mary Lynn announced, "Mr. Lurch was writing on the blackboard, then he turned and threw the chalk at Jane Prescott. It hit the wall behind her and broke into a whole bunch of tiny chalk pieces."

"Mr. Lurch. He is always very friendly to me when I'm at the school," Vivian said.

"What did Jane do to provoke such a reaction?" Pete asked.

Ernie sounded the alarm and said, "That is a dangerous practice—throwing chalk!" He exhaled, "Could very well put someone's eye out."

Mary Lynn looked at her grandfather with a new appreciation and said, "Grandpa, Jane even had yellow chalk dust in her hair."

"Hmmm…that teacher needs a reprimand," Ernie said.

William piped up, "At mornin' class attendance, Mrs. Johnson tol' us we had a new classmate from the country of

Ireland. She said his name is *Seen* O'Brien. He tol' Mrs. Johnson that his name is spelled S-e-a-n but sounds like *Shawn*." Mrs. Johnson laughed.

"I knew a couple of Seans growing up in London," Vivian said.

"And a second boy joined our class from the country of Quebec."

"Quebec is a province in Canada," Vivian corrected.

"Mrs. Johnson called him *Guy*. But he tol' Mrs. Johnson his name sounds like Pee but with a G. The whole class laughed."

Vivian looked around the kitchen table and said, "Well, I also had an interesting week. On Monday, I drove with Hillary Tuttle to a knick-knack store and a shoe store." She shook her head. "On a whim, any day of the week, Hillary may decide to leave home and go for a drive, visit a friend, or go shopping…" She glanced at Pete, "Oh, that must be so wonderful."

She breathed in the comforting aroma of the apple pie. "Tuesday morning, I walked around the corner to Sally's for tea with the clutch; it was nice to catch up on all the gossip. Wednesday morning, I met the other committee ladies at Gilwood School. It was an especially productive morning. And then Thursday, I was very industrious around the house." Vivian stared at Pete. "And Friday, well…a day Americans will remember and talk about for years."

"I meant to ask you about your school meeting on Wednesday. How was it?" Pete asked.

"Well…" Vivian said excitedly, "After three months of hot dog Fridays, we have enough money to buy drapes for the windows on the west side of the building. Those classrooms are like ovens during the afternoon. How those poor kids take instruction and learn under such extreme conditions…"

Vivian then glanced at William and said, "The principal joined our meeting and said that during Friday morning recesses, an older student is moving around the playground stealing kids' hot dog money. Have you seen anyone threatening the other children?"

William dropped his eyes and shook his head.

"All right. Well, if you see or hear anything…what sort of mean child steals hot dog money? My goodness," Vivian said.

"A kid that really likes hot dogs," Pete volunteered.

She sighed, "Based on the success of our hot dog Friday campaign, the committee has decided in the New Year to try pizza Wednesdays. Our goal is to raise enough money to purchase playground equipment." She smiled, pleased with the committee's agenda.

"Let me get this straight. The schoolyard bandit will now be able to line his pockets two days a week?" Ernie said, bewildered.

"You don't throw out the carton because of one bad egg," Vivian insisted.

Randy Cooper, the bad egg, William thought.

"We believe we have a solution. Every four weeks, a form will be sent home. The parents will decide on the number of lunch meals their child will participate in and then return the completed form with a cheque covering the cost of meals," Vivian explained.

Ernie nodded and acknowledged, "An admirable solution to a sticky problem and the children are doubly rewarded: they get hot dogs, pizza, and new play equipment. Viv, well done. They are truly fortunate to have you on their school committee."

"Well, thank you, Ernie." Vivian pushed her chair back, looked at Pete and said, "I have been thinking for some time now…"

Pete noticed a discernible change in the pitch of Vivian's voice. He eyed her as she got to her feet.

"…with Timmy in school half days and starting full days next September, I have decided to look for part-time work."

Pete's eyes flipped from Vivian to Ernie and back, "We are doing well…better off than many families," he replied quickly and added, "You're not happy at home?"

"I suppose we are, Pete." Vivian stood erect beside the table. She sighed. "I want to work outside the home and buy *stuff* with my own money—"

"I give you an allowance…" Pete cleared his throat and tried again, "I'm sure if I went to Mr. Grisham, he would approve some overtime, and then I would be able to supplement what I give you every two weeks."

"You already work long hours." She looked around the table and smiled, "Who wants apple pie?"

"Some of my girlfriends' mums work," Mary Lynn said. She jumped up from her chair, "I'll help you."

While Vivian and Mary Lynn dished up pie for everyone, the talk around the table ground to a halt.

William stirred in his seat. He looked sideways at Timmy fidgeting and eyeballing the ice cream on the counter. He then looked to his right. Ernie's eyes were closed, his arms were crossed, resting against his rising and falling chest. He vaguely recalled that his grandpa wanted to tell him something…something important. Oh well, he would ask Grandpa later.

He peered across the table and watched Mary Lynn add a scoop of ice cream to each slice of pie. Some slices were bigger than others; he licked his lips, crossed his fingers and hoped he would get a big slice.

Pete sat upright, his arms crossed. William thought he looked unhappy or annoyed, like when his mum gets annoyed when he quarrels with his sister.

Mary Lynn dropped two bowls with pie and ice cream in front of the boys. Ernie got a large slice of pie with a generous scoop of vanilla ice cream, while Pete's pie included a slab of cheddar cheese.

"I'll make a pot of tea," Vivian said. "I hope the pie is good."

Between bites, Ernie said, "Viv, your fruit pies are always delicious, and the crust is so flaky and golden."

"It's the lard," she smiled.

*   *   *

"Timmy, you've eaten all your ice cream and haven't touched your pie," Vivian said, shaking her head. She then gazed at Pete for a long moment, exhaled and said, "Last week Sally had an appointment at the bank. She enquired about a loan to buy new appliances and a chest freezer. She has worked in retail for the better part of ten years, she's a wife and mother, yet the bank officer said they required her husband's signature to approve the loan. It's just scandalous how the bank treated her."

Pete placed his fork on the plate and met Vivian's gaze.

She vented, "If I were in her situation, I would argue tooth and nail with the bank officer. I would demand to speak to the manager. I should be able to get a car loan just like any other working person."

The kettle whistled. Mary Lynn jumped up and unplugged the kettle.

Vivian ignored the disturbance and continued, "Pete, imagine how much easier our lives would be with two vehicles. Certainly, I need a job first."

"But Vivian…it's not just the price of the car," Pete said. "There are continuing expenses: gas, insurance, maintenance costs…operating a car is expensive."

"I understand all that, and once I find employment, well, I would keep working."

Pete looked across the table. Ernie was oblivious to his surroundings as he devoured his dessert.

Pete dropped his eyes to his half-eaten pie. The taste of cinnamon lingered on his tongue. "It's not that I'm against you getting a job or buying a car, but…"

Vivian appreciated that her husband accepted his role as the breadwinner and her role as a *housewife*. She was sympathetic to his concerns, but it was the 1960s after all. "Certainly, there may be times when Susan or Mary Lynn would be expected to help in the kitchen or with other household chores…regardless, more and more families cope just fine with both parents working outside the home—ours will too." She countered.

Silence overwhelmed the kitchen. Sensing a shift in mood, Mildred emerged from under the table and sat on her haunches beside Ernie. Her tail drummed against a table leg.

Well, that went better than I imagined, Vivian thought. Pete wasn't completely against the notion of her working…and buying a car. She glanced at the clock and said, "Where does the time go…the Ed Sullivan show is on in five minutes."

Ernie stirred in his chair, "Viv, that was a lovely dinner. Thank you."

"Please…Ernie, no need for thanks. Now, if everyone wants to move to the living room, in a few minutes I will bring in a pot of tea."

"I will help you clean up," Mary Lynn said.

Perplexed, she stared at her daughter, "Well, thank you, dear."

Ernie slid the chair back. He placed one hand on the table and slowly stood up. He shuffled to his right and then moved around the table. William sprang out of the chair, while Timmy landed on the floor and then popped up next to his dad. The boys followed their grandfather to the living room with Mildred a step behind.

Pete wiped his mouth with the napkin and said, "The pie was delicious." He eyed Vivian, "…Why not hold off cleaning up until after the Sullivan show? We can tackle the mess together after the boys are in bed."

Vivian, meanwhile, had plated the last two pieces of pie.

Pete walked to the counter, placed the dessert plate and fork in the sink, cleared his throat and said, "I believe I have established why Mildred latched onto Dad and hasn't left his side this whole time."

Vivian tilted her head and raised her eyes to him.

Pete heaved a sigh of relief, "It's because…he's wearing my moccasin slippers."

"Oh…of course, that must be the reason," she smiled, then turned to leave the kitchen with a dessert plate in each hand.

Ed Sullivan's distinctive voice carried into the kitchen.

"What are you doing with the last two slices of pie?" Pete asked.

Vivian's smile broadened, "I thought Susan and Trudy would appreciate a break from their school assignment and enjoy a warm slice of apple pie and ice cream."

Will wrinkled his nose as a sudden smell of ammonia, mixed with a tangy, sweet scent, invaded the passenger cabin. He coughed and squirmed behind the wheel. His eyes burned.

"That was 'Smoke on the Water' by Deep Purple. And folks, a little bit of trivia for your next get-together. 'Smoke on the Water' was on the B-side of the *Machine Head* album, released in March of 1972. I am Donny Mercuri, and you are listening to ROR 101.3 FM broadcasting the old and new hits you want to hear."

He kept his eyes on the highway and tried to ignore the unpleasantness. "Ronnie, did you know that Deep Purple's lead singer, Ian Gillan, wrote the lyrics after the band witnessed a fire at a casino during a Frank Zappa concert in Switzerland. The smoke on the water…"

A prickly sensation settled on his skin. He coughed again, then glanced over his shoulder at the empty passenger seat. "What the hell…" he stammered to the empty cabin. "Where am I? This isn't the Tempo…" He looked down at the large steering wheel, the shifter on the column and three large round dials set in a wood-trimmed dashboard. He eyed the blue interior and the rope obviously securing the passenger door. The vehicle slowly veered off onto the gravel shoulder. He jerked up his head and quickly eased the car back onto the four-lane highway. His mind whirled; he was behind the wheel of his 1973 Pontiac LeMans.

"Welcome back to the May 2-4 long weekend—celebrating our 10th anniversary on the air. And looking back ten years, drum roll please…the No. 1 hit on the Billboard Hot 100 Pop Chart from 1972 was 'Oh Girl' by the R&B vocal quartet the Chi-Lites."

While the 'Oh Girl' song filled the cabin, it clashed with the jarring commotion happening in Will's head. The radio host spoke over the song, "This is Donny Mercuri signing off, leaving you with the smooth vocals of the Chi-Lites. You are listening to ROR 101.3 FM."

"Mr. Greene." The female voice drowned out the Chi-Lites. Will glanced in the rearview mirror, then stared hard at the radio. The voice repeated, "Mr. Greene." The radio emitted a crackling sound, and the voice again said, "Mr. Greene…Will."

"What the fuck is going on?" he yelled. He reached for the volume knob and twisted it until it clicked. Silence. He had an overwhelming urge to reach down, yank the radio from the dash and throw it out the window. He swivelled his upper body, glanced at the back seat and down at the floor. He recognized the duffel bag and the small suitcase on the back seat, as well as the pair of running shoes and the insulated lunch box on the floor. He turned back and concentrated on keeping the vehicle from careening off the highway. The only noise in the cabin now was his heart thrumming in his ears.

Will stared into the distance beyond the empty highway. He had to know—did the voice calling his name really spring forth from the radio? His eyes fluttered as he anxiously tried to keep one eye on the road and the other on the radio. He maintained a tight grip on the steering wheel as he slowly reached and hovered his trembling hand over the radio knob. He held his breath, counted backwards: 'two…one,' and then turned on the radio.

"And that was 'Bette Davis Eyes' by Kim Carnes. And next up, Julia with the up-to-the-minute weather—"

Will breathed in deeply, then hastily shut off the radio. He rolled the window down. The fresh, warm air was invigorating. He turned his head and peered through the passenger window across a field to the St. Lawrence River and spied three islands on the horizon.

Of course it's Sunday, he thought. That's why my duffel bag and suitcase are in the car. It's the Victoria Day holiday, and I'm on my way to Cedar Landing to relieve the other SAR crew at noon. A sense of relief washed over him as a trickle of sweat ran down his temple. He swiped his hand across his sweaty forehead. His grip loosened on the steering wheel as he began humming 'Oh Girl' by the Chi-Lites. Why that song? He wondered. Will then reached over and switched on the radio.

*   *   *

The mid-morning Sun rose in the hazy pink sky as he continued eastbound down the highway toward his destination. Two weeks, he thought—stationed in a small town for fourteen days working with hydrographic surveyors and, if required, performing secondary Search and Rescue duties. He always felt melancholy leaving Veronica alone at home. It could be worse—instead of spending the shipping season in Cedar Landing on the St. Lawrence River, he could have been assigned to a hydrographic survey on Lake of the Woods, Manitoba, or be sailing the Great Lakes for twenty-eight days on one of the buoy tenders. Then again, there are always openings on the Arctic icebreakers.

"That was 'Emotional Rescue' by Mick and the boys, and following the News Flash, we have a doubleheader: 'Against the Wind' by Bob Seger and the Silver Bullet Band and 'Heartache Tonight' by the Eagles. You are listening to ROR 101.3 FM broadcasting the old and new hits you want to hear."

Sundays were inevitably the most tranquil days to travel along the highway; traffic was light, and there were fewer trucks. Will yawned, rubbed his face and yawned again. While he sped along the highway, he kept an eye out for the next guide sign. A minute later, as the Eagles' song faded away, a signboard appeared in the distance:

Lancaster, 27 miles

Salaberry-de-Valleyfield, QC, 60 miles

The settlement of Cedar Landing was still ten minutes east of Lancaster. Will checked the time on his black Casio Calculator watch: 10:20 a.m. He nodded, satisfied. He would arrive at the White Cedar Marina by 11:00 a.m. A reciprocal favour during crew change allowed the on-site crew to leave the base for home an hour early. The SAR trailer would be cleaned; the guys would be packed and waiting for the relief crew.

Will glanced down as a new vibration crossed the steering wheel into his hands and rattled his elbows. The LeMans 350 V8 engine, noisy on a good day, grew louder as metallic-like drumming echoed from under the hood. Suddenly, his feet began to bounce off the footwell as if the engine were trying to burrow through the floor pan to escape its fate. He quickly removed his foot from the gas pedal. A piercing screeching erupted from the engine and was abruptly silenced by a loud bang. The dashboard shook violently. His vision jiggled and bounced as he scanned every which way; he glanced at the rear-view mirror to see a large cloud of swirling blue smoke pursuing the car. A final high-pitched whirring noise passed through the footwell into the cabin. The vehicle slowed and limped onto the gravel shoulder. His mind raced, well fuck me…now what! He maneuvered the rolling car to a flat grassy area clear of the highway.

Will pulled the hood lever, unbuckled and jumped clear of the car. As he waited for signs of fire or smoke, he looked in both directions along the highway. It was deserted. He moved to the front of the car and tapped the hood. It was warm to the touch. He inhaled, reached under the engine hood, pulled the latch, yanked up the hood and jumped clear. He examined the engine from a distance. It was dirty, rusty, and caked with greasy oil everywhere; it looked like any other nine-year-old engine.

He sighed, relieved no flames were rising from the engine. He leaned against the car to gather his thoughts. Since he had owned the LeMans, the engine had performed faithfully. Even though the odometer just passed 146,000 miles, he suspected the car still had plenty of life—many more miles to burn. He smirked. He pushed off the car and decided to look underneath. He opened the door and activated the four-way hazard warning flasher. Dead.

He dropped to the ground, rolled over and inched his upper body under the chassis, pausing beside a small puddle of engine oil on the grass. Burnt oil assaulted his nose. With minimal clearance, he slowly turned his head and eyed the engine, the oil pan and the undercarriage. Thick black oil coated the undercarriage. He then noticed blue puffs of smoke rushing along the exhaust pipe to the muffler.

He hurried to distance himself from the smouldering exhaust pipe. His cheek dragged along the grass as he eased out from under the car. He rolled to his side, then onto his knees in a semi-crouched position. He sneezed twice just as a shadow fell over him. He looked up. Standing before him was a fellow in his late twenties, wearing a soiled full-length linen robe with sandals that showed many miles of wear. The fellow looked like an advertisement for 1970s communes. Startled, Will sprang to his feet and stepped back. He glanced at the highway as an eastbound car zoomed by without slowing. He noticed that there were no cars stopped along the shoulder.

The fellow smiled pleasantly and, with an open, guileless face, said, "Bless you. My apologies…my friend. I am not in the habit of alarming people." He peered at the broken-down car, then raised his hand in front of his nose, waving aside the smell of burnt oil poisoning the air. "Do you anticipate serious car problems?" he asked in a circuitous manner. "My friend…I will blissfully support you in every way to remedy this problem to set you on your way," he said congenially.

"Well, thanks, I appreciate the offer. But what I need now is a tow truck," Will said. He quickly decided he preferred the smell of burnt motor oil over the dank-smelling stranger.

Will watched the fellow for a moment and decided he was harmless—odd, eccentric, but harmless. The fellow tried to run a hand through his matted, shoulder-length hair. In his other hand, he held a six-foot gnarly yet smooth wooden staff. Its straw colour was accented by many dense black knots. It was a strikingly impressive *stick*. His long scraggly beard, Will imagined, would rival Billy Gibbons' of ZZ Top. Gibbons' beard, though, was meticulously trimmed.

Will pondered whether the *hippie's* clothes aimed for pious or more mystical, a wizard on a quest to Mordor! He stifled a grin.

"If I were you, I'd take a couple of steps back from the car…best to be safe," Will said. He then ducked into the front seat, gathered his gear and threw it out on the grass. He rifled through the glove box, retrieved his wallet and sunglasses. He stepped away from the car, reconsidered and decided to check the trunk. He popped the lid and discovered two boxes filled with non-perishables. He shook his head, sighed and realized he had no recollection of packing or putting the boxes in the trunk.

Meanwhile, the hippie had fallen back to the duffel bag and was staring toward the highway; he looked like a shepherd tending to his flock. Will dropped the boxes of non-perishables beside the rest of his gear.

"Thank you for considering my well-being," the hippie said, then laughed. "Most people prefer to pass me by and not enter into a reasoned exchange of thought. Regardless…once their vibe is revealed to me—I may then propose they find their peace and savour every blessed day." He laughed again. "Some people, frankly, tell me to go fuck myself." He pointed at Will's neck and said, "That is a remarkable pendant you are wearing. May I?" He took a step forward.

Will looked side-eyed at the hippie. He had never worn chains or any jewellery, for that matter. He lifted his hand, to his astonishment, he felt a thin chain around his neck. He immediately removed the chain and eyed the crumpled silver chain and the attached blue oval pendant. He frowned and stared at the pendant. He felt like an outside observer, as if he were disconnected in time. His hand trembled as he recalled it had been many years since he had seen his dad's World War II memorabilia.

The hippie sidled up beside him. He leaned in and said, "Your pendant is exquisite. An extraordinary depiction of the Mother Mary."

Will pulled his eyes away from the pendant, stepped back and said, "My dad was given this pendant during the Second World War. And, in fact, it represents Saint Christopher, the patron saint of travellers." He tried to rub the nasty smell away from his nose, then said, "I find it problematic to accept that the original owner was mistaken or misguided about the pendant's image and what it symbolizes."

"I am a devout follower of the Mother Mary and the patron saint of travellers, and I am saddened to say—I mean no disrespect to your kin—the pendant represents the Mother Mary." He smiled sincerely.

Will took another step back, hesitated, then slid the pendant back over his head and said, "Well, I am not Catholic…but, next time I see…"

The hippie's smile disappeared, and his expression turned grave. He raised the wooden staff toward the heavens and bellowed, "My friend, we are now connected. I grok our Chi is ONE. Be forewarned, you are surrounded by turbulence…your psychic vibes are in disarray." He looked up at the sky and announced in a booming voice: "William, I empathize with your inner turmoil." He dropped his head and was silent.

Will stared unblinking at the hippie. He was at a loss for words and unsure what to say or how to react to this new development. A moment later, the quiet was shattered as a semitrailer truck decelerated and pulled to the side of the highway. The passenger door swung open, and a voice from inside yelled, "Grab your stuff, I'll drop ya at the next stop."

Will inhaled the oily-smelling air, then cleared his throat as a weariness pressed against his chest. A sudden thought occurred: He said *William!* How the fuck does this robed guy know my name? A chill rolled down his back. He tried to shake off the unsettling sensation as he looked down at his gear and the two boxes of non-perishables. "Hey, you want these boxes of food?"

The hippie nodded. "That is very generous of you, friend." His pleasant smile had returned, and his staff once again was planted on the ground at his side.

"It's just some staples—*survival rations*: boxed noodles, canned beans, soup and stuff."

The hippie looked at the filled boxes and said, "Thank you for your benevolence." He kneeled, laid his staff on the ground and peered into one box. "Brown Beans...and Froot Loops," he said happily.

Will reached into the other box and removed a container of Lysol disinfectant spray. He dropped the spray into his duffel along with his running shoes, threw the bag over his shoulder, grabbed the suitcase and the lunch box. He eyed the hippie, hesitated, then said, "I could ask the driver if he'd be willing to give us both a ride to the next town?" Will wondered if he and the truck driver could stomach being cooped up in the cab with the smelly hippie.

The hippie got to his feet and casually said, "I am home."

Will scanned east and west across the field and along the distant treeline for a tent or other shelter.

Amused, the hippie watched him and then said, "You best motor...my friend."

Will nodded. He did not want to keep the trucker waiting any longer. He feebly said, "Take 'er easy." He turned and jogged toward the truck. He climbed into the cab, dropped his gear on the floor and shook the driver's hand. "Thanks for pulling over."

"Sure, happy to be of service…you leavin' them boxes behind? I got time. Bring 'em along," the truck driver said.

"It's just a few supplies. Anyway, I offered them to the hippie."

"The hippie?"

"Standing over by my car."

"Hmmm…all I seen, son, was the oil skid on the highway and you beside the Pontiac. Of course, I'm keeping this big rig runnin' on the road." He laughed. "I haven't seen a hippie 'round these parts…bin years."

Will turned and looked out the side window to see the hippie walking back to the treeline, holding his staff in one hand and the box of Froot Loops in his other.

As the semitrailer slowly picked up speed, the truck driver said, "All that oil back there on the road, I'd say your oil pan gasket blew out."

Will sighed and said, "The car's undercarriage is covered in black oil." He smirked, "Just last week…getting ready for this trip, I had the engine oil changed, and new spark plugs installed."

The truck driver glanced at him and said, "The motor is probably kaput…on the plus side, there's a truck stop, second exit ahead, two minutes off the highway. It's a full-service garage with a draggin' wagon on-call 24/7."

*   *   *

Jeremy Steele drove the green government station wagon slowly along the main street. Sitting on the passenger side with his arm resting on the windowsill, Will looked out the window at the town sign:

Welcome to Cedar Landing, Est. 1832 Pop. 650.

He constructed a mental image as they moved through the downtown. On the north side of the street, he counted five stores: Herb's Hardware, a laundromat, Keeler's Video Rental and a Scotiabank. At the end of the block, a general store also functioned as a Post Office.

He turned his head. A mobile trailer, locally known as the In and Out store, was stocked with liquor and beer. Sheets of plywood attached around the bottom of the trailer lent the structure a sense of permanence. A vacant lot next door was designated for vehicle parking.

Back across the main street, a clothing store with 1960s mannequins dressed in the latest fashions waved at the non-existent shoppers. Next door, Henby's Shoes was having a going out of business sale.

He turned back as the car trundled by a dilapidated two-story building. A 5-pin bowling alley covered the ground level, and on the second floor, a weathered sign affixed to a window implored: "Studio Apartment for Rent--Price Negotiable." A one-story building next to the bowling alley, The Jubilee Five-Star Emporium, with its intriguing name, enticed would-be shoppers to venture inside. He tried unsuccessfully to see through the hazy, blemished windows.

Jeremy signalled right, preparing to make the turn down the hill to the White Cedar marina. Across the street, the Royal Hotel was the only drinking establishment in town that had endured since the late 1920s. It was also the tallest building at four stories.

Driving down the hill, Will eyed the forty-slip marina, crammed with motorboats and sailboats. Two aluminum buildings housed the marina office and the service garage. To the west, he spotted the three white hydrographic trailers positioned perpendicular to the shoreline. And twenty feet further on, he studied the Search and Rescue trailer with an attached VHF Marine antenna that rose forty feet into the sky. He glanced at his watch at 2:05 p.m.

*   *   *

The Search and Rescue trailer ran parallel to the shoreline, situated thirty feet from the water's edge. The thirty-two-foot trailer had an office/bedroom at the east end, two bedrooms at the opposite end and a shared central lounge area.

Jeremy parked the station wagon behind the trailer next to the office/bedroom. Will exited the wagon and walked along the back of the SAR trailer, occasionally ducking to look underneath. The trailer was about three feet above ground, level and on multiple stacks of concrete cinder blocks. He eyed the above-ground holding tank, located a mere five feet from the back bedroom window. He shook his head and grumbled, "Oh, for fuck sakes."

He walked back and retrieved his duffel bag, suitcase and lunchbox from the back seat. As he trekked through the wet sand, he looked out at the calm green water lapping against the shore. As he approached the precarious-looking steps to the SAR trailer door, he paused and dropped his gear in the sand.

Jeremy rounded the trailer and yelled, "Careful going up those steps. They need some reinforcing." He caught up to Will and said, "Charlie the coxswain told me to take the back bedroom…something about seniority." He raised his eyebrows. "Doesn't matter to me which room I have…" he laughed and went on, "I measured, and both bedrooms are just over six feet long and three feet wide."

"A word of advice: keep the sliding window in the bedroom closed at all times," Will said.

Jeremy looked confused.

"On a warm day, the *honey tank*, and this one is only five feet from the window, can get pretty ripe," Will scowled and scrunched his nose.

"Oh…shit!"

"Literally." Will grinned. "Oh, and Charlie Ryder, he prefers to be called Chuck. He can get, well, let's say a little prickly if you call him Charlie."

"Okay…thanks."

"Hey guys, glad to see you made it." The tall, athletic-looking man held out his hand, "Chris Stock. I'm one of the survey hydrographers." He looked at Will, "Jeremy mentioned you had car problems?"

Will extended a hand, "Yeah…afraid the engine in my old LeMans is fried. The mechanic at the truck stop said he'd contact me later in the week with the diagnosis…I don't hold out much hope, though." He exhaled.

"That's a bummer, man."

Will reached into his duffel bag for the Lysol spray and said, "Well, I guess I have two weeks to decide what to do with the car."

Chris stared at Will and said, "You look really familiar."

"I thought I recognized you, too." He gave the Lysol container a quick shake and added, "I grew up in north Millington, the veterans' subdivision."

"Oh…really. In high school, I was on the Blue Crows football team with Frankie Malone. He always talked about hanging with the orchard gang, kids who spent time in the old orchard under the hydro towers. In fact, I was there a few times to play some pickup ball." Chris lowered his head in thought, "…and there was a girl, Frankie talked about constantly…Donna?" He grinned, "Frankie was hot on her heels."

Will chuckled and said, "Donna Moore. She was popular. Everyone liked Donna."

Chris nodded, "Donna Moore." He went on, "I knew Lenny, Stuart, Dean Henderson and…" He eyed Will. "You were buddies with Dean's younger brother, Slim Jim." Chris shook his head, "Sorry, man…that's what some of the *dipshits* called him…fuckin' kids."

Will ignore the jibe—he had heard much worse. "Yeah, Jimmy and I were buds for years, lived on the same street and then, well…the last time I saw him was about a year ago at Dean's Stag and Doe."

Retired navy sailor Chuck Ryder, sporting a crew cut, a neatly trimmed white goatee and wearing his government issue jacket, beige slacks and polished black military boots stepped out of the nearest hydrographic office trailer, marched over to the SAR trailer and said, "Heard you had car problems. Luckily one of the guys from the other crew and this guy," he pointed at Chris, "stayed around until you two decided to show—two hours late." He shook Will's hand, turned to leave and said over his shoulder, "Don't let it happen again."

"Great to see you too…Chuck." Will smiled.

Jeremy watched the exchange, concern outlined on his face. He eyed Will and said, "Did I just witness the prickly Charlie, er, Chuck?" He dropped his head and grumbled, "Damn, we're sharing quarters with this guy for the next fourteen days…shit!"

Will shrugged, tipped his head to the side and then gave the Lysol container another quick shake. He inhaled and said, "All righty. No time to waste. I'm goin' in, boys."

"What do you mean?" Jeremy asked. He raised his eyes, "What's with the Lysol?"

Will replied, "It's part of my treatment to eliminate insects, pests and rodents. These thirty-year-old trailers sit out all winter in a back lot, a refuge for every type of fuckin' creature. And have you seen the old, stained, decrepit mattresses?" He shook his head, "Before I hang my hat and unpack my socks in one of these coffin-sized bedrooms…I neutralize any critters that have taken up residence during the winter. I spray the mattress, ceiling and walls with Lysol, then close and stuff a towel under the door. Then I give the room about two hours to chill." He looked at Jeremy, "We should also pick up a couple of mouse traps for the kitchen cupboards. I hope this year we don't encounter any rats."

"Really," Jeremy said, frowning.

Will started up the wobbly steps, Lysol container in hand.

"Um…could I use the Lysol in my bedroom…that is, if you have any spray left?"

"Sure." Will nodded. "Don't forget to hold your breath while spraying." He opened the trailer door and stepped inside.

CHAPTER

TWENTY-EIGHT

Holding a two-four of Molson Canadian, Will stepped through the front entrance into the swanky foyer. Large Italian marble tiles, white with grey veins, covered the floor. Two half-walls with square columns reaching to the ten-foot ceiling separated the foyer from the great room. He turned to Jimmy, raised his eyebrows and said, "Geez, man, the front entrance is bigger than my parents' living room."

The opulent, glossy tiles continued throughout the great room. Six circular columns added strength and character to the large open space. At the far wall, the diffused early-evening light entered through three levels of stacked rectangular windows. Long shadows stretched from the circular columns to the foyer.

Jimmy stepped inside, shook his head in disbelief and said, "Christ, what an amazing space. The living room alone covers more area than either of our parents' homes." They both chuckled.

"Hey, Jimmy. Hey Will. Awesome, you guys could make it to my twenty-first birthday bash," said Gerald.

"Of course, man, wouldn't miss it," said Will.

"Cool home, man. Did your father design it?" Jimmy asked.

"This is their third house, and each one has been built according to his designs. This house, though, transcends the other two by a fuckin' long shot."

"Truthfully, man, I'm amazed your parents are okay with you having a party, even considering it is your twenty-first birthday," said Will.

Gerald laughed, "Technically, they aren't…they are hopping around some Caribbean Islands on a business trip." He air-quoted, *trip*. "Pass me the beer, Will. I'll put it in the fridge." As Gerald moved toward the kitchen, he turned back and said, "You guys can leave your shoes at the door."

"Roger," said Will. "Hey Gerald…last Saturday was Jimmy's twenty-first!"

"No way. See you in a sec."

Jimmy and Will stepped back to the door and removed their shoes.

"Interesting that his folks take a powder the weekend of his birthday," said Will.

"Evidently, they didn't forget it was his birthday. In the garage, Dean told me there's a new, right off the assembly line, 1977 Dark Red Corvette Stingray, 350 4-barrel V8, 4-speed manual transmission with Smoked Grey leather seats and an AM/FM stereo radio with an 8-track player," Jimmy said enviously.

Will shook his head, "A brand new Vette. Must be nice to have rich parents." He then raised his head, looked around and curled his lip, "Jimmy, do you smell that…smells like bleach?"

"It's chlorine. There must be an indoor pool."

Gerald appeared holding three full shot glasses and said, "Jimmy is right, that's chlorine you're smelling. I treated the pool this morning and forgot to close the door on the natatorium."

Will squinted at Gerald, then glanced furtively at Jimmy.

"Reminds me. I should also lock the pool door. I don't want someone taking a leak in the pool and falling into the deep end. That would not be very agreeable…for anyone." Gerald laughed and offered up the shot glasses.

"A shot of Jägermeister…for the birthday boys." Gerald said and raised his glass to Jimmy, "Salud! Cheers!"

Will and Gerald downed the spicy liqueur.

Jimmy stared at the chestnut-brown liquid, hesitated, relented, and downed the shot in two gulps. He suddenly fought the urge to regurgitate the liqueur.

Gerald retrieved the shot glasses. The doorbell chimed. Six people wandered into the foyer and in unison said, "Happy birthday, Gerald."

"Thanks much," he said and turned to Will, "I'll talk to you guys later. Make yourselves at home. Hey, there are folded blankets in the great room. Would you mind throwing them over the couches and chairs? We don't want red wine on white leather."

"No problem," said Jimmy.

"And check out my album collection. Spin whatever you want." He walked away.

"Jimmy. I'll see you in the living room. I'm going to find the kitchen and grab a beer." Will eyed him, "You want one?"

Jimmy shook his head.

*   *   *

Will was on his knees in front of a massive white oak shelving unit that supported hundreds of hardcover books, knick-knacks and a stereo system with multiple shelf speakers. He continued to peruse Gerald's extensive album collection. Uriah Heep's *Demons and Wizards* record was on the turntable, flooding the great room with the sounds of "Traveller in Time."

"I saw them live," Larry said from a couch. "An English band that didn't get enough credit—in my opinion."

Will nodded, spied Led Zeppelin's double album *Physical Graffiti*, pulled it aside and placed it next to Fleetwood Mac's *Rumours*, Rush's *Moving Pictures* and Boz Scaggs's *Silk Degrees*. Tired of looking at albums, he walked over to the couch, flopped down next to Larry and said, "Did you catch the playoffs?"

"Yeah, man. The Montreal Canadiens put on a formidable performance to win the series 4-0 over the Boston Bruins—gotta be one of the greatest NHL teams ever."

Will sipped his beer and said, "Their twentieth Stanley Cup. Mighty impressive." He scanned the great room and counted at least twenty people sitting and milling about, chatting and drinking. A quartet standing nearby shared a joint. He couldn't decide which smelled worse, the joint or the chlorine. He turned and watched a guy remove the Heep record and queue up Zeppelin's *Physical Graffiti*. Not his style of prog rock, he guessed.

Larry sipped a Coke and said, "Will, what did you think of the RCMP raiding Keith Richards' Toronto hotel suite, confiscating heroin and cocaine. Scuttlebutt is he could spend eight years behind bars."

"Yeah. Gnarly stuff. The Stones have been in the news a lot this year. And, how 'bout the other big story in March…carried in both the national and international papers, about Margaret Trudeau being spotted with Mick Jagger at the El Mocambo in Toronto…then it was leaked she spent the night at the same hotel as the Stones." Will shook his head, "Wonder what Pierre thinks of his wife hanging with the Stones. The bad boys of rock."

"Yeah, man. What a scandal. A national embarrassment." Larry downed his Coke and sprang off the couch. "You want another beer?"

"Thanks. I'm good…time to explore this big house." Will stood up, pulled the blanket back over the armrest and slowly wended his way through the crowd, the chatter and Jimmy Page's guitar riff. He worked his way past the enormous kitchen and toward the hubbub of laughter echoing through the doublewide hallway. Moving along the hallway, he gawked at the impressive indoor swimming pool behind the glass partition. On the opposite wall, vibrant acrylic portraits of dogs and horses eerily kept their eyes on the moving target.

Will entered the rustic family room and paused at the majestic floor-to-ceiling fieldstone fireplace. He eyed the black timber beams that spanned the twelve-foot ceiling, then scanned the crowd, glimpsing Jimmy on the other side of the room next to a set of French doors. He was beside a heavyset man, using a cane for support.

A hand reached through a group of revellers, grabbed Will's arm and thrust a beer in his hand. "Hey buddy, how's it hangin'?" Will smiled at Dan Hearn, his sister Carol and another woman he vaguely recognized.

*   *   *

Her two girlfriends were late to the party. Standing in the foyer, Donna Moore unzipped her platform boots, dropped them by the door, then moved next to a square column on the half-wall and surveyed the countless people enjoying themselves in the great room. She felt relieved—she recognized many faces. She then leisurely scoped out the spacious room with its Italian flooring, circular columns and white leather couches and accent chairs. Burgundy and slate grey features were judiciously placed throughout the room. She nodded her approval and thought the great room should be featured in *Canadian Homes* magazine. She did, however, question whether the interior designer was leaning toward elegant or pretentious.

*   *   *

Will threaded his way through the partygoers, the smoke and Carl Douglas' disco song, "Kung Fu Fighting."

Meanwhile, Phil Berger hugged the walls of the family room, pushed and maneuvered around the perimeter until he reached Jimmy. "Hey Jimbo, have you seen your brother or Randy?" he asked.

Will emerged from the crowd next to Jimmy.

"I haven't seen Dean, but I was just talking with Randy; he's outside in the courtyard," Jimmy said.

Will turned his head and looked through the French doors at Randy Cooper sitting in a Muskoka chair, his cane lying across his lap. He stared at Coop and thought for a guy in his mid-twenties, he could easily be confused for someone much older. "Christ, he does not look well," Will said, taking a swig of beer.

Phil looked outside at Randy, then said, "Guess you guys haven't heard, 'bout a month ago, he told me he has a curve in his spine causing him lots of pain and…bunch of other symptoms. Coop said it's called lumber scoliosis, and he's had the disease for most of his life but was only diagnosed four months ago."

"Poor bastard," Will said, glancing outside.

Jimmy sipped a cream soda, nodded in agreement and said, "A couple of weeks ago, he asked Dean and me to drop by his house…which is certainly out of character for him. Anyway, he revealed his lumbar scoliosis diagnosis, and in addition to physical therapy, he is a candidate for surgery. Given the circumstances, the prognosis is positive."

Jimmy eyed Will, "According to Randy, throughout his teen years, he was only truly happy and pain-free while he was holed up in his bedroom, hunched over his table, lost in his elaborate fantasy illustrations."

"He's like a changed man since his diagnosis," said Phil.

Jimmy continued, "He also told us about his other *news*. He just completed his second term at Birchmount College, enrolled in the Graphic Arts, Design and Animation program."

Will smiled and said, "Huh. I hope it works out for him. Looking back…I can't help but see a bully moving around the schoolyard, threatening and snatching the other kids' hot dog money."

"Will, the real bully was his older brother; he made him steal the other kids' change so he could buy smokes." Phil shook his head, "Coop didn't have a choice."

"Jimmy, did he tell you why he finally decided to see a doctor?" Phil grinned wickedly. "He's been seeing a girl in class, and she convinced him to seek medical help."

Jimmy nodded, "He did mention her…and he's stoked about the possibilities."

"Randy showed me a few of his fantasy illustrations inspired by his idol, Frank Frazetta. Will, you would be blown away. His artwork is phenomenal," Jimmy said.

"Ah, switchin' gears…I bumped into the lovely Donna Moore in the living room. She's here with two girlfriends. Man…they are easy on the eyes," Phil laughed. "Anyway, talk later." He moved toward the French doors.

"Jimmy, a few minutes ago by the fireplace, I ran into Dan and Carol," Will said. "Might be a good night to chat her up. Just sayin'. We both know she has a thing for you."

Jimmy frowned, "I'll think about it."

"Uh…yeah…you do that, buddy. Don't wait too long, though. For some unknown reason, Carol is attracted to that big brain of yours," Will grinned and had a swig of beer.

"Remember the philosopher blacksmith—strike while the iron is hot."

Jimmy chuckled as he looked out over the partygoers. "Will, I see Donna Moore. She's by the fireplace…wait, she just waved." He waved back. "She's heading this way."

*   *   *

Will glanced around the room as he thought back to the last time he crossed paths with Donna. Nine years ago, he realized. It was late autumn, and it must have been a Saturday. He was in the Safari station wagon with Mary Lynn, Timmy, and his mum was behind the wheel. They were bound for the big city of Barriston for an exciting day of shopping at the Eaton's department store. In his mind's eye, he watched twelve-year-old William move along a well-lit hallway toward an elevator. It would be his first time riding an elevator.

Vivian and Mary Lynn held two shopping bags apiece as they waited for the doors to open. The boys, empty-handed, stood silently, eyes on the half-moon dial indicator located above the elevator doors. They watched as the indicator arrow swept northward, passed number two and stopped on number three.

The elevator access door slid open, revealing an inner black iron scissor gate. The open weave of the gate allowed the elevator operator to see when the car was in alignment with the floor. After a quick check, the operator, an elderly man wearing a grey suit and white cotton gloves, manually pushed the scissor gate to his left, allowing access to the elevator. Timmy and William barely waited for the gate to open before they barrelled into the elevator, followed by an apologetic

Vivian. Mary Lynn stepped aboard, head down, embarrassed to be seen with her two younger brothers.

The operator pulled the scissor gate closed and pulled a lever ninety degrees to his right. He broke the silence and said, "Going Up." He kept his eyes on the scissor gate as the elevator moved between floors. As the elevator slowed, he said, "Fourth Floor: Cosmetics and Jewellery, Children's Clothing and Footwear."

Vivian's hand rested firmly on William's shoulder until the elevator stopped shaking and the operator had opened the scissor gate. As she stepped off, the operator said, "Madam. For the kiddies, on the fifth floor, we have Toyland with Santa's Village complete with reindeer and elves, and at 3 p.m., old Saint Nick himself will arrive from the North Pole."

*   *   *

The light streaming through the windows blended with the instrumental music, creating an energetic shopping environment. The spacious fourth-floor layout easily accommodated the many shoppers with room to maneuver.

Wherever Vivian turned her gaze, there was an abundance of merchandise displayed on fixed furniture, counters and racks, smartly organized and easily accessible. And with the friendly, helpful salesgirls around each corner and in each department, she was thrilled to spend the afternoon browsing and shopping.

She spotted another directional sign suspended from the ceiling. She turned to the boys and said, "We're almost there. The Children's Clothing department is just ahead and around the corner."

Trailing behind them, Timmy sidestepped and wandered away from the aisle over to a circular, multi-tiered display.

"Mum," Mary Lynn said and pointed, "the Cosmetics and Jewellery department is just over there. I'll hang out by the cosmetics while you and the boys are looking at the clothes."

"All right, dear. Pass me your shopping bags. We won't be too long…we shouldn't be more than ten or fifteen minutes."

Timmy held his arms out, stepped cautiously back toward the aisle and said, "Hey William…check out my hairy mask."

Vivian turned, eyed Timmy and grimaced at the sight of a wig covering his face. She hissed, "Timmy, take that wig off your face. You march right on over there and put it back on the display shelf." She noticed the disapproving looks from two shoppers.

Mary Lynn looked on disapprovingly.

William laughed and watched as his brother, shoulders slumped, moped back to the circular display.

Vivian waited, then put her hand on Timmy's back and steered him toward the Children's Clothing department.

*   *   *

Vivian had dropped the four shopping bags next to a clothes rack. Timmy, tired and whiny, sat on the floor under a rack of long-sleeved shirts. He had had enough and wanted to go home. "We are almost done, dear," she consoled. A moment later, she turned her head toward the boys' changeroom, "Come on out, William. I promise, this will be the last pair of slacks. Come on out and model them for me in front of the mirror."

The mellow instrumental music drifting down from the ceiling grated on her nerves.

"Mum, how many pairs of pants do I need?" William asked. He walked over, stood in front of the full-length mirror and looked at his reflection.

"I have only put aside two pairs. Now, turn around and look at me," she instructed.

He turned, eyed his mum, then, over her shoulder, he noticed a well-dressed woman and a girl perusing a display of boots. He stood at attention and watched the couple while his mother inspected the slacks. He squinted and bobbed his head back and forth, trying to get a better look at the girl.

"Well, the slacks are too long…I can turn up the legs and hem them, that's not a problem." Vivian continued to assess the fit of the slacks against his slender body. "William…stop fidgeting, stand still."

Disbelief and dread spread across William's face as he recognized Donna Moore. She held up a white, knee-high go-go boot. He watched her as she turned her head and said, "Mom, these are the boots! The Nancy Sinatra boots."

Meanwhile, Vivian had stepped closer, "Dear, I'm afraid these slacks are too loose. They are sitting too low…hike them up to your belly button," she instructed. William stared straight ahead as he fussed with the waistband. He watched Donna. He silently begged her not to look in his direction.

Vivian said, "I give up…these slacks don't fit your slim build…they are too long and too baggy around your waist."

"Mum!" William gawked at his mother, mouth hanging open. Despondent, he wanted to bolt for the changeroom. He exhaled heavily.

She continued, "They are just too baggy. There is just too much room in the crotch."

"Hey…William."

"No, no…" he moaned.

Revealing a dazzling smile, Donna playfully waved.

He dropped his head and covered his eyes, "No, no…no…"

* * *

"Hey Will…you're zoning out there, buddy," said Jimmy.

"Hey, bucko, how are you? Long time no see," said Donna.

Will looked around the boisterous, packed room, reined in his bearings, eyed Donna and said, "Oh, hey Donna…been a long time. How are you?" He inhaled, regrouped, "So, you know Gerald."

"His folks and mine go way back. I knew him even before we moved across town. It's great seeing so many familiar faces and catching up with old friends," she smiled. "What a totally awesome party. Gerald sure knows how to throw a bash."

"He sure does. I heard he hired a catering company with a chef, and tomorrow, a cleaning service will arrive to perform a deep clean. Like, who would think to do that?" Will said, laughing as his stomach growled, owing to traces of his childhood infatuation.

Donna laughed, "Chalk it up to Gerald. Anyhoo, you boys are looking good. Jimmy, I hear you and Dean have an apartment, and I assume you are now enrolled at U of Toronto? And Will—"

"Did I…hear my name?" The unsteady host slurred.

Donna turned and looked at Gerald with a sidelong glance, then said, "Oh, Gerry, it's still so early in the evening, chum. Maybe…you should slow down." She put a hand between his shoulder blades. "Come on, let's go to the kitchen, I'll make you a sandwich," she offered.

Gerald smiled goofily. "Chef has 'rived…and he's gettin' prepped…need to go and ignite the barbeques." He did an about-face, took a step and was swallowed up by his guests.

Donna sighed; she was perturbed. Nevertheless, she turned back to Will and said, "Oh snap! I wanted to ask you something…Gerry sidetracked me…, and now it's gone." She shook her head. "Damn it! Oh well…fuck it." She smiled. "How is that cute little brother of yours?" Before Will had a chance to answer, she said, "Hey, if you guys are into a disturbing, decently scary movie, you gotta see *Rabid*."

"The movie about a woman with a blood-sucking appendage under her arm?" Will said, surprised. He laughed and drained his beer. "You like horror movies?"

"Of course, why not…girls like scary movies."

"It's a Canadian movie written and directed by David Cronenberg," Jimmy volunteered.

"What I really want to see is the new space movie *Star Wars*," said Will.

"May the Force be yours…or something like that," Donna smirked. Her eyes lingered on him. "I like your flared jeans,

Will. They look so good on guys. I have a couple of pairs of bell-bottoms, but I prefer my flared jeans."

Jimmy interrupted, "Donna, I think a friend of yours is trying to get your attention. She's outside frantically pointing and waving."

She turned, looked over Jimmy's shoulder into the courtyard and said, "Yeppers. That's Lindsay. My other friend must be having another meltdown. Last week, her boyfriend told her he needed some space. I thought a party would do her good. Oh well." She signalled and waved to Lindsay. "I'll catch up with you guys later."

She moved toward the French doors, looked back and said, "Will, those flared jeans look good on you…not too loose." She smiled, flashed him a peace sign and went through the doors.

Will stared after her, then it struck him, "Oh shit. Jimmy, I gotta make a call…there must be a phone in the kitchen?"

"Hey, don't sweat it, man. I heard someone say that if you want privacy, use the telephone in Gerald's bedroom on the second floor."

"Okay. Great. Do you know where I'll find the stairs?"

Jimmy nodded, "At the back of the kitchen, you'll see the circular stairs to the second-floor landing."

Suddenly, Will's head throbbed, party noises withered, and an intense white light pierced his eyes. He strained to listen to Jimmy's directions.

"…second-floor landing, turn right at the Royal Hotel, hike a short distance along the sidewalk and tucked in an alley between two buildings, you'll see a telephone booth…"

TWENTY-NINE

Will walked up the steep incline, the green government-issue winter jacket tucked under his arm, then paused at the top of the hill beside the Royal Hotel and wiped the sweat from his brow as he gathered his breath. He checked the time on his Casio Calculator watch: 8:20 p.m. He turned and looked down at the marina and the government trailers at the base of the hill, then stared out over the lake. The St. Lawrence River at Cedar Landing, known as Lake St. Francis, extended twenty miles downstream, where the lake narrowed to the Beauharnois Canal.

As the sun slipped below the fiery horizon, he could still see a couple of barns and a silo five miles away on the southern shore. The spectacular view was picture-perfect—postcard material, he mused.

He turned and peered along the main street. Shadows stretched across the street to the far sidewalk. He walked past the steps to the Royal Hotel, continued to the end of the block and stopped at the narrow alley.

Will slipped on the winter jacket, zipped it up to his chin, careful not to catch his pendant, and pulled the hood over his head. He entered the telephone booth and placed the portable two-way radio on the shelf below the telephone. He left the bi-fold door open. After talking to the Bell operator, he waited until he heard Ronnie's voice accept the charge for the long-distance call.

"Hey, babe. Sorry, I'm calling so late. We had our first SAR call this afternoon. Someone on shore reported seeing a flare out over the water and figured it must be a distress signal from a broken-down boat. We searched for more than four hours, and no vessels were reported overdue. Turned out it was a non-event. The Regional Ops Centre then called off the emergency response."

Will listened, then said, "Right. But, at some point, you have to end the search. Chances are someone was messing around with leftover fireworks from the Victoria Day long weekend. You'd be surprised…it happens all the time. Anyway, how are things at home?"

After a couple of minutes, he said, "Sounds like a lot of blood…poor dog." Will nodded at the handset, "I know, I know…never fails. Shit always happens when I'm away. And the one time you call the bat phone, I'm out on a SAR call. Alright…so, Chinook's scheduled to have her torn dewclaw snipped and stitched next Tuesday, and while she's under, the vet will remove the other three?" Will hesitated then asked, "How much? Damn, this is gonna be an expensive month." He shook his head and mumbled incoherently.

"Hey, shifting gears for a moment, I prepared a home-cooked meal for four tonight. One of the hydrographers, Chris Stock, joined us for ham and scalloped potatoes." Will dropped his head, grinned and replied, "Yes, Ronnie. I followed your recipe, and the potatoes were perfect, tasty, and not too runny. I also cooked a bag of frozen corn and peas, and we had pineapple rings and hot mustard for the ham."

He listened for a moment, "The guys enjoyed the meal—no leftovers. Chris and Jeremy both scarfed back second helpings. Jeremy is the twenty-one-year-old deck hand; his father is a director of operations in Ottawa." Will nodded, "He's bright, and he's ambitious…although his master plan is to be a cruise ship captain, failing that, he wants to race cigarette boats."

He grinned, "I know…but it's good to have a goal. And Chuck Ryder, the SAR coxswain, well, he polished off one plate. I suppose he enjoyed the meal…though being ex-navy, it's an insult to the ship's cook if you don't clean your plate."

He shifted the handset to his other hand. "Yes, I know…but that's above my pay grade. Anyway, it has been six days, and from what I've seen, Chuck is still riding the *Coca-Cola wagon*. No booze, no worries. That's my new motto."

The telephone booth's overhead lamp buzzed, flickered, then bathed him in light. Will hesitated, then tipped his head back and eyed the ceiling panel. He stared at the spider webs and desiccated insects covering the entire panel just inches above his head. He debated with his inner voice—was it time to hightail it out of the booth?

"…Sorry, Ronnie. Yes, I'm still here, got sidetracked. I was thinking about an old lighthouse I entered last week. I really didn't want to go inside, since no one had set foot in it for almost two years, but the hydrographer needed help to geoposition it. The Coast Guard usually only enters these old lighthouses when a lamp is burned out."

Will sighed, "Well, Ronnie…you could not believe the intricate network of spider webs throughout the inside of the structure. It was so dense with cobwebs and detritus that it seemed like the spiders were trying to conceal the ladder to the lantern room." Will smirked, "I'm serious! I could barely see through the webbing and the hanging, decomposing matter."

He wiped the sweat beading on his forehead and went on, "Anyway, I fought my way to the top of the lighthouse, opened the trapdoor to the catwalk and attached the reflective prisms onto the railing that circled the glassed-in lantern room. Tony, the hydrographer, was about three hundred yards away, where he had set up the laser equipment over a landmark. When I signalled, he fired the laser at the prisms and recorded the distance. According to Tony, the last time the lighthouse had been geographically positioned was with a sextant way back in the early 1900s."

The booth's overhead lamp hummed and ticked; a constant reminder that before long, the ceiling panel would be alive with activity.

"Anyway, Ronnie, as I scrambled down the ladder, I lost my footing on the bottom rung and tumbled out of the lighthouse. When I got back to the truck and removed the jacket, the hood and the left sleeve were covered with a grey web-like material.

I grabbed a stick and scraped most of the scabby stuff off the jacket." He twisted his face into a lopsided smile, "Gave me the heebie-jeebies."

Will watched two old men loitering nearby, eyeing him. He covered the mouthpiece and said, "I'll be finished in a couple of minutes."

The men mumbled something, shook their heads and drifted along the sidewalk.

"Hey, Ronnie, sorry, say again…two old boys leaving the hotel wondered why I'm in a telephone booth wearing a winter jacket in late May." He tilted his head to the side and smirked, "No…no, wearing the jacket has nothing to do with spiders…it's just a cool night. Anyway, it's almost nine o'clock. I should be getting back to the SAR trailer."

*   *   *

The coxswain's bedroom, in addition to being larger than the two bedrooms at the opposite end of the trailer, included a bedside table and a small work desk. Chuck sat hunched over the desk, a cigarette burning in a makeshift ashtray. A small desk light illuminated the paperwork. He checked his wristwatch: 8:50 p.m. He glanced down at the single, oversized desk drawer, then eyed the curling smoke rising from the cigarette and grumbled, "Well, that was a fuckin' waste of four hours; check that, call it five hours—Goddamn Incident Report kept me stuck here for an hour." He dragged on the cigarette and exhaled sharply, "And for what! A fuckin' four-hour search because some little shit fired off a flare!"

Chuck removed his reading glasses and ran his hand over his crew cut. He then rubbed the back of his head, prompting his neck to pop and crackle. "I'm getting too old for this bullshit," he groaned. He lifted his head and stared at the smoke-stained ceiling. Through the closed door, he could still hear TV voices and the VHF radio hissing and buzzing.

He reached into the desk drawer and removed a three-quarter-full bottle of Wild Turkey, Chuck's bourbon of choice. With practiced ease, he spun the cap and poured two ounces into his *water* glass. The smooth amber liquid raced down his throat. He eyed the turkey on the label and knew one fundamental truth: Chuck Ryder deserved a second shot.

After his third shot, he hid the bottle in the drawer, stubbed out the cigarette, then removed his beige jacket from the back of the chair. He hiked up his beige slacks and tightened his belt one notch. He popped two breath mints, dropped the roll of Certs back in his pocket next to the Rolaids and opened the bedroom door.

*   *   *

Will peered through the telephone booth's glass panels at the darkened buildings across the street. A Closed sign hung in the window of Henby's Shoes. Next door, the lights were on in the display window. The clothing store mannequins, in waving poses, had been stripped of their clothes and wigs. An evolving beach scene with a portable ice chest, two lounge chairs, umbrellas, and striped beach balls was taking shape in the display window. The exposed mannequins appeared to move erratically under the flickering ceiling lights.

An eastbound train blasted its horn.

"Standby, Ronnie, the nine o'clock freight train is passing by…hell, I can't even hear myself think."

He continued to watch the clothing store as the display window lights dimmed and an employee stepped out onto the sidewalk and into a car. The mannequins now resembled eerie shadow figures.

The clatter of the train receded into the distance.

"Ronnie, before we hang up, I did hear from the mechanic. He said there was no oil left in the engine, which caused it to seize up and the engine block to crack. The engine is kaput—it's toast!"

Will listened…

"Yes, I thought about a new car purchase, but then we're stuck with a five-year car loan. I don't know, babe."

A moment later…

He nodded, "I agree, our joint savings are for a down payment on a home. Well then…we're on the same page, so we have two choices—buy used or replace the engine. The mechanic has called around to local wreckers, and he found a replacement engine with only sixty-eight thousand miles."

Will exhaled, "Three hundred and fifty is the price for the engine installed. As I said, it's gonna be an expensive month. And for another thirty bucks, he'll replace the passenger door lock mechanism. Then we won't have to both slide into the car through the driver's door," he grinned, "although I do enjoy watching you shimmy along the seat." He held the image in his mind. "If he gets started on Monday, the car will be ready by Friday in time for the Sunday crew change."

Will nodded, "I'll tell him to go ahead. Oh yeah, he said, whoever changed the engine oil two weeks ago didn't notice the old filter gasket was stuck to the oil pan, so the new oil filter never sealed. From now on, Ronnie, I will do my own damn oil changes!"

Two spiders slid down their silk and eyed the big green intruder. Will pitched back and bashed his head against a side panel of the booth. "Fuck. Ronnie, the spiders are on the move," he groaned. "Gotta go, I'll talk to you in a couple of days…love you too, miss you." He replaced the handset, grabbed the two-way radio, scrambled out of the booth and, relieved, stared up at the brilliant night sky. He sighed, pulled the hood back, unzipped the winter jacket and thought, home in eight days.

*   *   *

Chuck closed the bedroom door as he stepped into the shared lounge area. He stood by the door, arms crossed and glanced around the old office trailer converted to living quarters for three people. To his left, sitting on the lumpy couch, Jeremy was reading a novel, legs stretched out to the dinette table. A window above the couch afforded a view of the lake. An old armchair, planted next to the couch and draped in a yellow crocheted blanket, hides years of abuse. Chuck smiled to himself; someone had brought the blanket to add a touch of hominess. He appreciated the sentiment.

"Where's Stock?" he asked.

Jeremy looked up at him and said, "Chris left with some of the survey boys to see a band in Cornwall."

He nodded and then glanced at the two bedrooms; both doors were closed. "Greene in his room?"

Jeremy inhaled, dog-eared the page and said, "He left about thirty minutes ago to call his wife."

The blare of a freight train passing through town signalled it was nine o'clock.

Chuck looked over his right shoulder at the clock radio sitting atop the refrigerator. His eyes drifted to the stove, then to the kitchen sink centred in a small cabinet. He peered out at the station wagon through the small window above the sink. The dinner dishes were stacked and drying in a tray next to the sink. Satisfied, he nodded. He turned his head and eyed the dinette table. The black SAR telephone sat in the middle of the table, exactly where it should be according to Chuck.

Above the table, a corner shelf held a VHF marine radio and three charging cradles for the two-way radios. An upper corner shelf supported a Zenith nineteen-inch colour TV and an RCA video player. He moved toward the refrigerator. Jeremy immediately pulled his legs back, or else Chuck would be required to step over them. He was learning how to maintain the peace in Chuck's world.

He opened the fridge, had a look at the contents, then closed the door. He turned toward Jeremy and pointed with his chin, "Sure is a thick book. What are you reading?"

Jeremy held the book aloft and said, "*The Stand*. A fantasy novel by Stephen King. It's more than eight hundred pages." Assuming Chuck was interested, Jeremy enthusiastically continued, "After a virus wipes out most of the world's population, the stage is set for an apocalyptic battle of good versus evil…the 'Walkin' Dude'—"

"Huh…sounds like dribble to me; what a fuckin' waste of time. Well, smart guy, do you know that last month, on April 17th, the Constitution Act, 1982, became the law of the land

and now our great country, finally, has full independence from the Brits." Chuck watched for a reaction. "I didn't think so…just what the fuck do they teach you in school!" Then, pointing again with his chin, "Are those your videos and books on the table by the SAR telephone?"

Jeremy frowned, looked at the table and responded, "I rented a couple of movies for tonight, and Chris loaned us a few novels."

Chuck barely listened as he moved to the kitchen cabinet, halted and eyed the empty sink basin. He inhaled loudly, his cheeks suddenly burned crimson, and contempt curled his mouth into a sneer. He squared his shoulders and, with his back to Jeremy, barked, "What the fuck is this?"

"What's…what?" Jeremy asked, confused. He dropped the novel and stood up.

"Goddamn it. When you begin a task, you complete it."

Jeremy stood, mouth agape, his hands out to the sides, palms up. He had washed the dishes, wiped the table, and even cleaned the window above the sink. And earlier in the day, after he dropped by Keeler's Video store, he had purchased, with his own money, the yellow blanket covering the cruddy, beat-up chair. He believed he had fulfilled his evening housekeeping duties. "Come on, man—"

"Don't call me *man*," Chuck rebuked. He reached into the sink, turned and held the sink strainer at arm's length, waving it back and forth in front of Jeremy's face. "See…see that."

Jeremy didn't know where to look. Instead, he stepped back and almost fell onto the couch.

"Look…look here, you didn't empty the fuckin' strainer…see, two peas and four kernels of corn!" Chuck spat out.

Will walked into the trailer. He quickly sized up the situation, pitched his jacket and two-way radio onto the chair and with one long stride, positioned himself in the middle of the fracas and said, "What the fuck, Chuck!" With his back to Jeremy, he stared hard at Chuck and then ordered him to put the strainer back in the sink. Chuck eyed the object in his hand, turned and leaned heavily against the counter, then dropped the strainer in the sink. His head and shoulders slumped as his mercurial bluster weakened along with his unsteady legs.

Will glanced at Jeremy, slumped on the couch with his head resting in his hands. Will moved to the chair, picked up the two-way radio and returned it to the empty charging cradle. He reached up, switched off the TV, keyed the mic on the VHF marine radio and adjusted the volume.

With his head held high, Chuck pushed by Will on his way to the coxswain's bedroom. He entered the bedroom, snatched up his wallet, tucked it in his back pocket, grabbed the package of cigarettes, and marched toward the front door.

"Chuck, you'll want to take a walkie-talkie…the two nearest the radio are fully charged," Will said.

Without looking back, he reached the door and said, "Don't need it. I'll be on the boat."

Will watched him leave, then stepped to the sink, grabbed a glass from the drying rack and filled it with water. He downed the drink, refilled the glass and asked Jeremy if he wanted a drink of water.

Will handed him a full glass, then sat on the couch and said, "I'm sorry it came to this. On Monday, I'll speak to Landry and ask him to assign you to a different survey boat."

Jeremy turned his head and eyed Will, concern written on his face.

"Don't worry, I'll play it like the three of us need some distance from each other during the day. Landry will understand. He's a good head."

"Will…I almost popped him. I was this close."

"Hmmm…well, it's good you practiced self-restraint. You're twenty-one, and he's in his sixties…that would be tough to justify. And don't get me wrong, we all know Chuck can be an asshole, nevertheless…"

Jeremy stared at the floor for a moment, "Did you know that Canada has a new Constitution?" he asked.

Will raised his eyebrows, "Yeah…but, only because the nightly news has been weighing the pros and cons of patriation." Will sipped some water, "I don't know much about it other than the Constitution Act is the highest law of the land, and now there's a new section about protecting individual Rights and Freedoms. Why do you ask?"

Jeremy shook his head, "No reason."

Will suspected Chuck was behind the question. He looked up at the clock on the refrigerator at 9:20 p.m. He thought Chuck was likely on his way to the Royal Hotel. He was sure he smelled alcohol on his breath. "Don't let him get to you; he's an angry, broken old man," he sighed. "You know he's retired from the Navy."

Jeremy responded with a weak head nod.

"Two years ago, we were on the same Lake Erie survey. It was mid-summer, and I was up late, sitting outside the motel, when Chuck dragged a chair from his room and joined me under the stars. He doesn't talk much about his years in the Navy or that he fought in the Korean War; however, during that late-night conversation, he confessed that 'it's just too painful chewing the cud and dredging up old memories.' He then volunteered that he and his third wife had just celebrated ten years of marriage. I suppose that's why he was in a talkative frame of mind."

"Canadians fought in Korea?"

Will nodded, "The war began in June 1950 and dragged on for three years. Twenty-six thousand Canadians served as part of the United Nations mission to prevent communist North Korea from taking the South."

Will glanced at the closed door to Chuck's room. "That night, I promised him that I would spend some time learning about Canada's contributions during the War. I figured I owed it to him—when people make sacrifices for the greater good, I believe it should be noted and shared."

"You sound like my high school history teacher, Mr. Bigelow," Jeremy said. "Were any Canadians killed during the war?"

"More than five hundred lost their lives."

Jeremy sat upright, stretched his legs and downed the glass of water.

"Chuck was a crew member on a Canadian Tribal-class destroyer, the HMCS Nootka. In the spring of 1952, the destroyer was in the Yellow Sea off the west coast of Korea, supporting the South Korean troops fighting on the islands. Chuck piloted one of the destroyers' in-shore patrol boats, running missions up the rivers delivering supplies, equipment and troops to the front lines."

Chatter on the marine radio interrupted Will's thoughts. A couple of boaters were gabbing on channel sixteen. If they didn't wrap up their conversation in the next few seconds, he'd remind them to move to another working channel.

He went on, "That night Chuck revealed that he still struggles with the death of his bride, a Canadian nurse he met while stationed in Korea."

"How'd she die?"

"A military chaplain married them while she was in a Korean hospital fighting brain cancer. Two weeks after exchanging rings, she took a turn and passed away." Will glanced over at the clock. "I'm betting you haven't been around long enough to have heard about the collapse of his second marriage."

Jeremy shook his head.

"About ten years later, Chuck married a woman who lived in the same building. For reasons unknown, he takes pleasure in telling the story. He and his second bride spent their honeymoon in Sussex Corner, New Brunswick, where he spent his youth. During their second week, they stayed with his brother and his family. According to Chuck, the day before they were going to leave, he walked in on his bride in bed with his brother."

"Oh, geez."

"The best part, though, according to Chuck, was that five minutes later, he was in the car, driving back to Ontario, and that was the last time he laid eyes on either of them."

"And today, wife number three tolerates his grumpy old-man bullshit?"

"Well, he's been married twelve years. Third time's the charm."

Will eyed the videotapes and the three novels on the table. He stood up and scooped up the novels. He thought about Chuck for a moment, then said, "Tonight was all about Chuck; you just happened to be collateral damage."

"I'm good, man. Thanks."

"Okay, good. Chuck does have his demons. I'm sure he has a deep mistrust of humanity, and it's left him calloused, cynical and hostile. I suspect his drunken convictions will hound him to his grave."

Will sighed, then held up the books. "I see Chris dropped off Stephen King's *Salem's Lot* and *The Shining*." He then tapped the novel *Shibumi*. "I'm gonna crack this one open tonight. I read *The Eiger Sanction,* and it was a real page turner, written by the same author, Trevanian." He glanced again at the clock, then grabbed a two-way radio, "I'll be back in twenty…going to check on the boat."

CHAPTER

THIRTY

Will stood on the landing at the front door of the SAR trailer, turned and looked out over the water. The day's forecasted heavy downpour and high winds had lived up to expectations. By the evening, the winds had dramatically subsided; nevertheless, the river was a mass of roiling whitecaps. He turned and stepped light-footed into the trailer.

"Everything copacetic at home," Chris said.

Will nodded. "All good, thanks." He eyed the closed bedroom door, "Chuck in his room?"

Jeremy said, "He skipped out about 7 p.m. when we started watching *Animal House*. He said since it's Saturday night, our last night of SAR…he decided to have dinner at the Royal Hotel." Jeremy jumped off the couch and gathered the three videos from the dinette table. "Well, I also rented *Alien*, *Caddy Shack* and *American Werewolf in London*."

Will laughed, "I watched *Alien* four times on the big screen…but, whatever you guys want to see, I don't know how long I'll last…I'm bushed." He eyed the movies, "A four-movie marathon?"

Jeremy said, "Probably not. At the video store, Edith said it was two-for-the-price-of-one movie night. I don't believe it's a thing, Edith is just nice and—"

"Oh…you're on a first-name basis." Will smiled and flopped down on the chair.

Chris laughed. "I told him she's interested."

Jeremy shook his head, "No…her parents own the video store, and she is always working. Every time I'm in the store, she's behind the counter. Turns out, though, we're both twenty-one and just finished our second year of university."

"Well, you've got all summer to get to know each other," Will said.

The blare of a freight train passing through town signalled it was nine o'clock.

Chris said, "I've never seen the London werewolf movie."

"Will?" Jeremy asked.

"Gotta be one of the best werewolf movies. It has great makeup effects, lots of gore, horror and funny scenes," Will said.

Jeremy laughed, "All right. That's settled. I'm gonna make some popcorn. You guys want a pop?" He slid the video into the RCA player and dropped the other two onto the table. He moved to the fridge, removed three Cokes and from the freezer a box of Pillsbury microwave popcorn.

Will stood up and said, "You're right, Chris, microwaveable popcorn is the best. And it never burns."

"I know, eh."

The SAR telephone came to life.

Chris looked at Will. "Guess that puts the kibosh on movie night."

Jeremy glanced at the telephone, then peered through the microwave window as sweat ran down the sides of the popcorn box. He hit the pause button.

Will reached for the telephone, "Cedar Landing Search and Rescue." He picked up a pencil and wrote: Regional Operations Centre, 9:05 p.m. Saturday, June 05, '82. He held the pencil poised over the notepad and listened intently to the person on the line.

Chris turned his head, trying to eavesdrop on the conversation.

Jeremy crossed his fingers and hoped they were being sent out on a legitimate call and not just an endless search.

"Roger that. Could you repeat the lat and long?" Will scribbled down the two sets of numbers, then he repeated them to the operations person. He nodded and said, "Roger. Once we're in the shipping channel heading east, I'll radio in with an ETA." He glanced at Jeremy, nodded again and said, "Thank you…We will." He replaced the handset and opened the door to Chuck's room. He stepped in and scooped the two keys hanging on the wall. Each key sported a yellow float.

Chris jumped off the couch and said, "Well, guys. I'll get the fuck out of your way."

"Will, should I run up to the hotel and look for Chuck?" Jeremy asked.

Will exhaled, "If he's at the hotel, he'll be of no use to us."

"Uh…ok…ya, right."

Chris piped up, "Hey, if you guys need a third? I'm right here."

Jeremy looked expectantly at Will.

"Could be a long night." Will eyed him for a moment, "I'd feel a whole lot better with three of us out there."

Jeremy laughed. "Great. The three musketeers."

"Coast Guard got the call at 2100 from a guy who swears he saw a flare go up and for a few seconds could see a sailboat. He said the boat is in the shipping channel off Cote's Landing. He estimates it was 8:30 p.m. when he saw the flare," Will said.

"Took him thirty minutes to call it in…" Chris said.

"He had just docked and had to drive into town to find a telephone booth," Will said. He reached for Chuck's winter jacket and passed it to Chris. "Just in case the temp keeps dropping." He moved to the stove, plugged in the kettle, and handed the keys to Jeremy. "I'll be at the boat in five. I'm going to build some peanut butter and jam sandwiches and bring a thermos of instant coffee. I sense a long night." He stifled a yawn.

"I'll grab some granola bars," Jeremy said.

"I'll head down to the boat with you. Anything I should take?" Chris asked.

Jeremy said, "Nope. We have our gear onboard." He glanced at Will, slapping peanut butter on bread, and said, "See you down there."

Will had placed ten slices of bread on the counter. He stuck the peanut butter-covered knife into a jar of Strawberry jam. A minute later, he had five sandwiches wrapped in wax paper and stacked in his lunch box. The kettle whistled. He filled the thermos and grabbed three cans of Coke from the fridge. He glanced at the clock on the refrigerator, 9:14 p.m. He picked up the lunch box, tucked the thermos under his arm and grabbed his winter jacket from the chair. He reached for the door just as it flew open. Standing on the landing, a winded Chris gasped, "Chuck's on the boat…out cold."

Will sighed heavily, "Oh…for fuck sakes."

*   *   *

Chris stood on the dock next to the survey boat. A lamppost cast a pale light across the area as Will jumped on the deck to the smooth thrum of the engines and the smell of diesel. He stepped through the narrow doorway into the wheelhouse, looked at Jeremy, then followed the loud snoring to Chuck lying in a fetal position under the chart table. He dropped his lunch box and thermos in the corner and threw the jacket on the back of the coxswain's seat.

"I guess we could just leave him under the table." Jeremy volunteered.

Will thought for a moment. "We're protected here in the basin, but as soon as we clear the breakwater, it's gonna get rough."

Jeremy looked out the window at the flags hanging limp from the top of the marina office building.

Will exhaled, "Don't let the flags fool you—winds were out of the west and blowing ninety for most of the day, it's gonna be a bouncy, thrill ride out there…in his condition, he could put us all in danger." He squatted and tried to rouse him.

Chuck groaned and swore.

"Let's get him to the trailer," Will said. "Worst case, we take an arm each and drag his ass back to the trailer."

They struggled to get Chuck out from under the table. Finally, they got him upright, out of the wheelhouse and off the boat. Chris grabbed his legs while Jeremy and Will held his arms. They carried him to the trailer and dumped his intoxicated, limp body on his bed.

A minute later, Will was sitting in the coxswain's seat while Jeremy and Chris released the bow and stern lines secured to the dock cleats. Chris dropped onto the deck, coiled the stern line and yanked in the fender, protecting the boat's hull from the dock.

Jeremy jumped on the bow, removed the line from the bow cleat, untied the fender and walked back along the gunwale. He dropped down to the deck and entered the wheelhouse. He took two steps and ducked as he squeezed through the hatch beneath the console and into the bow storage area. He dropped both fenders and the bow line. He then backed out of the storage area.

Will maneuvered the twenty-three-foot Bertram survey launch away from the dock, pointed the nose south and slowly flanked the breakwater until they reached open water. As the Bertram cleared the breakwater, he opened both throttles halfway and pointed the bow southeast toward the shipping channel.

Jeremy sat in the hydrographer's swivel chair on the port side. A rack of electronic survey equipment was behind the chair within arm's reach. To his right, he had access to the echo depth sounder fastened to the console above the hatch.

Chris stood between the two seats, eyeing the depth sounder. The graph paper moved slowly to the right within the sounder display window as the electrically charged stylus burned a thin horizontal line through the paper.

Chris sneezed as the unpleasant smell reached his nose. "Will, we're at a depth of six feet…eight…and dropping," he said.

"Thanks, Chris," Will said as he stared at the white caps off the bow.

"These old sounders…don't think I'll ever get used to the smell of charred paper and chemicals," Chris said and sneezed again.

As the bottom fell away and the shoreline receded, the rollers increased in magnitude and began to buffet the boat's hull. Will grappled with the wheel as he tried to keep their heading southeast.

Chris turned, reached for a ceiling grab rail and stepped back to the chart table attached to the back wall. Chart 1432 was laid out on the table. The navigation chart covered the St. Lawrence River from Cornwall, Ontario, to Rondeau Bluffs, Quebec.

Chris had just enough clearance to squeeze in between the chart table and the marine radar. The radar was mounted at waist height on a makeshift plywood base fastened to the floor behind the coxswain's chair. He removed the sun shield hood, looked down at the display, and watched from a bird's-eye view as the green images on the screen refreshed every ten seconds. He adjusted the concentric range rings to include the northern shore. He then watched as the shoreline and breakwater appeared on screen, disappeared and reappeared. "Radar image is sharp, except for a bit of clutter," he said.

Will glanced at Chris and then at Jeremy. He checked his Casio Calculator watch. The resin glass crystal protecting the watch face was shattered. God dammit…must have happened when we were wrestling with Chuck under the chart table, he thought.

He squinted at the digital numbers on the watch face and said, "It's 9:35 p.m., one hour since the boater noticed the distress flare." He glanced out the side window into the darkness and shouted, "Hang on." Wave after wave pounded against the boat's hull. The churning water overwhelmed the bow, flowed up the windshield across the wheelhouse roof and poured down on the deck. Will switched on the wiper blades. The port wiper blade began to move, stuttered mid-sweep and ground to a halt.

Jeremy cursed and banged on the windshield. The wiper hung suspended midway through its arc. He glanced to his right and said, "At least the starboard wiper's still working."

The boat pitched and rolled. Chris quickly closed the wheelhouse door and watched through a back window as sheets of water rained down on the deck. He nervously glanced around as the wheelhouse walls seemed to contract and close in around him. He felt caged.

Jeremy cracked the port window open just enough for air to circulate in the cramped, confined space.

The bilge pump rattled loudly, then began pumping out water. "I hear the pump running," Chris yelled.

Jeremy flashed him a thumbs-up.

Will held the Bertram's speed at half-throttle—any faster, they would be bouncing off the ceiling. He tried not to fight the wheel as the waves crashed against the hull, forcing the bow to drop like an elevator as the boat rolled precipitously to port, lingering on its side until the turbulent water released its embrace, only to repeat the sequence.

Will swivelled the chair, enabling him to look over his shoulder and down at the radar. He watched the image refresh twice, then returned the chair to its forward position. He inhaled deeply and said, "There's a port channel buoy about three hundred yards out…soon as we pass the buoy, we'll head east for Cote's Landing. It should then be a smoother ride. Once we're in a following sea, we won't have to stomach this constant pounding."

"Fuck…that's good," Chris said. "I've never been out in seas this rough. I hate to admit it, but my guts are churnin'."

"Hang in there…won't be long." Will dimmed the ceiling light.

Jeremy flicked on the searchlight mounted on the wheelhouse roof. He reached above his head to the handle and manually rotated the searchlight while scanning the horizon. Water trickled down the handle and dripped on his jacket sleeve. "What's the bulb strength on this light?" he asked.

"Under ideal conditions, the light has a one-thousand-foot beam distance," Will answered.

"I think this one big green speck I'm looking at on the radar screen is the channel buoy. Looks to be about two hundred yards out, just off our port side," Chris said.

Jeremy kept the searchlight arc to about fifteen degrees. After a couple of moments, he spied the buoy. Five minutes later, the boat was in the shipping channel heading east.

Will said, "Jeremy, you mind taking the wheel. I'll radio the Coast Guard with our ETA." Jeremy was out of his chair and ready to move into the coxswain's seat before Will had finished his request.

Will swivelled the chair, reached for a ceiling grab rail, dropped to the floor and moved back to the chart table. He quickly marked their current position on the chart. The Bertram rode up a wave and surfed down the back side. Will leaned against the chart table and grabbed the parallel rulers as the tool skidded across the chart.

"There might be a problem with the radar; there is now a green mass covering a good quarter of the screen," Chris said.

"Try adjusting the brightness and contrast. If that doesn't help, then try adjusting the gain," Will said.

Using the dividers and the parallel rulers, Will measured the distance between their current position and the sailboat's last known position as indicated by the ROC. He stepped back to the console, reached for a grab rail and with his other hand, freed the mic from the marine radio. He squinted and eyed his shattered watch face at 9:55 p.m.

He keyed the mic:

"Prescott Coast Guard…this is the Canadian Survey Launch, Robin…CLS Robin…CLS Robin on sixteen."

"CSL Robin…go channel seven eight…seven eight."

"Roger, seven eight…This is CSL Robin on seven eight."

"Go ahead, CSL Robin."

"We are five miles from the vessel's last known position, proceeding at a speed of ten knots. Allowing for heavy seas, our on-scene ETA is 2240."

"Roger, CSL Robin…will continue to monitor channel seven-eight. Call back when on scene."

"Roger, CSL Robin out."

Will replaced the mic, looked down at the display screen and watched as the green mass grew larger with each sweep of the radar antenna. He glanced ahead at the mist building on the windshield, then looked again at the display screen.

Chris glanced over his shoulder and said, "What do you think that green blob is?"

Will adjusted the radar range rings, "I think it's a fast-moving front carrying a lot of moisture." He studied the range rings as the image refreshed. "In about thirty minutes, we're going to run into some weather." He dropped a hand on Jeremy's shoulder, "You okay behind the wheel?"

"No prob, Will. My folks' twenty-eight-foot Cuddy Cabin has twin inboard motors, twin screw, same configuration as this survey launch."

"Good to hear. Okay…we stay on this heading until we reach the green channel buoy off Cote's Landing." Will turned, reached for a grab rail, moved around Chris, then leaned over the table and placed his elbows on the navigation chart. He stared at the mark on the chart indicating the sailboat's location as of 8:30 p.m.

He quickly considered several scenarios. First, the spotter was mistaken—the flare streaking through the sky is just a distraction. Second, the boat hit bottom, took on water and sank. Doubtful, he thought, based on the water depth at the last known position. Third, the vessel is without power, in distress and is at the mercy of the river. He turned his head and watched as the radar display refreshed.

He turned back to the chart. He knew the lake's surface currents flowed northeasterly at three to four knots, and the six to seven-foot storm waves rolled along in an easterly direction. Using the parallel rulers, he extended three lines eastward from the sailboat's last known position. He estimated the vessel would be drifting toward Rondeau Bluffs.

A rocky bottom extended well offshore from the Bluffs. He was concerned that if the sailboat drifted for two hours, it might run aground in the shallow waters off the Bluffs. In this scenario, it would have broken apart under the heavy pounding. He rubbed his forehead and hoped that if the vessel was in distress, they had the wherewithal to drop anchor while still in deep water.

Will pulled his eyes from the chart and looked down at the radar display. The green mass was closing in on their position. He opened the wheelhouse door and stepped out onto the deck. He grabbed a handrail next to the door and held tight as the boat rode up a wave and slid down the other side. He stared out over the stern at the astounding display of stars in the pitch-black night sky. He shook his head in disbelief at the thought-provoking sight.

Chris joined him. He moved uneasily on the deck.

Will watched him grow paler by the second. "Chris, we're about two miles from the north shore. Can you see the lights dotting the shore? Try to concentrate on the horizontal line of lights and control your breathing, slow and deep breaths," he offered. He then leaned over the gunwale, looked eastward beyond the bow and stared into a void of misty blackness.

Something was concealing the stars, and they were steaming into it.

"Will, I think I'll stay out here in the fresh air…the seesawing and the smell from the sounder…I'm gonna hurl if I go back inside. I'm sorry to say, but this roller coaster ride makes me feel worse than the pounding we took earlier."

Will eyed him, "Concentrate on your breathing and stay next to the door, okay." He swung the door wide open until it rested against the outside wall and then secured it. "I will be right out. I'll fetch the Gravol from the First Aid kit."

*   *   *

A minute passed before Will reappeared from the wheelhouse with a can of Coke in a bucket and a lifejacket. Chris was sitting on the deck with his back against the wheelhouse wall, his head upright, watching the churning water off the stern.

"Put this lifejacket on and if you're going to puke, do it in the bucket, okay…don't try to hang over the side of the boat," Will instructed. He reached into his pocket, "Here's a couple of Gravol."

Chris reached into the bucket for the Coke.

"Looks like the fog bank is almost on us. I gotta get back inside. Hang in there, the Gravol should help settle your stomach." Will stepped into the wheelhouse.

"How's Chris?"

"He's goin' to stay on the deck for now."

Jeremy nodded and said, "Fuck me. This fog is getting thick."

The wiper blade slowly swept the windshield.

"Even with the searchlight showing the way…I can see at best, fifty feet in front of the bow. FYI, I dropped our speed to five knots."

Will nodded and moved to the radar. The massive green blob was now orbiting the Bertram. He adjusted the on-screen contrast, increased the brightness, and tweaked the gain to decrease the signal sensitivity. The *trick* eliminated some noise and clutter and allowed him to decipher a stretch of grainy shoreline, and three targets, he hoped, were a channel buoy and two inshore fairway buoys. A moment later, the green blob and clutter obscured the screen. He eyed his watch at 10:45 p.m.

"Jeremy, I think we're on scene," Will said. "Cote's Landing is about two miles off our port, and Rondeau Bluffs is dead ahead three miles. If we maintain this course, we should intercept a channel buoy in the next ten minutes or so." He reached for a ceiling grab rail and moved to the port side chair.

Jeremy wiped his hand across his forehead. "It sure is a mind fuck looking through the windshield into a sea of blackness. Kinda spooky and unnerving."

Will agreed. "I know. Even without the fog, when you're on the water late at night, far from shore in total darkness, it's easy to imagine you're not even on the planet but on a distant, remote world."

"Definitely," Jeremy agreed.

"Give me a second…" Will said, "I'll call the Regional Ops Centre and then relieve you at the wheel. You ready for a sandwich?" Will opened the lunchbox and handed Jeremy a PB&J and a Coke. He glanced back at Chris, still sitting against the wheelhouse wall with his legs pulled up and the lifejacket around his shoulders.

A minute later, he keyed the radio mic:

"Prescott Coast Guard…this is CSL Robin on seven eight."

"Go ahead, CSL Robin."

"We are on scene and will begin our search for the sailboat. We are currently two miles due south of Cote's Landing. Be advised, we are in a heavy fog bank…visibility less than fifty feet."

"Roger. We are monitoring the fog bank. Thank you for the update."

"Prescott…based on the sailboat's last known position and the timeline, there's a possibility the vessel was pushed into shallow waters. Are you able to check with the Quebec provincial police regarding any marine calls this evening between Cote's Landing and Rondeau Bluffs?"

"Roger. Stand by one."

Jeremy grinned and said, "I've noticed sometimes at the trailer, you call the SAR telephone the bat phone, is that because the boat's name is Robin?"

"Um…not really. The bat-signal is how Gotham City Police summon Batman. The black telephone is the ROC's method of contacting SAR personnel. That's all, just silly shit."

"Oh…okay. Too bad the boat wasn't named after a bird of prey like a Hawk, Eagle or Falcon…"

"…or the wise bird of prey, the owl." Will smiled.

Jeremy eyed him and said, "Do you know that the scientific name for a Robin is Turdus migratorius?" He laughed. "It is, I'm serious—"

"CLS Robin."

Will keyed the mic:

"Go ahead, Prescott."

"Be advised that the SQ have not received or reported any marine incidents."

"Thank you, Prescott. CLS Robin out."

Meanwhile, Chris stood in the doorway and said, "I think I'm slowly getting my sea legs."

"Have a seat, Chris." Will swivelled the chair, reached for a grab rail, stepped down and moved to the radar.

"Thanks, but I'll stay here. The fresh air helps my queasy guts."

Will nodded, "I think the dense fog is also having an impact—the waves are dropping in intensity and speed."

The three of them braced as the boat rode up the front of a large wave and slid down the back side.

"Not counting that wave," Will smirked. He lowered his head and, for a moment, stared hard at the radar display. He adjusted the control settings, trying to improve target visibility. The images on the display remained suspect. He lifted his head and glanced from window to window to window. He again dropped his head and studied the display through several refreshes.

"What is it, Will. The sailboat?" Chris asked. He pivoted from side to side, peering intently into the blackness.

Jeremy held the wheel firmly as he stared ahead into the night and said, "I don't see a damned thing."

Will reached for a grab rail as he moved next to Jeremy. He leaned against the armrest and said, "The reflection coming back from the radar would indicate something huge just off the port side, then it's off our bow, and last look, it was starboard. Must be…gotta be the weather interfering…" he exhaled as he continued to search the blackness.

The wiper blade slowly swept the windshield.

Chris, meanwhile, had entered the wheelhouse and was concentrating on the radar display. "Well, shit…according to the radar, there's something fuckin' huge just in front of us," he said through a shaky voice.

Jeremy gripped the wheel tighter, leaned forward, stared into the abyss and whispered, "Goddamn, you guys see this, suddenly, it's darker…pitch black. Is that even possible?"

Three heads tilted up as they stared wide-eyed at the eight-story wall of steel bearing down on them.

A loud, thunderous blast echoed in their ears.

"Turn," Will roared.

"Ship," Chris shouted as he reached for a grab rail.

"Port, turn to port," Will said, grabbing the armrest.

Jeremy spun the wheel to the left, reached for the starboard throttle lever and pushed it to the stop. The Bertram turned as the bow dropped and nosed into the trough of a wave. The starboard propeller screamed as it breached the water. He pulled back on the starboard throttle and eased the port throttle ahead. The stern dipped as the boat lurched forward, then rolled to starboard as a wave slammed against the hull. As the boat bounced back, another wave hit and crested across the bow. The Bertram slowly rebounded.

The danger receded into the murky darkness.

Will placed a comforting hand on Jeremy's shoulder.

"Holy fuck…fuck me!" Jeremy said.

The boat rolled to starboard.

"Jeremy, that was some phenomenal driving," Chris gushed.

"Saved our bacon," Will said.

Jeremy exhaled, then said, "The chair is yours…" He laughed, then sighed.

Will moved into the coxswain's seat and took control of the boat. After steaming north toward shore, he course-corrected. Once again, they were heading east, riding a following sea.

From the hydrographer's seat, Jeremy said, "Strange that the Laker's horn sounded the exact moment we were at its bow."

"I wonder, was the Laker under power or at anchor?" Will said, staring into the blackness.

Chris stood on the deck, leaning against the door frame. He swept his head from side to side as he maintained watch.

Will glanced at his watch, "It's 11:13 p.m. If we employ a grid pattern, staying short of the foul area off the Bluffs, we should be able to cover the search area to shore in under three hours."

Jeremy and Chris agreed.

Will succumbed to a yawn. He rubbed his face vigorously.

"I could use a cup of coffee, how 'bout you guys?" Jeremy asked.

THIRTY-TWO

Will piloted the boat westward, slamming into the waves while maintaining a course one mile offshore. Chris stood on the deck, peered out over the heaving waters, and, over the thrum of the engines, yelled, "Guys, the fog's thinning, it's breaking up. I can now see the humpbacked moon, stars to the west, and the air is definitely warmer."

Jeremy looked out the port window, reached for a grab rail, dropped to the floor and stepped through the doorway next to Chris. They both looked out into the darkness toward shore. "I can see lights on shore," Jeremy said enthusiastically.

Will stretched and reached for the ceiling. He inhaled deeply, glanced at his shattered watch face, thought of Chuck grappling with him under the chart table, turned his head toward the open door and yelled, "It's Sunday, 12:25 a.m."

Jeremy stepped back into the wheelhouse, grinned and said, "Figures…we'd get a SAR call the night before going home." He raised his hand to his forehead. "Damn, I wouldn't mind some Pillsbury popcorn about now. I should have just let it finish popping."

"Have another sandwich," Will said.

"I have a craving for salty, buttery popcorn. How 'bout you, Chris?"

Meanwhile, Chris had stepped into the wheelhouse to watch the radar display. He looked up, "Hmmm…with the wind picking up, I'll wait until we're back on solid ground before I eat anything." He dropped his head and watched as several new targets appeared on the display. He grabbed the binoculars and stepped out on the deck.

Jeremy followed him through the doorway and asked, "You see something?"

Chris scanned the wave tops and said, "Might be a fairway buoy," he pointed, "off the bow, about two o'clock."

Jeremy opened the storage box strapped to the wheelhouse. He picked through the marine equipment and retrieved a handheld searchlight. He moved to the starboard side and shone the light beam across the water. He tried to hold the light steady as the waves crashed into the bow.

Moments later, he saw a flicker of light—then another. He rubbed his eyes, stared at the surging waves, steadied the light and waited. Another glint of light sputtered and vanished. "It's a sailboat. I see the mast and…holy shit…the boat is low, really low in the water," Jeremy yelled.

Chris repositioned the binoculars. "I see it! Three people are on top of the cabin, squatting next to the mast. Looks to be two adults and a kid."

Will squinted as he looked out the side window. He brought the boat around and glanced at the depth sounder. The lake bottom was seventy feet below the stern-mounted transducer.

"They're waving like mad," Chris said.

Jeremy ran into the wheelhouse. "The vessel is almost submerged…water is up to the gunwale, only the bow and stern railings are visible, and the mid-cabin is only about two feet above water. The three of them are hunkered down on top of the cabin, holding on to the mast."

"Fuck…if not for the wind picking up, we never would have spotted the sailboat in that thick fog—less than two hours ago, we almost collided with a laker!" Will said, astounded.

Jeremy glanced at the depth sounder and said, "Sixty…sixty-two feet, Will." He then leaned into the hydrographer's chair, reached and turned the searchlight handle, illuminating the sailboat's cabin.

Will cut the engine's back, slowed to a crawl, and positioned the boat fifty feet off the sailboat's stern railing. He fought the waves to maintain a safe distance. He peered across the wheelhouse, through the port window. The waves again and again broke over the submerged bow and the cabin, as if trying to overwhelm the three people crouched around the mast. The woman and child were both wearing lifejackets, he noticed.

Will's mind charged ahead. He wondered how the sailboat was still afloat. He knew at any moment the vessel would be on the bottom of the St. Lawrence River. He checked the time, 12:40 a.m. He shook his head, realizing the family had been living this nightmare for four hours.

Jeremy ducked into the forward storage, grabbed three lifejackets and unclipped the first-aid kit from its bracket.

"Jeremy, grab the hundred-foot tow line and tie a fender and a lifejacket to one end. Better grab the valise life raft, too. I sure hope we won't need it," Will said.

"Okay, gotcha."

Chris glanced into the wheelhouse and said, "I can't imagine their rain gear is keeping them dry. They must be chilled to the bone." He stepped back and steadied himself on the deck. He watched the sailboat rise and fall with the waves.

He yelled through cupped hands, then resorted to hand signals; he wanted to offer the family hope… to let them know their ordeal was almost over. He mumbled, swore at the wind, the waves, the fog and then imagined…these poor people, stranded at sea in the dark of the night, huddled together on a sinking boat, a mile offshore in fog so thick they couldn't see the top of the mast! My God…they must have thought they were going to a watery grave. He shivered involuntarily.

Jeremy slipped on a lifejacket and joined Chris on the deck. He tied a fender and a lifejacket to the tow line, then stood ready to throw the hundred feet of coiled line.

"I'll try to inch up on their starboard," Will yelled and then cautioned, "We risk sinking the sailboat if we ride up on its deck. If we get too close, I'll back off and try again." With his right hand, he eased both throttle levers ahead and turned to port.

He eased the bow past the sailboat's stern just as a large wave crested and collapsed on its cabin. Jeremy reacted, throwing the coiled line. It landed on the cabin beside the man.

The woman waved and grabbed for the line. Will fought the waves trying to hold the boat steady, but it rolled and pitched toward the stern railing. He countered, pulled back on the starboard throttle and kicked the boat into reverse. Too late—he listened as the railing scraped along the Bertram's hull.

Jeremy and Chris exchanged worried glances.

The family remained huddled around the mast. As the first rescue attempt failed, the woman stood, gestured and yelled. Her voice was lost to the wind. Chris held a hand to his ear and shook his head. He then pointed at the young girl. The woman vigorously waved, then put her hands on her daughter.

Will realized his mistake. He needed a steeper approach angle to the sailboat. He maneuvered the Bertram into position, preparing for a second attempt. He waited for the next wave to pass, then inched the boat toward the sailboat's bow railing. He quickly turned the wheel to port and reversed both engines. The stern obliged and nudged over next to the swamped hull. The cabin was now in alignment with the boat's deck.

The woman scooped up her daughter and held her out over the water into Chris's outstretched arms. He turned and handed the girl to Jeremy. Will struggled to hold the boat alongside as it dipped and rolled. He watched the exchange and smiled tightly…now the adults.

Jeremy put the girl on the deck, turned and saw the woman patting her chest as her husband nodded in agreement. Chris yelled something just as the woman stepped onto the Bertram's gunwale and fell into his arms.

Will had no choice; the waves had seized control. He had to get the boat clear before it struck the cabin or mounted the sailboat's submerged deck. He pulled the throttles back and reversed the engines.

Grasping the mast, the man rose to his knees, then painfully gained his feet. Standing alone on the swaying cabin, holding the mast, his left arm hanging awkwardly by his side, he waited anxiously for his turn.

Jeremy brought the young girl and her mother into the wheelhouse. Tears streamed down the woman's face while her daughter clung to her leg. Will turned and noticed the girl's face was ashen, her lips blue. Jeremy offered the woman their winter jackets, then knelt and turned on the cabin heater.

The woman and her daughter removed their raincoats and wrapped themselves in the cumbersome jackets. She sat on the floor beside the equipment rack, her daughter on her lap. Jeremy handed her a lifejacket as a cushion. She smiled weakly, glanced at Will and said, "My husband…" She wrapped her arms tightly around her daughter, "he's hurt…when he fell, he broke his arm."

Jeremy calmly said, "Don't worry. We'll have him on board in a minute." He stepped out onto the deck.

Chris eyed him and said, "The guy is definitely hurting."

"His wife thinks his arm is broken."

Will waited for a wave to crest, then slowly moved the boat back into position. He stared through the windshield at the looming cabin. He felt the bow touch the sailboat's gunwale; he spun the wheel to port and reversed the engines.

Grimacing, the man jumped; one foot landed on the boat's gunwale, the second missed. His weight propelled him into Chris, knocking him back. Jeremy lunged and grabbed Chris's lifejacket; the three of them hit the deck. The man groaned loudly as he landed on Jeremy. Chris jumped up and helped the injured man to his feet.

"Thank you, thank you. I can't express my gratitude…I am forever indebted…" he sighed heavily.

The woman appeared on the deck, the winter jacket zipped up to her chin; her hands hidden inside the long sleeves. Grief, relief and happiness were evident on her face as she draped the long, floppy sleeves around her husband. She turned to Chris and said, "I think his arm is broken."

*   *   *

"Roger Prescott, Cote's Landing…ETA 130, CSL Robin out."

Will replaced the mic.

Chris stuck his head into the wheelhouse and said, "I looked away for a few seconds, looked back, and just the mast was sticking out of the water…then it was gone." He looked over his shoulder, "The boat fender and lifejacket are bobbing up and down on the surface." He stepped back, pulled the hood up on the winter jacket and closed the door. The boat's movement and the warm, dry heat inside the wheelhouse played havoc with his stomach.

"I just gave Prescott our position, and with our make-do floats marking the vessel's position, a salvage crew shouldn't have any problem finding your sailboat," Will said. He glanced at the man sitting on the portside chair. Jeremy was putting the finishing touches on a sling to support his left arm. The consensus was that he had a broken wrist and collarbone.

The man slowly turned his head, looked weakly at Will, groaned and whispered something inaudible. Will was sure he was in shock. Jeremy draped a metallic space blanket around him.

"The Coast Guard is sending two ambulances to meet us at Cote's Landing. We're about twenty minutes out," Will said. He turned his head and looked down at the woman and girl sitting on the floor, wrapped in a space blanket. The girl was enjoying a peanut butter and jam sandwich. Will smiled and exhaled. Her cheeks and lips were rosy red.

He turned back, looked through the window at the wealth of stars in the night sky and set a course for Cote's Landing.

*   *   *

Fifteen minutes later, the woman stood up, tucked the space blanket around her daughter and moved next to Will. She put a hand on his shoulder.

Will eyed a fairway buoy off their port. He smiled at her, then pointed to the lights at Cote's Landing and the flashing red-and-white lights of the ambulances waiting on the wharf.

"I found this on the floor by your chair," she said, holding out her hand. His pendant lay in her palm. She smiled, "Will, it is time to go home."

THIRTY-THREE

Doris sat on the edge of Will Greene's bed. During the past forty-eight hours, he had uttered incoherent sounds, experienced more reflexive limb movements, and yesterday, it was noted on his chart that he was semi-responsive for twenty minutes.

During her Sunday afternoon shift, Doris had routinely checked on him, hoping and wishing that he would emerge from his coma while she was on duty. Her shift as Charge Nurse had just ended, and as she passed by the door to her favourite patient's room, she heard him call out her name. She had spun around and entered the darkened room. Truthfully, she thought her mind was playing havoc with her tired senses.

Doris stroked his unresponsive hand. Disappointed, she slid her leg off the bed and gently squeezed his hand as she stood up. He squeezed back. She dropped her head and looked into his eyes. She whispered, "Will, if you hear me, squeeze my hand." Her eyes never left his. There was no response. She repeated, "Will, if you can hear me, please…squeeze my hand." She waited in the dark…then a tear appeared and ran down her cheek. His eyes slowly closed, then reopened. His lips twitched and moved slightly. "Are you smiling?" she said while trying to contain her excitement.

He squeezed her hand and opened his mouth, but his voice eluded him. He closed his eyes, and a moment later, a thick gurgling noise escaped his throat.

Doris gently squeezed his hand and said, "Slow down…don't strain. I will be right back…" She ran into the washroom, returned to his bedside and said, "Will, I'm going to place a damp face cloth in your mouth." She slipped the folded face cloth between his teeth. "That's great…now close your mouth and gently try to suck some water out of the cloth."

She watched and smiled warmly, "Nice and easy." She removed a small penlight from her uniform pocket. "Will, I am now going to shine a light into each eye to see how your pupils react." A moment later, satisfied, she said, "Excellent…both pupils are the same size, and both respond to the light." She slowly removed the damp cloth, patted his mouth dry with a tissue, then applied Vaseline to his dry, chapped lips.

Doris eyed her watch. She adjusted his bed covers and said, "Will, it's 11:30 p.m. My shift has ended, and I need some rest. I will be back first thing in the morning. Before I leave for the night, I'm going to instruct the nurses to check on you every thirty minutes." She smiled. "Now, don't take this the wrong way, but try to get some sleep. Tomorrow will be a long day."

She turned to leave, stopped and looked back at him. "In the morning, I will call Veronica with the great news."

Will squinted as the silhouette left the darkened room.

*   *   *

A lovely, warm sun-bleached Monday morning greeted Veronica as she left the house. She kept wiping away happy tears as she drove to the hospital. It was so nice of Doris to call this morning, she thought. And then she wondered why the Neurologist was so insistent on meeting her first thing. She parked the Toyota Camry and placed the parking pass on the dashboard. She entered the hospital lobby and followed the signs to Neurology and Dr. Pierce's office.

Veronica was surprised to see Doris sitting on one of the two chairs in front of the doctor's desk. Doris rose and hugged her. She couldn't help but notice Veronica's drawn face and puffy red eyes. Doctor Pierce walked around the desk, pulled a chair back and said, "Please, ladies." He stepped back and resumed his seat.

Doctor Pierce retrieved his clipboard from the desk drawer and took a moment to review his initial observations jotted down after sifting through the night-shift nurse's report. He then raised his eyes to Veronica, "Nurse Carter mentioned that she talked to you earlier this morning. I will only take a moment of your time, Mrs. Greene. First and foremost, your husband is doing exceptionally well. During the night, he had a lengthy conversation with one of the night-duty nurses." He dropped the clipboard on the desk and placed a hand on his scrawled notes. "I felt it pertinent that we discuss a couple of matters before you see your husband."

Veronica looked at the doctor, concern etched across her face. She held back tears.

"We need to be cognizant that emerging from a coma is a gradual process that often begins with the person being quite agitated and confused. This is expected and is not unusual behaviour. As we previously discussed, full recovery from brain trauma depends on many factors: the patient's age, overall health, underlying cause, and receiving timely medical interventions. Your husband, I assure you, has a solid foundation for a successful recovery."

He allowed Veronica a moment to digest the information. "Now, Mrs. Greene, there are signs your husband is experiencing retrograde amnesia; however, it is early days. Indeed, he may find it difficult to recall memories or experiences prior to the onset of amnesia. A word of caution…his memory loss may be permanent. However, twenty-four hours from now, we will have a much better grasp on his neurological condition."

Doctor Pierce dropped his eyes to the clipboard. "Now, Will mentioned to the night-duty nurse that he has four siblings?"

Veronica raised her head, looked at the doctor, hesitated, then said, "Yes. He has three older sisters and a younger brother."

He nodded, ran a finger across several lines of notes and asked, "Pete and Vivian are his parents, and his grandfather's name is Ernie Greene?" He looked at Veronica with a raised eyebrow.

"Yes…that is correct."

"Excellent. Parents can offer a wealth of information, generational stories, meaningful moments and memories that may help him to access or recall pre-amnesia memories."

Veronica stared at the doctor, glanced at Doris, dropped her head and said, "Will's mum is a healthy, vibrant eighty-eight. His dad, though, passed seven or eight years ago, and his granddad, well, he died in 1948."

Doctor Pierce scribbled something down and said, "We must assume that Will believes his parents are still present in his life."

He stood up, signalling the conclusion of their meeting. As he moved around the desk, he said, "All right…although not required, I am going to insist your husband wear a sleep mask for the next seventy-two hours. He will be told it is to protect his eyes from the light. It is vital during the initial stages of recovery to ensure he is stable and gaining strength before we offer or introduce information that may be upsetting or difficult for him to comprehend." Doctor Pierce glanced at Nurse Carter, then turned to Veronica. He smiled reassuringly, "Mrs. Greene, any questions?"

Veronica's mind was spinning. She had a bunch of concerns and questions, but first, she ached to see her husband.

*   *   *

Anxious and trembling, Veronica stared at the closed door to room 437. Her breathing was rapid; her heart pounded in her neck. She closed her eyes, inhaled and pushed open the door. She stepped into the darkness and shut the door. Slivers of morning light seeped in around the drawn curtain. She quietly moved over to the bed, halted and watched Will's chest slowly rise and fall.

"Ronnie…that you?" he whispered hoarsely as he adjusted the mask covering his eyes.

"Yes, Will. I'm here. I have…I've missed you so much…" Tears cascaded down her face as she gently sat on the edge of the bed.

"Don't cry," he said, slowly raising a hand. She held it against her wet cheek. He whispered, "How long…how long, Ronnie?"

"Oh, Will…"

The door opened. Doris and Doctor Pierce entered the room.

Doris flicked on the light and said, "Good morning, Will. Are we ready for a busy day?"

"Mr. Greene, I'm Doctor Julian Pierce, the attending physician supervising your neurological recovery."

Veronica stood up, wiped her face with both hands, then backed away from the bed.

Doris moved over beside her.

Doctor Pierce smiled and said, "You are the talk of the town, Mr. Greene."

Two nurses entered the room carrying three folding chairs. "Thank you, Jill, Pamela," Doris said. She helped Veronica unfold the chairs by the foot of the bed.

The doctor pulled a chair close to the bed, dropped his clipboard on the seat and said, "All right, Mr. Greene…please take a big deep breath…and another." He reached for Will's right hand and said, "Squeeze…" He held his other,

"Squeeze…wonderful." He lifted the tucked bed sheet and said, "Wriggle your right toes…now left." He nodded and dropped the sheet. Pleased with his patient's progress, he nodded again and said, "…are you thirsty?"

Doris immediately stood up and left the room.

"All right. Now, I am going to ask you a series of questions."

Veronica pulled the chair closer to the bed and put her hand on Will's lower leg.

Doctor Pierce picked up the clipboard, sat on the chair and said, "All right. Ready?"

Will nodded and fidgeted with the sleep mask.

"Splendid. What is your full name?"

Will whispered, "William Ernest Greene."

"Your wife's first name?"

"Veronica."

"Do you have a pet?"

"A Heinz 57, we call her Chinook."

Veronica listened to every word as she stroked Will's lower leg. Concern registered on her face as he answered: 'Chinook.'

Doris returned with a glass of water. She placed it on the tray table and returned to her seat.

"How many children do you and your wife have, and their names?"

"Two children, Ellie and Adam."

"Can you name the province and country?"

"Ontario, Canada."

"Very good. Just two more questions. What year is it and how old are you?"

"1989 and…I am…I am thirty-three."

Veronica's hand froze on his leg. She inhaled sharply while fighting back tears. Doris reached over and held her hand.

"Well now, that's enough grilling for one day," Doctor Pierce said. He stood up and tucked the clipboard under his arm, glanced at Veronica, then back to Will and said, "I have scheduled an EEG, electroencephalogram for this afternoon and depending on the technician's schedule, you will also have a CT scan tonight or tomorrow morning. Later this morning, we will remove your feeding tube and catheter. In addition, the dieticians will assess your nutritional needs, tailor a diet plan and gradually reintroduce you to solid food. Now, let me see, Tuesdays, my rounds are in the afternoon. Therefore, tomorrow, after your noon meal, we will discuss the test results and my expectations for your immediate future. Any questions?"

Will struggled to stay awake. Sleep was knocking.

Doctor Pierce scribbled on his clipboard, turned to Veronica and said, "All right, Mrs. Greene, could I meet you by the nurses' station in, oh," he checked his watch, "let's say ten minutes."

*   *   *

Twenty minutes ticked by before the doctor appeared in the hallway. "Sorry about the wait, Mrs. Greene," the doctor said as he scrutinized the people milling around the brightly lit nurses' station. He stood beside Veronica, dropped some paperwork on the chest-high semi-circular counter, and said, "I do not see Nurse Carter; perhaps she is doing her rounds."

Veronica eyed him and said, "Doris is off duty today…she joined us this morning, I believe, to console and to be by my side. She's a lovely person, a wonderful, dedicated nurse."

"That she is." He looked Veronica in the eye and said, "All right. Now…your husband…he is experiencing retrograde amnesia. After we complete our tests and as he begins to experience familiar surroundings, we will have a better gauge of the extent of his amnesia. In most cases, retrograde amnesia improves over weeks and months. Now…as your husband just demonstrated, older memories are more resistant, and perhaps this is why he…Will believes it is 1989."

He looked down at his clipboard, studied his notes and said, "Last night, he talked about your two children, Ellie and Adam. Twice, he told the night-duty nurse that once he was well enough, he would take the children hunting for wild asparagus. Obviously, we are unaware of the context, but it was apparent to the nurse that he was talking about his own children when they were just little tykes. With that said, we don't want to subject your husband to any additional mental anguish or emotional distress. Hence, the sleep mask. We want to give him every chance to adjust to his…surroundings."

Veronica nodded. "I understand," her eyes began to tear up, "when he finally sees me…he'll understand that I am a much older version of his wife and the year is not 1989." She dropped her head and wiped away a tear, "I'll have to tell Adam and Ellie that they will have to wait to see their dad…for…for a few days."

"Now, Mrs. Greene, I want you to be prepared for the possibility that your husband may experience temporary or long-term memory loss for weeks, perhaps months…"

Veronica exhaled and stared at the floor, "For almost two weeks, he was sick with a viral infection and with walking pneumonia. I didn't realize at the time how sick he was," she shook her head and went on, "…no one was in the kitchen to witness his fall. Anyway, as he lost consciousness, he must have hit his head on the kitchen counter before hitting the floor." She inhaled, "There was so much blood."

He reached out and put a supporting hand on her shoulder. "It was an accident, Mrs. Greene. It was no one's fault. Will is very fortunate that his influenza, hypoxia and cerebral edema were assessed and treated within hours. Performing the craniectomy, administering medications and receiving oxygen support, his chances of a near complete recovery are quite promising," he said reassuringly.

Veronica sighed, "Thank you, Doctor. How many days do we wait before telling him…it is 2009?"

*   *   *

During Doris's Tuesday morning break, she checked in on Will. She reviewed his chart—he had had an uneventful night. The night nurse had cranked up the head of his bed.

Will raised a hand and said, "G'mornin' Doris."

She smiled, put a hand on his arm, and said, "How'd you know it was me?"

"By your footsteps. Your runners have a distinct squeak with each step." He slid a hand over his bristly scalp, yawned and said, "Last night a guy came in the room and mopped the floor. I swear he had bathed in Stetson cologne."

"That's Terence…usually works the 3 p.m. to 11 p.m. shift. He certainly likes to splash on the cologne. He often goes out to the clubs from work. For the life of me, I don't know where he gets his energy. By the way, my husband used to wear the same cologne when we dated."

"In my *coma dreams*…that's what I've decided to call them; I would sporadically smell Stetson cologne. Strange, huh?"

"That's wonderful, Will. Keep evaluating your dreams, your coma dreams."

Will nodded. "Doris, any idea when I can drop this eye mask?"

"That's up to Doctor Pierce. Initially, he said three days."

"One other thing, Doris. Do you mind a personal question?"

"Shoot."

He reached for the pendant around his neck, "Any chance you are Catholic?"

She knit her brow and said, "Well, raised RC, but don't practice much these days." She looked at him expectantly.

"This may be a strange question, but would you have a peek and tell me which saint is depicted on my pendant?" He lifted his head, exposing his neck.

"That's interesting, Will. I had this very discussion with Veronica just two weeks ago when she placed the pendant around your neck. It was on the day you were scheduled for extubation."

"I was on life support!" He said hoarsely, then coughed.

Doris cursed silently. "Will, I thought you knew." She hurried on, "A ventilator is quite common when someone is in a medically induced coma, with head trauma and respiratory failure. It assists the body's healing process, allowing the person to rest and recover. Two weeks ago, the healthcare team decided to disconnect you from the life-support machine and to reduce your meds. However, you didn't emerge from your coma—your body decided it needed another two weeks' rest."

Will breathed in deeply, "Christ. That is, um…nerve-wracking…disturbing to learn that I was on life support." He considered the implications. "I was on life support," he whispered to himself.

Doris watched his reaction. Well, all things considered, he took that quite well, she thought. Nevertheless, she silently berated herself. She stepped closer, "Will, I am so sorry. I don't want to cause you any additional stress."

"I'm not upset, Doris. Honestly, though, I really just want everyone to be forthright with me. Anyway…I would appreciate hearing your opinion on my pendant."

"Yes, of course. I understand that your father received it as a gift during the Second World War, and he believed the pendant represented Saint Christopher, the patron saint of travellers. As I told Veronica, without reservation, it is a depiction of the Virgin Mary."

Will rubbed the pendant and remained silent as an image of the St. Lawrence hippie formed in his mind.

Veronica walked into the room, hugged Doris, bent over and pecked Will on the lips.

"Brushed my teeth this morning." He ran his tongue over his smooth teeth, then flashed his pearly whites.

Doris said, "I should be getting back to my rounds. Will, I'll put in a request to have the ventilator removed from the room."

"Thanks, Doris."

She closed the door on her way out.

"Your mom, Ellie and Adam send their love. They want to give us a few days to reconnect before visiting," Veronica lied. She looked away from him, embarrassed by her deception.

"Oh…Okay. Thanks, babe. I was wondering why the kids haven't been in for a visit."

*   *   *

Will enjoyed a small bowl of lukewarm chicken noodle soup for lunch and Jello for dessert. A dietary aide entered the room and moments later left with the food tray. She left behind a second helping of Jello and a sealed plastic cup filled with orange juice.

There was a light knock at the door, then Doctor Pierce entered. Veronica, sitting close to Will, stood and pulled the chair back to the foot of the bed.

"You are looking well. In forty-eight hours, we will remove the mask, open the curtain, and let some daylight in. All right?" Doctor Pierce said.

"Fantastic…be nice to feel the sun on my face."

"Now, I have reviewed with my team both test results, the EEG and the CT scan and we are very pleased, everything looks normal. As a follow-up, we will schedule a second EEG in six months."

"Thank you. That is so wonderful to hear," Veronica said. Her legs were trembling. "Excuse me," she said.

Will listened as Veronica pushed back the chair, walked to the washroom, and closed the door; water splashed against the sink bowl. He turned his head toward the doctor. "Gotta say…I feel an enormous sense of relief."

Doctor Pierce nodded, " Later today, a physio team will assess your mobility and immediate needs. They will develop a focused plan and provide advice and various strategies to support your recovery."

"When do you think I can get out of bed?"

"That will be up to the physiotherapists. Depending on their assessment, they may want you ambulatory by the weekend."

Will nodded, "…three more days."

Doctor Pierce's pager began to vibrate in his pocket.

Will heard multiple beeps. He tilted his head up.

"I'm being paged." He pressed the function button multiple times, then slipped the pager back into his pocket. "Before I leave, Mr. Greene, any questions?"

Will exhaled deeply, "I have been lying here for two days and nights in total darkness, thinking about being in a coma and trying to analyze, come to terms with the sweeping, intricate dreams…I *experienced*." He inhaled and went on, "In my coma dreams…that's how I am defining them," he turned his head in the direction of the doctor's voice, "I seamlessly weaved between two tracks of time." He cleared his throat. "I thought I was living life with my wife and two kids, then on the flipside, I was an eight-year-old living life in 1963. Doctor,

I wonder…I wonder why…why did my dreams focus, why was I preoccupied with those two timelines?"

Will sighed heavily, "It leaves me," he chuckled nervously, "questioning my own reality…"

A powerful impulse enveloped him. He had a sudden need to glimpse, to touch the tangible, the authentic world that existed beyond the hospital bed. The constant pressure of the sleep mask was agonizing, the darkness intolerable. He shook his head and exhaled loudly, "Tell me, doctor, have any of your previous patients experienced anything similar?"

"The simple answer is, yes. Numerous studies have focused on understanding the underlying biology and physiology of brain impairment and comas. In many cases, a patient will emerge from a coma with vivid childhood memories and, quite often, memories of profound events that had altered the trajectory of their life. Conversely, some patients describe a comatose state, like a light that blinked off then on, devoid of any perception of the passage of time. Then again, there are a few cases where, upon waking, the patient claimed they had experienced a lifetime through another's eyes." He glanced at his watch.

"Frankly, when it comes to comprehending and unravelling the complexity and function of the human brain, we are continually breaking new ground. Indeed, the human body has a remarkable ability to rewire and to compensate for damaged areas of the brain. However, there is still much to discover—it is an extraordinary organ. Now, Mr. Greene. I must be on my way." He turned, eyed the closed washroom door, and left the room.

Veronica waited for the doctor to leave. Her guilt at lying to Will was overwhelming. She looked in the mirror and dabbed at her wet eyes. She exited the washroom, walked over next to the bed, and said in a feigned cheery voice, "How about some music. I've grown to appreciate one of your favourite groups, Super Tramp."

"There's a radio in the room?"

"The hospital staff were kind enough to place a table against the far wall for all my *stuff*. First order of business, I bought a turntable, it's here now with oh…twenty of your albums." Veronica touched his arm, then moved across the room to the table and asked, "Should we listen to *Breakfast in America*?" She opened the turntable lid and scanned the albums.

"Ronnie, Ronnie…look at me, babe."

Veronica turned her head and eyed him, "…Oh, Will."

"I've missed you…" He smiled weakly, "I like the bits of grey in your hair."

She turned slowly to face him. "You removed the mask!"

"Fuck it. I'm done with wearing this mask—enough is enough. My vision is kinda blurry though."

"That's because your glasses are at home. I didn't think to bring them to the hospital."

"I wear glasses?"

Veronica slid over and sat on the edge of the bed. She gazed into Will's sunken, dark-rimmed eyes. "I love you, Will Greene."

"I love you too, Veronica Greene." He squinted and asked, "Are those little laugh lines around your eyes?"

"I'd pop you if you weren't already down. These are stress and worry lines."

"Very sexy." Will then turned serious, "How long, Ronnie. How long have I been in a coma?"

Veronica stared at him. She struggled to reply. Her mind went blank.

"How many years? You look amazing, babe, but…you're not thirty-three. Please, Ronnie, tell me."

Tears streamed down her face. She blurted out, "It's Tuesday, June 09th, 2009."

Will stared at her. He tried to breathe, but his lungs would not cooperate. He moaned, "Twenty years…I've been in a coma for twenty years?"

"Will, I am sorry…I'm so distraught…you, you were in a coma for seven weeks and four days."

His mind spiralled. Bizarre images and sensations tumbled around his head. He stared at Veronica. He opened his mouth, but his voice failed; his tongue felt thick. His mind went dark. The hospital room blurred, turned grey. He gasped and, through the haze, mumbled, "Ronnie, I have so many questions…" He shrugged, "I feel like I am on some weird game show."

His irrational thoughts and questions raced and scrolled across his mind like a stock-market ticker. He lay back and wiped his moist eyes. He was spent.

Veronica consoled him.

Minutes passed.

"I am ready to listen to Super Tramp," Will said.

THIRTY-FOUR

Doris slowly opened the door to Will's room, stepped in and checked his chart. She was pleased with his progress.

Will had been watching the door, waiting for her to enter the room. "Mornin', Doris." He smiled in the semidarkness. He eyed Doris for the first time.

"Good morning, Will." She moved next to the bed, looked down at him and said, "Oh, my goodness. Your sleep mask...but it's only Wednesday. Oh my. Doctor Pierce decided it was time for you to see the world again. I am so pleased...do you mind if I turn on the light?"

"Please. And the curtain."

Doris brought light to the room.

"Ahh...there's nothing like the morning light."

"Would you like the bed raised?" She turned the crank.

Will exhaled, "Much better...it's nice to be sitting upright."

"How are you, Will...does Veronica know?"

"She was here when I removed the mask. I have lots to think about...I am alive...and I will get better!"

"I know you will. Once you're around family and have other prompts like home videos, family albums, or even a diary, you may be surprised how quickly memories return. And you'll have Veronica by your side to fill in the gaps. Your wife is quite the woman. I will miss visiting with her."

Doris glanced at the turntable, noticed an album on the platter, and said, "Veronica was here every day by your side, talking, reading to you, doing crosswords and Sudokus. Sometimes, she would be asleep in the chair, holding your hand. Regardless, she always had an album playing in the background, hoping against hope to stimulate your senses. It was a steady stream of reading and music."

Will listened and thought about the first time he laid eyes on his future wife at the Tiltin' Tavern.

"And, by the by, I met your sister three weeks ago. Doctor Susan Greene Brody. I was on night shift, and she came by your room at 2 a.m."

Will grinned and said, "Huh…she's my second-oldest sister. I remember she was determined to be a surgeon."

"She is, and a damn fine one, so I hear."

Doris eyed him and said, "I'm late for my shift." She walked to the door, turned and said, "I'll see you in a couple of days. I'm off for some needed rest."

"Doris, thank you…and thank you for being there for Ronnie."

*   *   *

Veronica walked into the room at 10:00 a.m. and said, "You're looking healthier every day, hon. I talked to your mum last night. She has a cold and is concerned she might pass the bug to you. I told her it's best to wait until next week to visit, when we hope you'll be home. Oh, yes, I brought your bifocals."

"How is she otherwise?"

"She's slowed down a little since your dad passed. But she's a vibrant woman, living on her own and still driving at the age of eighty-eight."

Will smiled.

"And tonight, I will return with Adam and Ellie."

He perked up, "Okay…great. Truth be told, I'm a tad nervous about seeing the kids…the adult kids."

"They are too. Memory loss or not, you're their father, it will be fine."

"I know…I know." He inhaled and said, "Incidentally, Doris checked in on me before the start of her shift. She said my sister, Doctor Susan Greene…" he struggled to recall.

"Doctor Susan Greene Brody. Don't you worry, we'll get you up to speed." She walked over to the table, eyed the albums, and the selection of books from Pierre Berton to Stephen King to Isaac Asimov. She gathered up three items, then dragged a chair over to the bed. As she sat down, she said, "Do you remember Randy Cooper?"

"I have early memories of him." Will tilted his head, "I don't think we were friends."

"Oh, no? Well, about a month ago, this wall calendar arrived in the mail." She slid the calendar from its protective sleeve. "Here. Have a peek at the August calendar page."

He reflexively put on his glasses, flipped to August, and stared at the illustration of a mysterious landscape with heavily muscled Romanesque soldiers and shapely women holding shields and swords, battling blue, three-legged winged creatures. "Amazing drawings."

"Will, look at the bottom, the handwritten note."

He lowered his eyes and read:

Will, when you're back on your feet,
you and Veronica should come to San Diego for a visit.
I'll take you on a tour of the animation studio.
Get well soon, buddy.
P.S. I have plenty of room.
Coop

He was at a loss for words.

Veronica carefully inserted the calendar into the sleeve, put it on the tray table and picked up an envelope. "I've kept all your Get-Well cards at home…this one, however, was hand-delivered by Donna Sadowski, the Mayor of Barriston,"

Will raised his eyebrows, confused.

"Donna Moore. A long time ago, you were fond of her—your first crush."

Will smiled, "Donna Moore, the Mayor of Barriston. A politician? Huh…I'm not surprised. I can see her as a woman of the people."

"Her future looks bright. She now has her eye set on provincial politics. Now…hon, I purposely set aside this magazine for last." She handed him the April edition of *Maclean's* magazine. "I have more copies at home."

Will stared at the magazine cover.

"Such a lovely family picture," Veronica said.

Will read the caption: "James and Amahle Henderson, The Dynamic Duo Reshaping the Work Environment While Raising Four Children." He chuckled, "I knew that boy genius was going places."

"In the article," Veronica said, "James talks about the *catalyst* that changed their lives twenty years ago—the night he and Amahle shared a late-night pizza."

Will's eyes grew wide. "I remember. It was a meat lover's pizza that sparked Amahle to reconfigure their presentations for the technology companies."

A tear ran down Veronica's cheek. "James called every Friday night looking for updates and always asked how I was holding up." She reached into her pocket, "He dropped by three weeks ago, made quite a stir with the nurses." She smiled knowingly and went on, "He wanted you to have this…"

Will looked down at the lustrous black obsidian Clovis point. His hand trembled as she placed it in his palm.

"James is utterly convinced the Clovis point is a good luck charm, a talisman that also possesses mystical or supernatural healing properties," she said, then shrugged. "He is unwavering in his belief."

*   *   *

Will had been staring at the Clovis point for the better part of an hour. Veronica had sat quietly next to the bed, watching her husband. She checked the time and said, "Will, your lunch will be arriving any minute, and you do have a busy afternoon with physio and whatnot." She exhaled, "I did bring it today. We can wait too…we could wait until you're up and mobile."

He handed her the trinket—the talisman and said decisively, "I'm as ready as I'll ever be…let's have at it."

"Keep in mind, you've lost thirty pounds." Veronica stood up, walked to the table and removed the compact mirror from her purse. Will watched her and waited. She returned to the bedside and handed him the round mirror.

He exhaled, glanced up at her, then flipped the lid and peered into the mirror. He stared at his shaved head. His eyes pursued the red crescent-shaped scalpel wound that ran from his hairline to behind his ear. He reached up, touched the raised incision and slid his fingertips along its length. He lowered his hand, dragging it across his sunken cheeks and grey five o'clock shadow. Shocked by his own reflection, Will stared into his hollow, dark-rimmed eyes and uttered, "So…this is what fifty-three looks like. Fuck me…I look old."

CHAPTER
THIRTY-FIVE

SUNDAY, JULY 05, 2009

Will could see the house in the distance, his mum's blue Honda Civic in the driveway. He held a cane in his right hand and a dog leash in his left. He stopped and looked down at the six-year-old black Labrador retriever. Mobi paused, then sat at attention. He bent over, stroked the dog's neck and said, "You sure are a well-trained dog." Mobi raised his head, drooled and swept his tail back and forth across the sidewalk. Will patted him on the head, straightened up and said, "Let's go home, boy."

* * *

The screen door closed behind him. He leaned the cane against the wall, then knelt and removed the dog's collar. Mobi sat, eyed him and waited. He stood up and limped into the living room. Mobi followed behind. Vivian was on the couch with a photo album open on her lap.

"Hey, Mum. How are you?"

"Top of the world, dear," she smiled and closed the album. "You are looking well. Your hair is coming in nicely, and I'm sure it won't be long before you will be walking without a limp." She leaned forward and placed the album on the coffee table.

"Physio three times a week certainly helps, especially the pool. Where's Ronnie?"

"She's in the kitchen getting us gals a drink."

Will sat on the couch beside his mother. Mobi flopped down on the floor next to him. He glanced at his watch, 2:50 p.m. "Well, the rest of the gang should be arriving soon."

Vivian eyed her son, "Are you sure you are up for all this company?"

"I am. It's family, and everyone has chipped in to help. Ellie and Adam made the burgers yesterday and picked up sausages, hot dogs, and buns. Caroline and Susan are bringing salads and desserts, and Mary Lynn is supplying the tables and chairs. She said it's no problem because she has a Chrysler minivan." He shrugged. "And Tim offered to be the barbecue chef."

"Well then, everyone is chipping in; that's wonderful." Vivian dropped her eyes to Mobi. "I see the dog is still your constant companion."

Will nodded, "I'm growing fond of him. Now that Ronnie is back at work, he is good company. Although I must be careful not to trip over him." He looked down at Mobi and noticed an old, stained banker's box, reinforced with packing tape. "Mum, what do we have here?"

"I'm excited to show you. But we should wait for Veronica, she will want to see this too."

Will studied the banker's box for a moment, then noticed his mum eyeing the old painting.

"The windmill painting looks splendid over the chesterfield," she said, pleased.

Will nodded, glanced at the painting and said, "We decided to move the *windmills* into this room; it just seemed…fitting for the painting to be hung on the living room wall."

He smiled, "Most mornings I'll wander into the room, sip my coffee and just stare and marvel at the mysterious scene. Oddly enough, I find myself wondering what was going through Dad's mind on that day in 1945 as he stood in the gallery eyeing the painting. The war had just ended, and he was days from embarking on a return voyage to Canada after five long years overseas. And his reunion with his war bride was still months down the road. One day, I may have the answer."

Vivian placed her hand on her son's cheek and said, "Your father would be happy; the painting meant the world to him."

"I miss him."

"I do too, dear."

Lost in thought, Will unconsciously touched the Virgin Mary pendant around his neck.

Veronica walked into the living room holding a serving tray with two drinks. "Oh, you're home. I didn't hear you come in. A pleasant walk?" she asked.

Will nodded as he patted Mobi on the head.

She placed the tray on the coffee table among the three photo albums, then sat beside Vivian.

"Thank you, dear." Vivian inspected the highball glass with a lime wedge. She sipped the rum and Coke, "…mmm, that's lovely."

"Hon, would you like a drink?"

"I'm fine, thanks."

Veronica picked up the Bordeaux glass and sipped the Cabernet Sauvignon.

Vivian put the highball glass back on the table and said, "Veronica, please hand me the box on the floor."

She leaned forward, picked up the banker's box and placed it beside Vivian.

"Is that your phone's ringtone, I hear?" Will asked.

Veronica ran to the kitchen. A minute later, she sat back down and said, "Doris and her husband are going to drop by for a drink. I am so thrilled she accepted our invite."

"Cellular phones. What remarkable technology…right out of Star Trek," Will said, amazed. "These small portable phones must be so liberating," he mused.

Veronica grinned slyly, tipped her head to the side and said, "Hmmm. I don't know about that."

Vivian moved the banker's box to her lap. She scrunched her nose, "Oh my, it smells musty."

Will eyed the faded writing on the box lid.

437 Binbrook Lane,
Ernie + Violet's stuff from Aunt May

Vivian said, "Your father kept this box in the basement for as long as I can remember, and after he passed, I didn't have the heart to throw it out, so I asked the moving men to put it in my storage locker at the apartment building." She removed the lid and went on, "The other day, while searching the apartment for family pictures," she turned her head and looked at Will, "to help jog your memory, I decided to rummage through my storage locker. My Lord, when I rediscovered this old box, well, it immediately brought back early memories of your father, Ernie and Violet."

Vivian sighed, "Inside the box, buried under some photographs, knick-knacks and a couple of old books, was this eight-by-ten photograph of your father in uniform, standing with his parents in Aunt May's kitchen." She reached into the box and handed Will a creased sepia-toned photograph.

"It must have been taken in December 1939, a couple of days before Pete shipped out. When I dug through the box, the photograph was loose, and the picture frame's glass was shattered. For all I know, the frame may have been damaged decades ago."

Will's hands shook as he studied the photo.

Veronica stood, moved around the coffee table and sat beside him. "Mobi, move," she ordered. She stared at the photo, then whispered, "Will, look at your granddad's clothes!"

"I know, exactly how I pictured him in my dreams…his white hair and goatee, his beige vest and—"

"When I saw the photograph, it gave me goose bumps," Vivian said.

Will pointed at the photo, "Look, Ronnie, there's a chain hanging from Grandpa Ernie's vest pocket. I think I can make out the outline of his pocket watch!"

Vivian's hand trembled as she passed Will a folded piece of paper. Speaking softly, she said, "Your grandfather wrote this letter to your father. It was obviously hidden behind the photograph…my goodness, I'm feeling weepy." She wiped away a tear, removed a tissue from her sweater and dabbed her eyes. "In late 1943, your grandfather underwent stomach surgery. I suspect he wrote this letter to Pete in the event he didn't recover from surgery." She reached for the rum and Coke. "I can only assume Ernie forgot that he stowed the letter behind the photograph for safekeeping." She tipped the glass back and had a swig.

"This is incredible," Veronica said, astonished. "We are the first to read your grandpa's letter, written over sixty years ago!"

Will read the letter. He then inhaled deeply, turned his head and gazed bleary-eyed at the photo albums on the table. Since he had been discharged from the hospital, he realized that as the days passed and he built new memories, his coma dreams grew weaker and more difficult to recall.

A moment later, in his mind's eye, he visualized eight-year-old William in his parents' small living room, sitting next to his grandfather. Behind them, the windmill painting appeared dark and ominous, obscured by the evening shadows.

Will snapped back to the present. He closed his eyes and wrestled to hold on to the fading image. As the memory sharpened, he saw Mildred lying on the turquoise broadloom curled around his grandfather's outstretched legs, snoring softly. As Grandpa Ernie was about to share the Greene family's set of core beliefs with him, they were suddenly interrupted and summoned to dinner. Will sighed heavily as he returned to the present.

Veronica leaned against him. Her voice quavered, "What's in the letter…what did your granddad say to your dad?"

Will slowly turned his head and stared at her. "I'm trying to make sense of all this—the photo, the letter…Grandpa Ernie died in 1948—yet he was in my coma dreams. Ronnie, he shared family stories with me!"

Will held up the letter and said, "He wrote about his philosophy of life, what it means to be a spiritual person and describes the Greene family's three cardinal rules." He lowered his head and eyed the letter. "He states *one* must labour to be *Present* to live in the here and now, to make the most of each day; secondly, *one* must endeavour to maintain a *Positive* outlook no matter the challenges, and lastly, *one* must have *Purpose* to guide and to motivate." He exhaled loudly, ran his hand gently along the incision on his head, then handed the letter to Veronica.

She refolded the letter and held it in her lap. She smiled affectionately, "Well, hon, that's a philosophy I could certainly get behind." She turned to Vivian and said, "Mom, what's your take…what's your opinion?"

"I think dear…thirty years ago, I may have had a very different answer; nevertheless, sitting here and closing in on my ninetieth year, well, I choose to believe Ernie paid his grandson a visit." Vivian dabbed her eyes with a tissue, picked up the rum and Coke and drained the glass in two gulps. She gently wiped each side of her mouth with the tissue. She smiled radiantly, "I believe I'll have a second rum and Coke."

Veronica's cell phone began ringing. "Damn, I left my phone in the kitchen." A minute later, she entered the living room holding a child's shoe box and said, "That was James. He and Amahle are running late; they'll be here in thirty minutes." She placed the shoe box on the coffee table.

"You keep your father's pocket watch in that shoe box?" Vivian asked.

"No. I keep Dad's watch in the bedroom under glass."

"James's good luck charm, his Clovis spear point, is in the shoe box," Veronica said.

Will noticed the bemused expression on his mum's face and said, "I decided that the Clovis point should be returned to Jimmy." He shrugged, "If by some manner this charm or talisman aided in my healing…well, it fulfilled its duty. All the same, it rightfully belongs with Jimmy."

Veronica nodded in agreement as she reached for the Bordeaux glass, gulped the contents, smiled, and said, "Mom, I'm also ready for a second glass of wine."

Veronica stood, looked out the window for a moment, turned back and eyed Will. A grin slowly crossed her face. "Hey, bub, don't be looking at me like that! Three times last week, remember," she said while holding up three fingers, "we're not as young as we used to be."

Vivian laughed heartily.

"That may be true, but I feel like I have been stationed on the far side of the Moon for twenty years," Will chuckled.

REVIEWS

I hope you enjoyed reading this book as much as I enjoyed writing it. If you did, I would appreciate a brief review on your preferred book website.

Please also feel free to drop me a line.

read.ike.j@gmail.com

ACKNOWLEDGEMENTS

Thanks to my better half. Her input helped me overcome many obstacles encountered throughout the writing process. I especially enjoyed her needling me to stay on track and not wander off into the forest.

Thanks to the *team* for their patience and sound advice.

A shout-out to my constant writing companion, Mobi. A handsome, gentle Labrador Retriever who left us too soon.

AUTHOR'S NOTE

I devoted many hours to researching various aspects of Canadian history; if I misrepresented any historical events or people, that's on me.

Mike J Read
May 04, 2026

* 9 7 8 1 0 6 7 5 7 2 5 1 8 *